# OUR LADY OF THE HIGHWAY

*a novel*

# OUR LADY OF THE HIGHWAY

*a novel*

## Hal Hartley

ELBORO

OUR LADY OF THE HIGHWAY
*a novel*
Copyright © 2022 by Hal Hartley



ISBN: 978-1-7379274-3-3

Published by Elboro Press

Elboro Press books may be purchased in bulk for educational, business or sales promotional use. Please address enquiries to:

office@elboropress.com

First Edition, 2022 – Fourth Printing

# OUR LADY OF THE HIGHWAY

ONE

The convent of Our Lady of the Highway has seen better days. A hundred years ago anywhere from fifty to sixty nuns lived here and had their meals together in silence at long wooden tables arranged in rows across this vast, cathedral-like kitchen opposite the massive black stove. But by the late nineteen-sixties, that cast iron antique was taken apart and sold as scrap. The tables were busted up, sawn into pieces, and hammered across the windows to protect the convent from the random violence running roughshod over this then worthless stretch of Brooklyn.

However, on this unseasonably warm winter afternoon in 2016 there are just four sisters living here. The mother superior, Sister Bernadette, is the youngest at seventy-one. She's at the ancient, warped, wooden counter cutting up a potato for the soup they'll eat this evening. She's distracted, though, by Sister Agatha's attempt to clean the windows.

Agatha is eighty-nine and nearly blind. She has punched her wet, palsied fist through the panes before. But she loves clean windows. She loves the light.

A third nun, Sister Catherine—in her early eighties, we

think—is sweeping the pantry. She pauses and looks around at the spotless concrete floor as if disappointed there isn't more dust and debris to wrestle into submission.

A small chime is heard and the three sisters look to the large clock high up above the doorway to the convent's main hall.

"Sisters," announces Bernadette, laying down her knife, "it's time for midday prayer. Leave your work for now."

"Yes, Mother Superior," replies Catherine quietly, setting aside her broom.

"I'll go and relieve Sister Dominique at vigil," the mother superior adds, drying her hands on a towel.

As Bernadette leaves, Catherine helps Agatha kneel down right there on the floor where she's working. The two old nuns turn to marked pages in their breviaries—small thick prayer books they carry with them at all times. They've recited these prayers a million times before and know them by heart. But following along in the breviary helps maintain the preferred rhythmic cadence. "God, come to my assistance," they begin. "Lord, make haste to help me."

Bernadette strides through the quiet, dilapidated, but perfectly clean main hall of the convent. It's as tall as a church but darker than it might be because of the wood still covering the magnificent windows soaring skyward above. She reaches the landing of a stairwell leading down to the lower level and pauses. She's not tired and she's not weak. She's just in the habit of preparing herself for the next problem to solve.

She continues.

The stone stairwell descends in a wide, proud spiral before reaching and, as it were, prostrating itself before the forbidding entrance to the basilica, the subterranean church that is the heart and soul of this cloistered convent. Opening and closing the basilica's monumental doors has been beyond the sisters' capacity for years. These days the six-inch thick, three-hundred-year-old wooden doors are almost always left ajar. The mother superior slips inside and pauses to confirm the prescribed order of things.

What is the prescribed order of things?

Sister Bernadette has no doubt about this at all. To her the universe itself is kept on course by virtue of the perpetual prayer cycle she and her sisters of the Order of Clementine have been maintaining for the past three hundred and forty-seven years in this stately underground church, the basilica. Since 1669, twenty-four hours a day, seven days a week, there is a sister of the Order lying face down on the cold stone floor of this private, spartan sanctuary praying for world peace.

Right now, Sister Dominique, the ninety-eight-year-old prioress (the convent's second-in-command) is lying motionless, with arms outstretched, in the attitude of a cross. She is nearing the end of her own six-hour session of prayer, begging the lord of the universe to intercede and end humanity's ceaseless and violent quest for vengeance and prestige.

Reassured, Bernadette starts towards the prioress.

The basilica is half a city block long and has colonnades running along the left and right walls. There are three small windows high up on either side looking out at ground level, letting in a weak and dappled light. At the far end is the high altar, situated patiently in its semicircular apse. There are no pews. The place is a wide-open underground plateau consecrated to faithful submission to the Almighty.

Without any fuss, Bernadette kneels beside Dominique. She makes the sign of the cross and taps her sister on the shoulder before lying face down on the floor herself. Though Dominique hasn't responded, Bernadette begins praying immediately, in Latin: "*Defende me Domine Deus, et discerne causam meam incredibili—*"

She pauses, though, and looks across at Dominique. Only now does she see that the old woman seems to be asleep. Bernadette lifts herself up on one elbow and comes closer. "Sister," she whispers, "Sister Dominique?" Getting no response, she listens for breath. Hearing nothing, she reaches out and lifts Sister Dominique's hand.

It falls flat and lifeless to the floor.

The old woman is dead.

"Shit," the mother superior sighs, though she automatically glances at the altar and nods an apology.

But Bernadette is not surprised. After all, the prioress had been fading daily. She hopes her sister's passing was easy, but there's no time for sentimentality. She's already in problem-solving mode. That's been her job for decades. She'll have to get Sister Catherine to soldier on with the vigil for an hour or so while she herself carries Dominique upstairs and arranges for the sacraments to be administered. But who will administer them? There's a new priest over at the parish of Saint Ann's, she's heard. But priests are always trying to interfere with her management of the convent and she prefers not to ask for help if she can avoid it.

Standing, she crosses to one of the small gated windows high up in the wall looking out into a garden. She locates a simple wooden chair and stands on it.

Outside, the wiry middle-aged groundskeeper, Jesus Ortiz, is tending to the vegetables.

"Mister Ortiz," Bernadette calls hoarsely.

Jesus stops and looks around, not certain what he's heard,

if anything. Bernadette calls again. "Mister Ortiz! Down here at the window." He sees her now, or at least her aged hand obscured by the grimy old shatterproof glass. He sets aside his rake and approaches.

"Sister Bernadette?"

"Yes. It's me," she announces dryly. "Sister Dominique is dead."

Likewise, Jesus Ortiz is not surprised. He stands back and looks around again, weighing the afternoon's upcoming hassles.

"Yeah," he mumbles, then, "where she at?"

"Down here in the basilica."

Jesus removes his cap and scratches his head. "Oh man," he growls, worried. No grown man has ever been inside the convent. And though Jesus was born and raised here, he hasn't seen Dominique face-to-face since he was twelve. "How you gonna get her outta there?"

"She's a hundred years old," Bernadette reminds him. "She weighs nothing. I'll carry her upstairs. But I need you to call the pastor at the church of Saint Ann's and arrange for her to receive the sacrament."

Jesus is glad she's in charge. "All right," he replies and starts to go. But then he stops and turns back. "You okay, Sister," he asks carefully.

"Mister Ortiz," Bernadette scolds, "death is part of life and is nothing to make such a big deal about."

But Jesus can hear in her voice the weight of her concerns and comes over to the window, shrugging his shoulders. "Yeah, I guess. You're the nun. Not me. Here—" He stoops down and passes her his hip flask of whiskey. She takes it and drinks while Jesus surveys the convent's property and tries to decide where to bury Sister Dominique.

"Thanks," the mother superior says, fortified, handing back the flask.

"I'll go call the church and find a backhoe to dig a grave with," the groundskeeper assures her as he, too, takes a hit from the flask.

"God bless you, Mister Ortiz."

As Jesus moves off, Bernadette steps down off the chair, faces the altar, genuflects, and starts praying while she stands and crosses back to Sister Dominique. "Holy Mary, mother of God, pray for us sinners now and at the hour of our death." Kneeling, she works her hands beneath the tiny old nun and lifts her from the floor. "Grant us the strength and patience to endure all obstacles." Standing with some effort, she starts for the doors and the formidable staircase beyond them. "And please," she begs, stopping, "send me someone—anyone— to help keep this busted up operation in business. Amen."

Tick, tick, tick—the clock on the wall of a conference room in the New York offices of the Rutledge Insurance Company measures the seconds of the day. Lola, an attractive junior policy adjuster, sits with half a dozen middle management executives around a large table listening to company policy being explained by their boss, Mister Richard Drake.

"Slice it and dice it anyway you want, ladies and gentlemen, but the fact is insurance is a business like any other and not a social service."

Lola is gazing out the window trying not to hear. The man disgusts her. She doesn't like her job. And she's not entirely certain health insurance should, in fact, be a business like any other. "Think nice things," she advises herself, "blue skies, puffy clouds, happy children…" But something in that particular avenue of reverie—happy children—complicates her efforts. She adjusts: "What will I have for dinner?"

Meanwhile, Drake notices. "Lola, you with us?"

She spins slowly back away from the window and leans an elbow prettily on the table's edge, a perfect picture of grace and competence. "Oh, yes, just—sorry. Please, continue."

And he does: "It's just as crucial to enhance shareholder value as it is to demonstrate plausible accountability in the settling of policy-holder claims."

Forced to pretend to be paying attention, Lola concentrates on the wall clock above and behind Drake's head. Her associate, Meg, a trim, middle-aged African American Baptist woman, is not fooled. Uneasy, she studies Lola watching the clock.

"Another way to boost earnings, of course," Drake continues, brightly, "is to dramatically increase premiums when policies come up for renewal."

The clock stops noticeably.

Meg lets out a stifled yelp and fidgets in her seat. The others look at her with concern. A sharp stab of pain pierces Lola's temple and she glances aside. Drake is oblivious to this deeply interior little drama, but he has noticed the stopped clock. He uses it as a convenient motivational talking point. "Could happen to anyone, right?" he suggests. "Just like that: functioning, not functioning. Is that our responsibility?"

Lola's associates all grin and nod amiably. They applaud. Lola stares at a glass of water across the table and, seeing this, Meg rolls her seat further away.

"Insurance," the boss concludes, "is not about prevention. It's about monetizing probability."

The glass fractures and falls to pieces, water flying everywhere. Meg screams, jumps out of her chair, and trips over someone's briefcase.

A bell is tolling in the convent's tower as Jesus puts his rakes and shovels away. He stops, makes the sign of the cross, and takes a sip from his hip flask. Tilting it towards the bells, he sadly toasts: "Happy trails, Sister Dominique." He's about to return to his work when there's a knock at the door.

The hollow metal door is small, cheap, dented, and retrofit into the eighteen-foot-high wall that surrounds the convent of Our Lady of the Highway. "That must be him," Jesus decides as he starts undoing the five different flimsy locks that secure it.

Outside the convent walls there is nothing but miles of deserted streets, garbage dumps, recycling plants, chemical factories, and bricked up warehouse buildings humming with unseen mechanical activity. A boyish looking thirty-three-year-old priest stands waiting as Jesus pokes his head out the door.

"Hey, Father Robert," Jesus asks, "from Saint Ann's?"

"Yes. And you must be Mister—" Robert consults a note-to-self and pronounces in what he believes is the proper Spanish, "Hey-zeus Ortiz?"

"Call me Jesus."

"Excuse me," the priest asks politely.

"I ain't Spanish," Jesus explains. "Born here and everything. I speak American. Call me Jesus."

"Okay," Father Robert agrees, amiably. "Jesus—can I come in?"

"Right this way."

Entering, Robert is happy and surprised to see greenery and a poor but well-maintained vegetable garden; in fact, a small farm.

"I thought they was sending over the new pastor," Jesus says.

"I am the new pastor."

"No way!"

"It's true."

"You're too young to be the boss!"

"Well, you know how it is: all hands on deck." But then, looking around at the garden, the young priest asks: "What do you grow here?"

"A little bit of everything," Jesus replies, proudly, adding: "It's all the sisters got to eat these days."

Father Robert expected as much and turns to consider the run-down building. "How many of them are there now?"

"Nuns? Well, now that Sister Dominique is passed on, that leaves three."

"And they continue the vigil?"

"Damn straight," Jesus confirms, shaking his head and reaching for his flask. But he desists and continues. "Twenty-four seven, eight hours each, nonstop prayers for world peace or whatever the fuck." Wincing at his own bad language, he holds up his hand. "Sorry." But the priest just smiles and Jesus concludes: "And not one of 'em under seventy years old at least!"

Robert has got the lay of the land now and wants to get started. He moves on: "Where's the body?"

"Inside. The others laid her out in the gallery."


Back at Rutledge Insurance, Lola runs into the ladies' room, drops her laptop, and hangs her head over a sink. Meg enters but stays by the door, keeping her distance. She wants the last word but doesn't want to get infected. "You've got the devil inside you, girl," she says. "I say you get yourself to some kind of exorcist."

Lola wants to apologize for making Meg look like a crazy lady in front of their colleagues. But she's still too unsettled to speak. Anyway, Meg's terror subsides and she sighs before turning to leave. "I'm moving to a cubicle on the far side of the office."

Left alone, Lola looks at herself in the mirror and splashes water on her face.


Robert and Jesus enter the convent's gallery. It's the old-fashioned term for what today might be called a reception area. But, on the other hand, one doesn't see many rooms like this these days. Not even in a prison, with which it has some similarities. It's a large, high-ceilinged room divided down the middle by a twelve-foot-tall partition of massive iron grille work—like an ornate fence. An inch inside this grille is another obscuring veil of wooden-slatted blinds, nearly closed.

The convent of Our Lady of the Highway is a cloister. Catholic nuns, sisters of the Order of Clementine, once convinced of the authenticity of their calling, enter in behind these bars and remain there for life, never to show their faces to the outside world again. This might seem extreme, even barbaric, to modern sensibilities. But women have been choosing this way of life throughout the centuries. Not a popular choice by any means. Though, for instance, in Europe and elsewhere, in eras of mostly masculine warlike insanity, choosing the cloistered life could seem like a smart move.

Our Lady of the Highway, legend has it, was founded by an independently minded nun who had had enough of the vicious, backstabbing, mercantile and political slaughter of the late 17th century in and around the Dutch West India Company's trading colony of New Amsterdam. The English had finally caught on to the money the Dutch were making hand over fist exploiting the local natural resources and were preparing to force a hostile merger, if not an outright invasion and takeover.

After that, the legend gets a little cloudy.

Who was this Sister Clementine anyway? Did she receive some sort of charter to found the order from the Catholic Church in Rome which was, naturally, woefully under represented in the very Protestant New World colonies? Had she wandered down from the much more French and Catholic colonies in the Montreal area hundreds of miles north? Interested parties were sure to have attempted to ascertain the facts. But one thing or another would come up and interrupt such investigation—usually war.

A hundred or so years later, the Dutch were long gone. The English colonists were now fighting their own government back home. If they were concerned at all about this quiet bastion of Catholic idolatry way out in the woods on the outskirts of Brooklyn, they might have consulted some of their revolutionary-minded French allies. And, in fact, there is some existing correspondence between a French diplomat and the Vatican on record addressing the issue of Catholic monasteries and convents in the New World dating from around this time. But it's inconclusive. Correspondence was slow, letters got lost, ships sank, messengers were executed. And, of course, the church had its own problems closer to home. No one really cared about a houseful of spiritualized virgins growing their own vegetables in a far-flung corner of the English empire.

So, the ladies endured, hardly noticed.

Now, the draped body of Sister Dominique is laying out on a bier in the center of the gallery, her hands clasped at her chest, her rosary beads entwined in her fingers. Father Robert sets down his bag, dons the sleeveless outer vestment called a chasuble, and prepares for the sacrament he is about to administer.

Just inside the iron grille and slatted blinds, Bernadette looks on. Agatha is with her.

"Is that him," the most elderly sister asks, squinting.

"I assume so," replies Bernadette, skeptically.

"He's young, I think."

"And probably incompetent."

Robert has heard this and turns. Jesus only now remembers to remove his cap.

By design, of course, it is difficult to see the nuns through the grille and the blinds. Robert comes closer, friendly and respectful.

"Mother Superior? That you?"

"Good morning, Father. Yes, it's me, Sister Bernadette. Sister Agatha is with me."

"Sisters, I'm sorry for your loss," the young priest says sincerely. But Bernadette surprises him with her calm but imperious reply: "Sister Dominique died well, praying," she insists, "a true bride of Christ. She's with God now."

Though he's touched, Robert is also placed on guard; this elderly nun is tough. Still, he likes strong personalities. He smiles. "Yes, that's true. I'll administer the sacrament now, if you please. We'll arrange for the removal of the body afterwards."

"There will be no need for that, Father. Thank you."

Father Robert is already on his way towards the body. He stops, turns, and hesitates. "Pardon me?"

Jesus steps forward, intruding carefully, raising a finger to indicate the delicacy of the matter. "The sisters, Father, they take care of their own."

"For almost three hundred and fifty years," Bernadette takes over, "the sisters of Our Lady of the Highway have been buried in the graveyard behind the tool shed."

Robert looks to Jesus and the grounds keeper shrugs: it's true. Then, choosing for the moment to stay out of the convent's business, the priest clears his throat and moves ahead:

"I see. Sorry. As you know I'm new to the parish."

Bernadette pulls rank: "Exactly."

But this irritates the young man. He's amiable and obliging, sure, but sees no reason to sustain insults. He's already got his hand raised to make the sign of the cross in the air before him and so begin the sacrament. But he lowers it and comes back towards the grille. "But do we even know if that's legal?"

"Is what legal," Bernadette asks in return, magisterially naive.

"Burying people in—well, behind the tool shed."

Jesus coughs and raises his finger again to make a point but Bernadette shuts him down. "Jesus, I'll handle this," she snaps. "Perhaps you can go to the post office and retrieve our mail."

The man shrugs, overruled, waves goodbye to the priest and shuffles back outside.

Bernadette glances at Agatha. "Sister Agatha, it's nearly time for you to relieve Sister Catherine at vigil."

"Yes, Mother Superior. I'll go now." And as she totters away, she calls out to Robert, girlishly, "Have a good day, Father!"

"Thank you, Sister Agatha. You too."

Bernadette waits for Agatha to depart then approaches the grille. On his side of the divide, Father Robert does the same. They're alone now.

"Mother Superior, I have no wish to interfere with your governance of this convent, but only to offer assistance."

"That's understood," she allows. Then, being unusually magnanimous, adds, "and appreciated."

Robert pauses and tries to evaluate what's implied by this. It's hard to gauge without seeing the sister's face. Sensing she has said all she intends to say for the moment, he carries on: "Since you've requested a new confessor, and since I have been assigned as that confessor, I must assume you are willing to hear some well-considered advice from people who care about you and your sisters."

He waits to see how this sounds to her.

Bernadette, in fact, does consider his point judiciously. She steps aside and sits in a chair beside the grille.

"Continue."

Robert suspects this curt little response is a positive sign and his only chance to make some headway. He pulls up a seat and sits close to the partition as well.

"First of all," he insists, "there are too few of you to continue the vigil."

"The vigil must be maintained!"

"Of course," he says, backing off.

"Not one interruption in three hundred and forty-seven years!"

Robert is genuinely amazed. He shakes his head and concedes: "I know. It's a miracle."

"No! Not a miracle," the mother superior insists, "determination, commitment, submission, discipline!"

"Of course," Robert agrees, though he's not entirely sure.

"But you need more and younger sisters to carry on with this."

"Easier said than done, Father Robert," she admits. "Far and few between are the women with the necessary mettle. I've tried for years. There aren't many of us left."

Here comes the hard part, he thinks—the crux of the matter: "Well, in fact, I've discussed this with the bishop and we've found a few good nuns who might be just what you need."

Bernadette is taken aback. She hadn't suspected this new young pastor would be so forthcoming about the convent. It's almost reassuring except that—

"The bishop," she asks, suspiciously.

"Yes."

"He can't be trusted," she states flatly.

Robert is stunned and, for a moment, he's at a loss for words.

"Why do you say that," he asks, finally.

"He's a politician. What's he know about being a nun?"

"Well, ah…" Robert fumbles.

But she doesn't require an answer anyway.

"A man of the world," Bernadette continues, "compromised by the *ways* of the world!"

Father Robert is suddenly exhausted. He looks across at the peacefully inert body of Sister Dominique and envies her.

Three weeks earlier, Father Robert is sitting in the hallway of diocesan headquarters, across from Sister Ellen, the bishop's devoted and battle-hardened secretary, arguing about parking lots. "But the parking lot is only for parishioners," the busy sister explains.

"Who only come there on Sunday, at best," Robert points

out, then: "What I'm suggesting…"

But she can't allow him to go that far: "The diocese is very clear on this."

"On what—the use of empty parking lots?"

"Yes. It must discourage commercialism of church property."

"But, if I may, we do pass around a collection plate during the Mass itself."

"That's different."

"Is it?"

"I guess. It's donations. I'm not an accountant, Father. It has to do with New York State sales tax or something."

By now, the priest is up on his feet, pacing, strategizing, reaching for solutions. "It's an empty parking lot six days out of the week," he resumes. "If we ask people, say, to donate a certain amount so as to be able to park their cars there we could parlay that into the funds needed to fix the daycare center's roof…"

But the phone rings.

"Hold on," Sister Ellen says, lifting the receiver. "Yes," she replies to some unheard question, then: "Right. Okay." She hangs up and looks at Robert. "The bishop is on his way up."

Down in the street, Bishop Thomas Frank steps out of a black town car and makes for the diocese building, smiling broadly, waving to his many fans, and muscling his way past angry journalists and invasive TV camera crews. Handsome, tough, and with a military bearing, he signs autographs, shakes hands with the faithful, and avoids microphones thrust in his face. There's a lot of screaming going on and he allows his three younger, more agile priest-bodyguards to guide him to the lobby. Once inside, his smile evaporates. He stomps up the stairs to the second floor. Reaching the landing, he heads straight for his office.

"Sister Ellen, get our publicists on the line. And leave a message with what's-his-name at the cardinal's office in Rome. Postpone the conference call—" He spots Robert and stops. "Father Robert! What are you doing here?"

Robert stands. "We have an appointment—I think."

"Do we," the bishop asks, relieved. "Excellent! I need to talk to a sane individual. Come on in here."

They disappear beyond Frank's office door.

Lola steps nervously into the cubicle she shares with Meg, who is clearing off her own desk and moving elsewhere. She grabs her coat and starts to leave, but Drake stops her.

"Lola, how's it going with policy 17,834?"

"That would be the Wilson family, Mister Drake, and their five-year-old daughter with multiple sclerosis."

"Don't let it get personal, Lola. It's just a policy."

Punching her fists into the sleeves of her coat, she decides for good: "I quit."

Drake has heard this before from a long line of fairly decent young people horrified by the reality of the insurance adjuster's job. He comes closer, amorously, and Lola stiffens with rage: "Easy," he coaxes. "Come on, Lola, you're up for a raise soon. What are you doing after work? Let's have a drink and discuss."

Lola backs away and knocks a computer monitor off a desk. She raises her hand, palm out, and stops her boss as she stares at the carpet. "Don't," she begins urgently, but then ends in almost a whisper, "…touch me."

Drake falls back in mock alarm, stands aside, and allows Lola to flee.

Bishop Frank's office at diocesan headquarters in Brooklyn is a sort of military situation room with strategic maps on the walls, a few globes, and computer screens displaying various real-time analytics. At sixty-four, he's got the energy and rough good looks of a man half his age. An army veteran, he's never really stopped being a soldier. The diocese is his theater of operations.

"What time is it," he asks Father Robert as he strides in.

"Three-fifteen," replies the priest, taking his first look around at the commander's inner sanctum.

"Good enough." The bishop grabs a bottle of scotch and two glasses from off a shelf. Pausing, he looks over and asks, "You?"

Though he likes his beer, Robert is not a whiskey kind of guy. But how can he pass up an opportunity to hang out with one of the few men of the cloth he's always looked up to. He nods affirmatively. "Sure."

"Grab some ice from the mini bar there."

So, they fix their drinks, enjoy them, and stand silently on either side of the bishop's counter-height map table where the progress of various campaigns of spiritual enlightenment are displayed. Time slows down. The pressure of events ease. These two thoughtful men acquire the necessary perspective. Finally, the bishop sighs and asks: "What am I going to do about this priest in Staten Island caught having sex with boys on the junior high school soccer team?"

The issue is as clear as day for Father Robert. "Cut him loose."

Frank looks up, pauses, impressed. "Excommunication?"

"Well, the church can have mercy. But you must allow the civil authorities to prosecute."

Frank agrees. He nods and turns away to pace the room, brooding. "The cardinal wants me to transfer him somewhere."

Five minutes ago, Robert would never have imagined he'd be venturing his own two cents to help the bishop reach a decision about anything. But before he can even think about it, he blurts out: "That's pointless," and immediately feels like an idiot.

"Yeah, I know," the bishop concurs, "it's weaklings like this who give the church a bad name." He drains his scotch, contemplates the ceiling, and shakes his head. "You know, you'd think a life of sexual abstinence was the hardest thing you could ask of a man."

Young Father Robert needs to look aside and think about this. It's true, it was not hard for him as a teenager to embrace a life of celibacy and devote his life to God. But maybe that was only because he'd never *had* sex and was so shy and awkward. It's easy to give up something you've never had and can hardly imagine. But by his late twenties, already ordained, he'd grown into himself, acquired an easygoing confidence and—as many people noted—was not at all bad looking. And by thirty years of age the molecules of his body realigned themselves somehow so that, all of a sudden, he saw the wonders of feminine beauty all around him. A girl's bare arm beside him on the subway was a wonder. Faces, ankles, knees; all cause for rejoicing. But he, of course, as a boy on fire with the revelation of God's promise of eternal life, had chosen to forego all that.

Robert dates his real dedication to the faith from about that time, his late twenties, when he was, finally, fully cognizant of what he had sacrificed. For now, though, he sighs, shrugs, sips his scotch, and quotes: "'Many are called but few may follow.'"

This simple old standby hits the bishop like the voice of the prophets themselves, like a book thrown at his head. He comes back to the map table. "Damn straight. And I know of what I speak." He pours himself another scotch and drops in an ice cube. "I'm not a holy man, Father, I'm just devout. I've been in love my entire adult life."

While the great man savors his second whiskey, Robert waits. The word love can be made to mean all sorts of things in the spiritual life, and he assumes he'll learn, now, what metaphorical relevance the bishop is referring to. The bishop, in fact, sees Robert's expression and moves to clarify:

"And not just spiritually. Not just emotionally. Sexually."

He takes a picture down off the wall. It's of a pretty nun, aged about twenty. Carrying it back over, he places it on the map table and allows the younger man to view it at his leisure. With no trace of pride or embarrassment, the bishop continues: "Sister Tatiana-Magdalena dos Santos e Ramirez. The best nun there is and the sexiest woman alive. I was a wreck. I joined the army. Went to war. Even that didn't help. But if I couldn't have that woman, I didn't want another. Finally, I took orders just to keep from committing sacrilege."

He takes the picture and hangs it back up on the wall. He stands aside and admires the love of his life a moment longer. Then, sighing, he turns and shrugs: "We were younger then, of course."


Lola hurries down Seventh Avenue in Manhattan and ducks left into Twenty-First Street. Rain is threatening. But she knows where she's going.

This otherwise unnamed Bar & Grill is empty at four in

the afternoon. It will fill up just after five when everyone gets off work. But Lola is relieved to be alone and slides up onto a barstool.

"What can I get you, miss," asks the bartender.

"I want a frozen margarita," she begins, "a pint of Stella Artois—draft—a glass of water with ice, a shot of Jameson's and a hot chocolate. But if you don't have hot chocolate a cappuccino will be fine."

The man has to process this. Then, politely, he asks, "You mean, like, all at once?"

"Yeah. And a straw, please. Thanks."

As the bartender goes about preparing this wild collection of drinks, Lola lays her bag on the stool beside her and rests her head on her folded arms. It's been ten years since she came to New York and somehow found a job—for a while. That ended and she found another job. And then another. And so on. There was waitressing that led to dog walking that led to cleaning toilets that led to table dancing which led to something she still suspects was a bona fide nervous break-down. About three years ago, though, after a month-long occupational training course in business administration, she wound up as a receptionist at Rutledge Insurance and found she enjoyed the work. She was good at it. Phone work was easy and natural for her. And she discovered she had a gift for inventory and expediting. All the postal workers and the Federal Express guys fell in love with her because she knew how to sort things out quickly and make their jobs that much easier.

Things were looking up.

Unfortunately, she responded to the attentions she aroused in her new boss, Richard Drake. He gave her a raise and moved her from her happy place in Reception to being a sort of company spy on the clients their product, insurance, was supposed to protect. She was handed a license and taught all sorts of ways to discredit a client's claim to compensation in order to save the corporation from having to pay what it owed.

This was about the time of the incident.

But just now, her boyfriend enters the bar.

Leo is forty, handsome, unassuming, and a junior high school math teacher. He's good with kids and that might explain something about how he's managed to deal with Lola for just over a year. He shakes himself free of rain, tosses aside his umbrella, and comes to her cautiously. He kisses her chastely on the neck and she clings to him like a life raft.

"You really did it," he asks, "you quit?"

"I couldn't take it anymore."

"It's okay. Good for you."

"I stopped a clock and I made a glass of water explode."

Leo loosens his tie and puts up with this. He's used to it. The bartender, though, has heard it too and, clearing his throat, politely looks away.

"Did you see the psychiatrist," Leo asks at last, sitting.

"Yeah. She said I have guilt issues I have to deal with."

"Right, okay," he starts, supportive, proactive, though he finds the professional advise a little lame, "that's a start. So, how do we go about that?"

"Well, Leo," Lola suggests, frustrated, "I guess I usually deal with my guilt feelings by shattering glass, making lights go out, stopping clocks, and even causing car accidents and the deaths of young children if I'm really particularly conscience stricken. I think. Right?"

He places his hand on hers. "You did not cause that kid to get run over by a bus, Lola. He ran into traffic."

"No. I wanted to hurt him. I was angry. And that's what happens."

The bartender waits for the right time and brings Lola's assortment of drinks. He backs away carefully, trying to make himself invisible. But Leo stops him:

"Can I get a beer? Draft. Thanks."

Lola takes the straw and sips alternately from one drink and another. The bartender pours Leo's beer and watches this strange ritual from afar. Leo, catching the man's troubled expression, throws down some cash. He takes the beer as it is slid across the bar. "Thanks," he says, lifting the mug to his lips. But he stops when Lola announces:

"I need to enter a convent."


Robert finishes the sacrament and makes the sign of the cross over the body of Sister Dominique. He removes his chasuble, sets aside his bible, and returns to the partition. Bernadette is waiting on the other side.

"So, Mother Superior, what do you think?"

"If the vigil were able to be perpetuated and the hours reduced for each of my sisters," she admits, considering the implications one more time, "yes, I'd welcome help from the bishop and from the parish of Saint Ann's."

"And…"

"And, yes, perhaps a new mother superior to replace me is a good idea."

"You've been at it a long time."

"It might be nice not to be the boss."

This is all good. These are major concessions and Robert is pleased. "Good," he says, thinking that perhaps this is enough to attempt on his first meeting with the cranky mother superior. However, Bernadette is curious and keeps him from leaving.

"But who are these nuns, anyway," she asks.

Father Robert is caught half out of his seat. He stalls a moment, casting about for possibilities. Bernadette waits and sits forward in her chair, an ear to the blinds. Robert sits back down and decides she doesn't need to know the whole truth.


The winter sun is setting over the diocese of Brooklyn. The bishop and Father Robert are comfortably aglow with their third scotch.

"Your reverence, I have in fact come to seek your advice about a convent in my parish going through some hard times."

"Which one," asks the bishop, jumping up from his seat and approaching the wall map. He loves a new crisis to confront.

"Our Lady of the Highway."

"Oh, yes. Order of Clementine. Mother Superior goes by the name Sister Bernadette, no?"

"That's her," admits the priest.

"Major pain in the ass, that woman. But a good Catholic. What's the issue?"

"They've been praying for world peace nonstop for three hundred and forty-seven years," Robert explains, as much for his own benefit as for the bishop's. He can hardly believe it. "Cloistered, cut off from the outside world, living with only the barest necessities."

"Tough broads, no denying it."

"But there's only four sisters left and they're all over seventy. The prioress, Sister Dominique, is almost a hundred."

The bishop wanders back to the map table, doing the math:

"Four elderly sisters doing six-hour shifts of prayer

twenty-four seven?"

"Exactly."

"There ought to be a law about this type of thing," the bishop decides and tosses back the last of his drink.

"They need more and younger nuns," Robert asserts, waiting while the bishop cogitates. There is a lot that goes through his head each day that he tries to spare his subordinates.

"This is bound to appear selfish and maybe misguided, Father," the older man admits, "but the person to solve our problems out at Our Lady of the Highway is, well—" He gestures to the framed photo on the wall, "Sister Tatiana-Magdalena."

Are red flags raised somewhere along the watchtower of the young priest's conscience?

Certainly.

Might it be a problem to bring to Brooklyn a nun the bishop is in love with?

Probably.

But in the seven years of his experience as an ordained Catholic priest, when has he not been forced to fix one problem by making use of another? What crisis has he avoided without causing a second crisis a little less urgent? Isn't it so that his vocation provides him with nothing but catastrophe? Calamity is the material he works with. Other walks of life deal in success. Being a Catholic, as he sees it, is to swim against the tide on principle. He can't let these four elderly sisters out in Brooklyn wear themselves out with an effort of mystical charity the rest of the world doesn't even know or care about.

"I wouldn't presume to doubt your judgment of her character," Robert allows. "And, in any event, we're not in a position to be terribly discriminating, are we?"

Bishop Frank likes this young man more and more every time they meet. "Exactly," he exclaims, slapping the map table. "It's an emergency and, besides, Sister Magdalena needs a place to hide."

Perhaps there are now many more red flags fluttering in the wind above the battlements of Robert's goodwill. He sips his scotch.

"Excuse me?"

"She's wanted dead or alive by various governments, ours included," the bishop explains, splashing himself another drink. "Her specialty is the destruction of armaments. She sunk a US cargo ship loaded with guns destined for a right-wing coup in Venezuela over a decade ago. She's also a genius at opening family planning clinics and organizing labor unions." He turns aside and paces. "Damn it, it's all I can do to keep the Vatican from excommunicating her. A US automobile manufacturer tried to assassinate her at least once."

By now, Father Robert is simply inspired. "Well, Our Lady of the Highway is a cloister," he points out. "Once she goes in, no one will see her again."

"The perfect place to hide," the bishop nods, way ahead of him.

"Where is she now," Robert asks.

"Hard to say. But we have a number."

"A number?"

Bishop Frank crosses to his desk and reaches for the inter-com, explaining as he goes: "Some lo-fi espionage to help her stay off the grid." Pressing a button and leaning forward, the bishop asks, "Sister Ellen, can you come in here a minute?" Leaning back, he gazes at Robert and adds: "This might become intricate."

Ellen enters. "Yes, Your Reverence?"

"Sister, can you dial the number, please?"

Sister Ellen has been by the bishop's side for years. Reference to the number causes her to make an adjustment to her customary loyal submission and, casting a glance around, she isolates the glasses and the half-empty bottle of scotch. She proceeds with cautious, gentle, respect. "Really?"

"Yes," he confirms, no worse for wear given the three and a half scotches.

Ellen hesitates, then comes into the room and dutifully straightens up, recapping the bottle and returning it to the shelf. "Are you sure," she asks, casting a withering glance at Father Robert.

"It's for the greater glory of God, Sister," Frank declares, staring a hole in his desk blotter.

"I'm sure, your reverence, of course. But—" She sighs, comes right around in front of his desk, and waits for him to look up at her.

He does.

"But think about your feelings," Ellen advises at last.

He nods. He trusts her. "I can handle it," he says.

"Remember last time."

"I know," he concedes, "it's dangerous. And if the cardinal finds out, we're done for."

Robert feels like a loser, an enabler, selfishly having taken advantage of the bishop's fondness for a midafternoon drink and friendly, manly, discussion. He puts down his whiskey and comes forward: "Maybe I can talk to her directly myself," he suggests, even pleads.

Back at the Bar & Grill, Leo is stunned, his beer still halfway to his mouth. "What," he asks.

"This lady I work with, Meg, she said I should see a priest," Lola explains. "She thinks I'm possessed by the devil or something."

Leo is getting angry on Lola's behalf. "And who the fuck is she when she's at home?"

"She's born again. Prays all the time. Always handing out pamphlets—crazy shit."

"Lola, you are not possessed by the devil."

"God, I hope not," she sighs and continues sipping her assortment of drinks.

"A convent... I mean, you're not even Catholic, are you?"

"I was, once, I guess. When I was a kid. I received my confirmation in the fourth grade. I wonder if it expires or something, like a driver's license?"

Leo has no idea. He was raised without religion. He shrugs and, finally, sips his beer. "I know a priest."

This surprises Lola. She herself doesn't know anyone even marginally Catholic. "At the school," she asks.

"No, at the bar around the corner from my place in Brooklyn. He's the pastor of this church called Saint Ann's on Metropolitan Boulevard."

Watching his profile, Lola remembers once again how good Leo is at calming her nerves. How does he do it, she wonders. She knows she's not easy. He's the only regular boyfriend she's ever had. "You know I'm not crazy, right," she asks. "I'm just emotionally challenged."

He turns to her, pauses, and wonders again how this young woman has changed his life. He hasn't got many friends, but the ones he does have think Lola is both stunning and out of her mind. They think Leo has the patience of a saint. "Honestly, Lola," he admits, "I don't know. But I'm willing to stick with you and find out."

She caresses his cheek, enjoying the fine stubble of his two-day-old beard. "You're handsome," she says with relief.

"Thanks," he replies.

Then her mobile phone rings and she reads the screen. "Oh man. I have to take this." It's one of the clients she needs to inform about her decision to quit the firm. She wants to give the man tips on circumventing Rutledge's tactics for evading claims. She kisses Leo and runs outside without her umbrella. He watches her go, admiring her figure, and then turns back to the bartender.

"I guess she's a lot of work, huh?"

Leo nods and lifts his mug. "She's special."

"She always order like that," the bartender wonders, nodding at the collection of beverages.

"Yeah," Leo replies, "that combination of stimulants and depressants keeps her in a zone where nothing happens."

"What could happen?"

"Oh, you'd be surprised how many streetlights I've seen go out just by her passing by below." He drinks, then: "Truly, it's unusual." He stands and works out a kink in his neck. "Yeah, and there is the breaking glassware. The bent spoons. The computers that crash when she's very emotional." He walks over to the window. "And like this. Look, it's pouring rain over there on Sixth Avenue and it's pouring rain out that way on Seventh. But it's not raining on West Twenty-First Street."

"It was just a minute ago," the bartender says, joining Leo. They watch as Lola has her phone conversation on the sidewalk twenty feet away from the downpour on Seventh Avenue. "Well that maybe can be explained possibly by some kind of rare weather pattern or, you know—whatever."

"Hmmm," Leo concurs, skeptically. "I read somewhere, too, about how collisions of radio frequencies in densely populated metropolitan areas have been known to deflect precipitation and reduce humidity."

This really impresses the bartender: "No shit."

"Yeah," Leo assures him.

"Amazing the stuff science can explain these days, right?" And he walks back to the bar, reassured, as Leo ponders his girlfriend's magic powers.

"Hmmm," he repeats.


Father Robert exits one of the ground floor service entrances at the back of the diocese building and crosses the street as the last rays of the winter sun warm the structure's heavy limestone facade. He makes for a neglected pay phone that hasn't been used in decades. Reaching it, he looks around warily and then back up at the building.

Up on the second floor, beside her desk, holding aside the window curtain, Sister Ellen huffs just slightly, annoyed. Confirming the priest is in position, she lifts a mobile device and punches in a number she reads from a slip of paper.

Enrique is working at a drill press in a loud and busy factory in Honduras. His mobile device vibrates in his shirtfront pocket. He stops, removes his goggles, and reaches for the phone. All he has to do is see the number and he snaps to attention in spite of himself.

"Sí," he answers dutifully.

Sister Ellen stares at the nearest wall for a moment, wondering if she should proceed or not. But then she responds as expected: "*de la cruz.*"

That's all Enrique needs to hear. He hangs up, looks across the factory floor to a woman named Susanna, and lightly pounds his chest with his clenched fist. Susanna nods, understanding. She switches off her machine, steps into the ladies' room, pulls out her own phone, and begins texting someone else.

Rabbi Lebowitz is shepherding a few torturously bored Jewish lads through their Hebrew lesson. He pauses, though, when his mobile device chimes. Standing back, he reads Susanna's text. He, too, knows exactly what to do, though he doesn't hurry. He finds a post-it note and scribbles on it: "*de la cruz*".

Moments later, Stephen Greenblatt, the most hopeless of the rabbi's Hebrew scholars, is speeding along on his skateboard through the windy streets of an American suburb, out of his mind with happiness, on a mission from God. He skids to a dramatic finish in the open doorway of a local mosque, interrupting a class of young people practicing their Arabic. The elderly cleric, Iman Said, approaches, amused, and receives the note. Studying it, he nods appreciatively to the boy and gestures for his class to follow him upstairs.

Up on the roof, the kids look on, fascinated, as Said attaches a tiny message to the leg of a pigeon and lets the bird fly away.

Elsewhere, an elderly Monsignor is drilling a class of young Catholic seminary students—men preparing for the priesthood—in ancient Greek. He notices the pigeon alight on the classroom's windowsill.

Moments later, he's got the miniscule note and sets the bird free. He reads it, rolls it into a spitball, and turns to one of his students.

"Let the sexton know our sister has a call."

The young seminarian sprints across campus, through cloistered walkways, and over well tended lawns.

The sexton is the man who takes care of the church and is in charge of ringing the bells. "So, it's one big one followed by two little ones," he instructs the young man, then adds, "twice."

The seminarian is eager to oblige though he has no idea what's going on. "Right."

"You do the little ones," the sexton continues, grabbing the ropes leading high up into the steeple. "Here goes." He tugs and a slow low-timbre gong resounds. Then he points at the kid who tugs the other rope twice, creating two higher pitched clangs.

Finally, in a nearby supermarket, a cashier pauses as she hears the church bells and glances askew at her present customer. "That's odd."

The customer agrees as she hands the girl some cash:

"Never heard the church bells ring like that before."

But in a nearby aisle, two plainly-dressed women are listening intently, responding to the bells as if alerted. Though unassuming and down-to-earth, Tatiana-Magdalena is pretty and sophisticated. Her companion, Evelyn, is younger and rugged. They drift towards one another from opposite ends of the produce section, practically huddling like little sisters in a thunderstorm.

In the distance, the peculiar sequence chimes again.

Tatiana-Magdalena and Evelyn glance at one another, nod in wordless understanding, and move towards the exit as inconspicuously as they can. Exiting, they have to look around before finding their younger friend, Veronica. She's studying fashion footwear in a nearby shop window. Evelyn grabs her by the wrist and leads the way. They weave through busy pedestrians and up the sidewalk of this small nondescript Middle American city. Finding a payphone, the women sort through their assorted loose change. Tatiana-Magdalena approaches the phone and Evelyn stands guard, scanning the middle distance for trouble.

Father Robert is reading his breviary when the pay phone rings in Brooklyn. Startled, and cold, he drops the thick little book. Picking it back up off the sidewalk, he lifts the chunky old graffiti-scarred receiver: "Hello?"

Tatiana-Magdalena pauses, but then turns out, away from the phone, and answers: "How am I needed?"

Two months later, at the convent of Our Lady of the Highway, Sister Catherine makes her way slowly down the stairs and approaches the basilica. Sister Bernadette lies prostrate on the floor before the large high altar, reciting prayers in Latin: "*Pater noster, qui es in caelis, sanctificetur nomen, dimit-timus debitoribus…*"

Catherine lowers herself to her knees, makes the sign of the cross, and taps Bernadette on the shoulder. She herself then lies face down on the floor and begins praying, taking up exactly where Bernadette leaves off: "*Fiat voluntas tua, sicut in cælo et in terra, da nobis hodie…*"

Bernadette raises herself stiffly from the floor, delirious with fatigue. Standing, she turns to the altar, genuflects, gets her bearings, and makes her way to the door.

Coming up the wide stone steps from the basilica and reaching the main hall, the elderly nun pauses for breath before crossing to a smaller staircase leading up to the dormitories. She frowns as she has to pass by the suspicious new young Sister Veronica, who is working hard but clumsily to remove planks of old wood covering the windows. Veronica pauses in her work, timid, as Bernadette stomps on by.

"So be it," the older nuns grumbles, "but that's where those godless miscreants broke in back in 1983." Then she stops and indicates Veronica's old, scuffed, slightly heeled boots: "Those are not regulation footwear."

But then they both look off at the sounds of some fierce demolition happening further along the main hall.

"What in God's name—" Bernadette mutters as she goes off to investigate.

In the vestry—the offices where the convent's simple business matters were once dealt with—Sisters Magdalena and Evelyn are busting up old furniture and knocking buckling plaster off the walls. They're wearing tool belts and sporting protective goggles. The air is thick with dust.

Bernadette arrives and takes all this in, tired but furious: "Sisters!"

Just barely able to wield an eight-pound sledgehammer, Magdalena checks her swing and looks over. She smiles carefully. She's been expecting this. Bernadette took an instant dislike to her the day she arrived. She's dropped the Tatiana from her name too, not wanting to risk burdening the older nuns with the knowledge they are harboring an internationally wanted outlaw.

"Ah! Sister Bernadette! Good morning."

"What's going on here? What are you doing to the vestry!"

The new mother superior sets aside the sledgehammer, removes her goggles, and approaches excitedly: "We're turning it into a brewery!

This knocks the the wind out of the senior nun. She finds a place to sit. "Oh, my Lord," she prays, "what is to become of your holy church on earth!"

Magdalena sits beside Bernadette and reassures her:

"Sister, the convent needs an income."

"Charity from the faithful has always sufficed."

"Well, not really. At least not for about forty years."

Bernadette finds this small statement of fact threatening:

"And what would you know about it?"

Evelyn, with an unlit cigarette clenched in her teeth, senses contention. "I'll take this junk outside," she says and drags some demolished furniture out into the hall.

"Sister Bernadette," Magdalena begins, "I'm aware you resent the bishop's appointment of me as Mother Superior. But we must make the best of it."

"That man's an idiot."

"Who?"

"The bishop."

"He has a difficult job."

"You've put a spell on him!"

"Oh! Please, Sister! Such superstition!"

Bernadette stands and paces, trying to control herself. She has decades of experience sizing up nuns. This one, she decided almost immediately, ought to be in the movies and nowhere near a convent. "It's your foreign ways. Your charm. You're progressive views. Your *joie de vivre*! Are you wearing lipstick? Anyway, the bishop is in love with you."

Magdalena wonders just how much Bernadette knows about her and the bishop. Great effort has been made to shield the older sisters from any knowledge of her radical activist credentials. But her and the bishop—that's something else all together.

"Sister, I assure you, the bishop is not in love with anyone and is wholly devoted to God's church on earth and all its servants, including this, the convent of Our Lady of the Highway."

Bernadette is at the end of her rope. So protective is she of the convent, she actually caresses the old brick wall she supports herself against as she launches into her regular and expected litany: "The convent's been here for three hundred and fifty years!"

"Yes, I know," Magdalena admits. She's heard this a lot before.

"Before the diocese was established!"

"Of course."

"Doing the Lord's work before there was even a country here!"

"Understood."

"And we never needed to open a brewery!"

Okay, at least this is new. Magdalena brightens up, hearing something she can finally argue with: "Well, times change," she announces sweetly.

"They certainly do," Bernadette replies confidently. "But we will resist it to the end!"

"There is a long, healthy tradition of nuns being industrious and producing a product to help support their spiritual aims."

"Beer?"

"Why not?"

"It makes people drunk."

"It makes them laugh, too. It helps them sing."

"And frolic."

"Pardon me?"

"You know what I mean. It's a sensual indulgence. It causes car accidents!"

And with that, Bernadette strides across the room and exits, slamming the door behind her.

Magdalena is weary. Her indefatigable optimism and can-do attitude has been harder to sustain of late. She checks her wristwatch. So much to do, and the days so short. And what does Bernadette know about herself and the bishop anyway? Of course, there is nothing to repent of in that chapter of her life but, nevertheless, there was a bit of a scandal. Still, that would suggest that Bernadette suspects who she, Magdalena, really is. No, that's impossible, Magdalena decides. This good, devout, conservative, veteran nun would never have allowed it.

But now she hears a commotion in the hallway.

Stepping out from the vestry, Magdalena is nearly knocked down by a teenage boy running frantically by. Something hits the floor and she sees it's a handgun. Startled, she reaches down and snatches it up as the boy, Xavier, climbs out a window at the far end of the hall and scrambles away across the roof.

Magdalena comes a few steps further up the hall, checking the firearm with casual expertise to make sure it is—as she expected—unloaded. She finds Evelyn and Veronica beating up another teenage boy, Vincent, who brandishes both a handgun and a pair of silver candlesticks. Evelyn wrenches the gun from Vincent and pauses when she hears a small bell chime. She glances at Veronica and the younger nun hurries off.

Veronica comes running into the darkened inner gallery. Jesus is waiting with Lola outside the partition. The blinds are closed and the young sister peeks out: "Hello! Sorry. Just doing some chores. I'm Sister Veronica."

"Sister," Jesus reports, "this girl here says she's got an appointment."

"How may we be of assistance and, of course, God be with you," Veronica greets her confusedly.

Curious but exasperated, Lola replies: "Hi. I'm Lola. I have an appointment with—"

But she and Jesus have to jump aside as Evelyn comes banging through the gate dragging Vincent. She throws the kid out on his ass and he slides across the outer gallery till he hits the far wall.

Jesus watches, wide-eyed—best not to mess with the new prioress, he thinks. Lola—for a second—sees Evelyn and Veronica plainly before they remember to slam the gate shut. Vincent scrambles for the exit and disappears with the candlesticks, Evelyn calling after him: "And be sure to tell your boss we have your gun!" She lights a cigarette, shaking her head, muttering: "Idiot." Then, exhaling, she gestures to the girl outside. "Who's this now," she asks. Veronica is peeking out through the blinds, studying Lola's feet.

"I really like those shoes."

Having overheard this, Lola calls, tentatively: "I have an appointment with the prioress."

Evelyn hands Vincent's gun to Veronica and looks out through the blinds. "That's me."


Eight blocks away is a place called Margaret's Bar. No one's really sure who Margaret is—or was. The place is run by a tough, young-seeming woman named Chastity who has a lot of tattoos. It's a clean but faded old Brooklyn beer hall sparsely populated with retired workmen. It's also just been discovered by a small gang of fresh-faced younger people with electronic devices. They look up as Father Robert enters, puts his briefcase down, and sits at the bar.

The natural leader, spokesman, and all-around savant of this low-key but stylish clique—Charles—looks positively challenged by the existence of a Catholic priest three stools away from himself.

Robert notices. "What," he says, trying not to appear defensive.

"For real," Charles asks, sincerely.

"Yeah," Robert admits, "I know the neighborhood's changing, but this is my regular place."

Just then, Leo walks in, nods to Chastity, and approaches the priest. They're marginally acquainted with one another by way of being the only Red Sox fans in the neighborhood who both use Margaret's as a place to wind down after work.

"Excuse me, Father," Leo begins, "are you on duty? Can we talk a minute?"

Robert drags the beer Chastity has just poured for him across the bar and sips. "Sure. You mind if I have my beer?"

"Not at all," he assures him. "May I join you?"

"Certainly."

"I'm Leo."

Charles and his crowd find all this terribly exotic and they observe from a polite distance as the men shake hands.

"Father Robert," the youthful priest introduces himself. "What's up?"

Likewise, Leo pulls his beer to himself, sips, and explains:

"My girlfriend wants to enter a convent."

Conversation stops. Leo and Robert have everyone's attention, old and young alike: aged plumbers, carpenters between jobs, real estate agents on the skids, the busy young hipsters. Robert and Leo pause and look around as everyone dives back into whatever it is they were doing.

But curiosity hangs like smoke in the air.

Over at the convent, Lola sits in a stiff-backed wooden chair in the outer gallery before the partition. Jesus is about to return outside to the garden but turns and indicates the lock on the door.

"When you're ready, you can unlock this and leave."

Lola hesitates. "Okay," she says, wondering if she should make a run for it now and forget the whole thing. But Jesus goes out, closes the door, and Lola listens as the key is turned in the lock. Then, all of a sudden, the blinds behind the iron grille ripple up and out of the way, revealing Sister Evelyn.

"Who knows you're here," the prioress asks, blowing smoke out one end of her mouth.

"I was sent by Father Robert of Saint Ann's Church," Lola replies obediently.

Veronica rushes in from further back in the convent and happily announces: "The mother superior will see Miss Lola now."

Sister Evelyn makes way for the mother superior who is heard striding up the hallway. Lola rises slowly to her feet as well, not sure what the proper etiquette is. But if she is scared, uncertain, or feels inadequate, all stress leaves her as the happy, quick-witted, and attractive mother superior appears in the doorway thirty feet away.

Confident, preoccupied, serious but smiling, Magdalena is uncomplicated, graceful and selfless even as she pauses to slip a handgun into her ankle boot. Lola finds herself drifting towards the iron grille partition to accept the mother superior's offered hand.

"You must be Lola," the mother superior asks musically. "I'm Sister Magdalena and welcome to Our Lady of the Highway."

TWO

Let's go back a little, to just before Lola is introduced to the sisters.

Leo has rented a car and is driving Lola to her interview at the convent of Our Lady of the Highway. It is far from the nearest subway and no buses have rumbled down these neglected streets in decades. Lola tries to stay positive but her face betrays a little more skepticism with each turn into yet another avenue of urban wasteland.

"What goes on around here," she wonders aloud.

"Waste management, I guess," Leo replies, glancing over at a parking lot full of garbage trucks. He's much less divided about this whole adventure. He's obviously worried about Lola coming to live in this godforsaken wilderness. "I don't know, Lola," he mutters ominously.

"I think that's it," she replies, pointing.

They pull up across from a little door in a vast brick wall that runs the length of the street. Far down on the right they can see the top of the convent building itself, though it could be just another derelict warehouse. Warily, Lola gets out and approaches, checking again the address she has written on a

scrap of paper. There is, in fact, a number on the door, scrawled in black Magic Marker and faded almost to invisibility.

"This is it, I guess," she admits without enthusiasm and
reaches up to a cheap little doorbell seven feet off the ground
adhered to the brick wall with nails, staples, and duct tape. It
glows feebly and a small weathered tag beneath it announces:
*visitors*.

Leo joins her and reaches up towards the button himself.

"You sure you want to do this?"

She's not. But before she can answer, the door is shoved
open and Jesus peeks out. They jump back. He sizes them up.
"Yeah," he asks, threatening, territorial, or just afraid—it's
hard to tell.

Inside the convent at this very moment, Sister Evelyn, wearing a tool belt and protective goggles, is about to toss some
rotted planks onto a refuse pile at the end of the hall. But she
stops when she sees Sister Veronica, pale and alarmed, silently gesticulating towards an adjacent hallway. Evelyn comes
forward, peeks around a corner into an old storage area, and
sees two teenage boys, Vincent and Xavier, brandishing
handguns and looking around for stuff to steal.

"Look, Vincent, these candlesticks must be worth something," Xavier says, the younger of the two.

His cousin is a braggart and must always have the last
word. "Nah, ain't no one uses candles no more but like my
grandmother."

But he takes them anyway.

Xavier is nervous. He doesn't know how to hold the gun
and tries to emulate Vincent's cocksure swagger: "Where
these sisters at, anyway," he tries on for size.

"Yeah, let's put some fear o' God into these brides of

Christ an' shit."

But as they step out into the hall, Evelyn and Veronica tackle them. Immediately overpowered, Xavier runs away and collides with Sister Magdalena. He drops his gun and she retrieves it as the kid reaches an open window and climbs back out onto the roof of the old carriage house. Meanwhile, Vincent puts up more of a fight and takes a few vicious punches before Evelyn gets his gun.

Now, as we've seen, she pauses when she hears a small bell chiming and Veronica is sent to see who's calling.

Out in the street, Leo is leaning back against the car, waiting. But something catches his eye and he thinks he sees some skinny little kid scrambling across the roof of the convent. He comes away from the car and drifts down the street to get a better angle. But Xavier is nowhere to be seen. Then, just as Leo is about to return to the car, the kid appears at the corner of the convent wall.

Leo stops and turns.

Xavier freezes.

They stare at one another.

Xavier turns and runs away down the adjacent street. Leo hesitates but then follows at a jog, mostly just curious about what's around the corner. Once there's a safe distance between them, Xavier slows to a walk, casting cautious glances back at the stranger. He recedes into the distance and vanishes into an alley. As far as Leo can see, there is nothing much to speak of in this second street either. The wall of the convent stretches for what looks like two city blocks before reaching some sort of a creek or canal.

He heads back down the street, wondering how his class is getting on, sixteen gifted seventh-grade mathematicians in a public junior high school he's been teaching at for three years. He likes the kids. Advanced Math, though, might be cut from the curriculum and his job cease to exist. He got a heads-up from one of his colleagues. It's been determined mathematics is better taught online.

But his thoughts now skew to more intimate concerns: how far is he willing to go for Lola? Pretty far, he suspects. If this experiment in living with the nuns helps convince her she's not psychic he might even want to move in together, have kids maybe.

Just as he reaches the car and leans back against it, he jumps forward again as Vincent bangs out through the little door with the candlesticks and staggers away, moaning. Alarmed, Leo runs towards the door but Jesus appears in it and blocks his way.

"Sorry, no more visitors today."

"Who was that? What's going on in there," Leo demands.

"He's just some dumbass punk. Don't worry, Miss Lola won't be long." And he slams the door shut before Leo can say another word.


Inside, moments later, Lola is seated across from Sister Evelyn, the wrought iron grille partition between them, the blinds drawn and nearly closed. Jesus is waiting just inside the door to the garden. Evelyn raises a slat of the blinds with her fingertip and studies the young woman.

"What are your qualifications?"

Lola is uncertain exactly where to address her reply:

"I attended a business administration course for a few months," she begins. "I'm a competent office manager and a really good receptionist. But somehow I got promoted to claims adjuster at this evil insurance company…" And without meaning to she goes on to describe stopping the clock and exploding a glass of water in the Rutledge Insurance conference room. It all comes out in a rush and once it's said, Lola looks away and regrets it all.

But Sister Evelyn is impressed. "Hmm. So does this kind of thing happen often?"

"It depends," Lola answers after a moment's thought.

"On what?"

Though she suspects it sounds vague, dissimulating, and embarrassingly sentimental, Lola finally admits: "Feelings."

Sister Evelyn has been around the block and seen a few things in her time. She knows a liar or a psychopath when she sees one. She doesn't think she sees either one here.

"You should meet Mother Superior," she says, gesturing as much to Veronica, who dutifully hurries from the gallery. Meanwhile, the prioress stubs out her cigarette and comes closer to the closed blinds. "Listen, do you know anything about beer?"

"Excuse me?"

"I mean, do you like beer?"

Lola just stares at the blinds a moment, wondering if these sisters have been running background checks on her. She answers honestly, though with something like an apology:

"Oh, yeah, I guess."

Having eavesdropped discreetly from far across the room, Jesus decides he can leave now. "When you're ready," he calls softly, "you can unlock this and let yourself out."

Lola looks over and sees Jesus about to exit, indicating the lock on the door. She should make a run for it. She's scared. But Father Robert has gone out of his way to help her and she doesn't want to appear ungrateful. It's been almost a month since she first went to see him—

Though the church of Saint Ann's is no longer what it once was, the neighborhood itself is on the way up again. After a generation or two of steady decline, younger, upwardly mobile families are buying houses and apartments throughout the area between the Brooklyn-Queens Expressway and the old Brooklyn Navy Yard. Businesses are coming back and schools are opening.

The regular parishioners at Saint Ann's can be counted on the fingers of one hand. But the church has managed to survive by way of weddings, christenings, and, mostly, the funeral business. For the most part, Father Robert ruefully acknowledges, people tend to remember they're Catholic only when a family member dies or some young bride-to-be insists on the pomp and circumstance of walking up the aisle on her father's arm. The new pastor doesn't let it get to him. That they come at all gives him something to work with. He's noticed a few young couples drifting in to try out mass on Sunday.

Now, it's a Tuesday, a month earlier.

In the lobby between the church and the parish offices, an exhausted older woman, Señora Diaz, sits with her seven-year-old granddaughter, Inez. She keeps her hand on a stroller containing her screaming infant grandson, Joseph. The church secretary, Patsy, comes and goes, busy with some filing. Though she smiles indulgently, it's easy to see this bawling kid is getting on her nerves.

Joseph pauses in his wailing for a second, but then resumes with a long, ear-splitting scream. He just won't stop. And Señora Diaz seems to have long since given up hoping he will. She fiddles with the blanket covering the boy and shakes her head.

Lola enters from the street and winces at the sharp pitch of yet another agonized howl. There's only one bench to wait on and so she sits close by Señora Diaz who looks to her for sympathy. Lola obliges. Then she leans over a little, sneaking a peek in at the crying infant.

Joseph locks eyes with her.

Lola smiles.

The kid stops crying.

We can hear a pin drop in this church all of a sudden. The little girl gets up and looks down into the stroller.

"Grandma," she calls joyfully, "he stopped crying!"

The old lady is terrified. She looks at Lola, falls back, and makes the sign of the cross. Lola falls back too, wanting to apologize. Patsy steps out into the foyer, startled by the quiet. Inez claps her hands and stomps her feet.

"He stopped! He stopped!" she sings. "Joseph stopped crying!"

Father Robert steps out from the office as well.

"Father," cries Señora Diaz, still looking at Lola, "it's a miracle!"

The good-natured priest comes over and stoops down over the infant. "Not really, Missus Diaz," he replies. "Despair gets boring. Right, Joseph?"

The infant chuckles and tries to devour his own fist.

Back to business, Father Robert stands up, looks around, and spots his new appointment: "Lola?"

"I'm sorry," she answers automatically.

Lola and Father Robert walk in the small park beside the church rectory.

"Has the little boy been ill," she asks.

"Nothing the doctors could diagnose," Robert tells her.

"But that little bruiser has been crying like that since the day he was born thirteen months ago. I christened him myself and practically had to wrestle the kid to the floor to get the thing accomplished."

This glad news just confuses and saddens Lola. It must be a good thing the boy has stopped crying, she thinks. But why did it have to occur just as she looked at him? This could mean nothing. Or everything. She's exhausted from never knowing one way or the other. She sits on a bench. "I think I need to enter a convent."

Robert remains standing, watching her from a few feet away. "Oh," he asks, encouraging her to continue at her own speed.

"I'm worried."

"About what?"

"Causing harm."

He decides this is enough to start with. Nodding, he sits on the bench as well. "This is about the boy who ran out in front of the bus?"

"Leo told you?"

"Yes."

Lola sits back and takes a long, well measured breath.

"He's right, of course. I can't prove I caused that to happen. But I was so angry at that boy."

"Why," Robert asks, cautiously, noticing how carefully she works to control her emotions.

"He was torturing this wounded dog," Lola begins. "The dog's leg was broken I think and it was trapped, stuck, with its hind leg caught in one of the holes of a sewer drain. And this boy he was… stabbing it with this stick… and flicking lit matches into the animal's face… I tried to stop him. I grabbed him by the collar of his shirt and dragged him away and he whipped me with the stick right across my eyes. I started crying and ran away. I couldn't even see anything for a while. But I called the police to come save this animal and when they were arriving the kid dropped the stick and ran... straight into a bus."

Robert has heard most of this from Leo already. "And you feel responsible for this?"

"I made it happen."

Concerned, the priest stands and takes a few steps away, composing his thoughts. Finally, he turns back to Lola. "No offence intended, Lola, but I want to do due diligence and move carefully through all the standard and accepted preliminaries before I start to have the kind of conversation with you that I am, in fact, qualified to have. Okay?"

She's a little surprised at his almost lawyerly manner but nods. "Okay."

"Have you spoken to a psychiatrist?"

"Yes."

"And?"

"She said I have guilt issues I have to deal with."

Robert looks aside, already irritated with this unknown psychiatrist. "Have you sought out independent third-party observation of these occurrences?"

Wow, Lola thinks, this guy doesn't talk like a priest.

"How do you mean," she asks.

"Well, science has studied the possibility of telepathy and psychokinesis and so on for over a century." He shoves his hands down deep into his jacket pockets, hunching his shoulders, as he looks off across the garden and thinks. "It could be helpful to have rational objective analysis of your experiences."

There's no response. He looks back over at Lola.

"That sounds embarrassing," she admits, glancing away at the stone walkway, adding, "I think I'd rather be locked up in a convent actually."

Now this is interesting, Robert decides, returning to the bench. "Why do you want to be locked up?"

"I'm a danger to society," Lola replies with certainty.

"Why a convent then? If it's just about being locked up, there are hospitals, prisons, the military."

This is a good point and she mulls it over: "The quiet. I imagine it must be quiet in a convent." She straightens up, composes herself, and adds: "And I might be useful in a convent. I'm a good administrator and I like waking up early."

"Lola, a person doesn't just decide they need to become a nun. They receive, to use old-fashioned language, a call; an urge from deep in the heart. And the call needs to be tested long and carefully until it cannot be mistaken for anything else."

Lola hears this loud and clear. It's almost like what she's been trying to articulate on her own for months and months.

"But maybe that's what all this is," she says slowly, staring at the ground, "my making stuff happen. I've tried to ignore it. But I can't."

Robert, now, is the one who is surprised and uncertain. He waits for her to complete her thought. She looks up at him and, she too, waits for the idea to come clear in her own mind.

"It might be a call."


Later that same day, Leo comes out of the junior high along with dozens of kids, many of whom are his students. One of them, a gangly Black girl named Sasha, races past him.

"Bye, Mister Haroldson!"

"Take care, Sasha," he replies, lifting his attention from an article he's reading. "See you tomorrow."

A boy runs to catch up. "Mister Haroldson," the kid calls shyly, "I finished the equation!"

Leo stops and turns. He accepts the sheet of paper the boy shyly extends to him. "Way to go, Ben," he says warmly. And he studies the equation Ben has scrawled over the entire face of the page as the kid hangs back, expectantly, with his noisier, goofier pal, Derek.

Leo is glad for this. Ben, he believes, is a natural mathematician of truly exceptional ability. But he's often too shy to make a greater effort. He suspects the kid comes from a home where being intellectually gifted is seen as unmanly or something. Happily, his friends in class encourage him.

"I proofed it twice," Ben offers eagerly at Derek's urging.

Leo smiles, enjoying the evidence on the page of the boy's thought process. It's clear his pen can hardly keep up with his thinking. "It's correct," he announces, slapping the sheet of paper playfully against the kid's chest. "Keep it up."

Ben and Derek rejoice, do a high five, and run off after the equation as it flutters away in the breeze.

Riding the subway home, reading a book about medieval female mystics he found discarded in the laundromat, Leo adjusts his reading glasses and rubs his tired eyes. He notices a woman seated opposite vacantly admiring him. Caught, she smiles and looks away. Leo returns to his book, smiling too. He's pretty sure he sees her from time to time on this train.

Night is falling by the time he reaches Margaret's Bar. Entering, he waves hello to Charles and his friends. They're huddled around a table having some sort of meeting. He's never seen unemployed people work so hard. They're always scheming and drawing up plans, comparing online research, and sharing their MetroCards as they dash around town on important but unspecified errands.

Father Robert is at the bar fussing with the TV's remote, skipping through channels to find tonight's game. Chastity has Leo's beer ready for him as he slides onto a stool.

"Tough day," she asks.

"Thirteen-year-olds, algebra. Do the math." After a satisfying sip, he turns to the priest. "How did it go with my girlfriend who wants to become a nun?"

Robert sets aside the remote and drinks. "Have you ever witnessed any of these alleged psychic events?"

"No," Leo replies. But then he adds, "well, maybe. I don't know. I'm a rational man. Perhaps I'm missing something."

"She's a fascinating person."

"Tell me about it."

"It'd be easy, I guess, to diagnose her as hysterical, obsessive-compulsive, or, I don't know: psychotic. But she might just have—forgive me for this oversimplification—a conscience."

Leo nods, considering this. Then: "I have a confession to make."

Robert pauses with his beer halfway to his lips and looks at his new friend again. He pushes back from the bar and stands. Looking around, he spots a quiet area in back.

"Step into my office."

Taking his beer, Robert heads to a table beside the old telephone booth way back beyond the pool table. Leo hesitates, uncertain, then follows.

But let us leave them here for now and jump forward a little—

It's a few days later and Lola is sitting in the offices of a convent in Westchester County, thirty minutes north of Manhattan. The prioress of this establishment is studying some papers before her on the desk as Lola waits and, of course, worries.

"Lola, I must say," Sister Miriam finally admits, "a recommendation from Father Robert at Saint Ann's is impressive. He's a hardworking priest and does much good for so many failing parishes in the area. But your answer to a number of the questions on the application for the novitiate are troubling."

Lola feels she should say something, but all she can come up with is, "Oh?"

"Like this one," says the sister, lifting the page and reading: "'Have you ever been convicted of a felony?' Your answer: 'Not yet.'" Lowering the page, she looks at the girl, stern but willing to listen. "What does that mean?"

Lola decides it's best to be straight with a nun.

"Well, Sister, I think I have psychic powers I'm not really in control of and I think I caused the death of this horrible little kid a few months ago. I gave myself up to the police but they didn't believe me and sent me home."

Sister Miriam has heard enough. She removes her reading glasses and drops them on the desk. Lola is politely led out of this august institution and the doors are shut loudly behind her.


Back at Margaret's Bar, Leo and Robert are huddled over a small table shoved up against the wall.

"I'm not Catholic, though," Leo warns.

Father Robert dips his fingertips into his beer and flicks some brew at his friend. *Dominus vobiscum,* the priest intones. "Now you are for fifteen minutes. I promise."

"How do I—is there a formula?"

"You say, 'Forgive me, Father, for I have sinned.'"

"Really? Just like that? You start out admitting everything right off the bat?"

"Those are the ground rules. We take it for granted you're guilty. More efficient that way. Come on."

"Forgive me, Father, for I have sinned."

"What is the nature of your transgression, my friend?"

"I started dating Lola because I thought she was insane."

Robert looks up, momentarily stymied. Leo is an easy guy to talk to, but he doesn't offer much information about himself unless asked. Moments into the sacrament of confession, the priest has learned more about his new friend than he has in a week and a half of barroom chat.

Leo continues: "I've done that sort of thing sometimes, sex with women who are out of their minds. It can be amazing. I mean, erotically." But he's suddenly afraid he's out of line. "Is this okay?"

Robert leans back and wonders if anything can be out of line in a confession. He decides not, sips his beer, and leans his elbows back on the table: "As far as the unsaved go, you're doing just fine, Leo. Please, continue."

Taking his friend's professional word for it, Leo does:

"But we've never had sex, Lola and I."

"Really? After what? Like…"

"A year."

In spite of himself, Robert blurts out, "Wow!"

"Because she believes crazy shit will happen if she has an orgasm," Leo explains.

Robert frowns, drinks, and buys time to imagine the implications of all this without, necessarily, conjuring up particulars. "Like what kind of crazy shit?"

"Oh, I don't know," Leo draws a deep breath, "like she'll give me a heart attack or something."

Robert ponders this and looks across at the television above the bar to see if the game is on yet. "Okay, maybe after all, she is insane."

"But I don't even care anymore."

"If she's insane?"

"About having sex," he clarifies, then adds, "or at least having sex with her *because* she's insane."

The priest studies the floor, tapping his foot. "I think we might consider this a kind of spiritual progress on your part."

They raise their beers and toast to this. After a long sip that feels somehow earned because of making it this far, the two men delve in deeper:

"This problem of hers," Leo continues, "this whatever we choose to call it—hysteria, delusion—it's so real a weight she carries around and struggles with and, for the most part, without even complaining—it's made a different man of me. I can't imagine life without her now. I've discovered this tenderness I didn't know I was capable of."

Robert sets down his beer and swivels aside in his seat. He gazes abstractedly down the dim hallway to the restrooms.

"Do you love Lola enough to lose her for a while?"


Sister Marie is the strict old prioress of the Convent of the Sacred Heart in Woodlawn, New Jersey. She reads from a list of questions on a page of paper: "Are you married?"

Lola likes the uncomplicated manner of this interview. She replies happily: "No."

"Do you have children under the age of eighteen?"

"No."

"Are you prepared to be celibate?"

This trips Lola up. "Prepared?" she repeats.

The sister already expects complications: "Yes," she confirms, dryly.

"What do you mean by celibate?"

"Abstaining from sexual relations, of course."

Lola wants to be careful about this and is not sure where masturbation, for instance, lies on the spectrum of sexual relations. "With, like, you mean, another person, right?"

Moments later, she's led out politely and the doors of this second convent are shut firmly behind her.


Leo and Father Robert are shooting pool. The priest thinks out loud: "I think it might be good for Lola to spend time in a convent as a lay sister, not taking the vows. She needs to be unplugged from the world for a while."

"But where?"

"I can make some inquiries, make some recommendations. Of course, she'll need to apply for a novitiate and be interviewed and so on."

Uneasy, Leo lines up a shot but then stands back: "A novitiate?"

"A novice can live in the convent of an Order for a while and then she and the Order decide if she's called to take the vow."

This worries Leo even more: "The vow?"

"That's the decision to move forward and become a nun."

"I don't like the sound of that," Leo admits and shoots. He sinks the wrong ball and steps aside.

"You afraid she really wants to become a nun," Robert asks, studying his options.

"What do I know! I'm in love with a girl who believes she can cause car accidents by wearing a certain skirt."

Robert shoots, misses, and stands back: "I don't think Lola wants to become a nun," he confidently asserts and sips his beer. "But time as a novice, fairly secluded, dedicating her days to meditation and to the service to others, this might help cure her."

Leo stays where he is, leaning back against the wall.

"How long?

"Few months. You could probably visit."

Leo comes over to the table, looks for a shot, but then decides to just lay down his cue. "What choice have I got but to support her in her decision?"

"You could walk away," Robert says, studying his friend. "You're still a young man. Handsome. Employed."

"Impossible."

"That's what I thought. Your sins are forgiven, go in peace and do not sin again."

"Pardon me," Leo asks, blankly, having lost the thread.

"That's how it ends—a confession," the priest explains. "I sign off and usually I give you some penance to perform but, you know, seeing as how the game's about to begin and all…"

Robert sets down his pool cue too and heads for the bar.

"Father," Leo calls, stopping him, "one last thing: what is it—does the body have a soul?"

This gives Robert genuine pause. Now they're really talking his language. He turns fully around and waits for Leo to continue.

"Or are the soul and the body two separate things?"

Father Robert pauses, then takes a step forward and lays his hand on Leo's shoulder. "No. The soul is embodied. And that's either the reason we're all so fucked up or the recurring melody behind humanity's greatest hits. You want another beer?"

"Sure," Leo says, looking off at the floor and letting all this soak in.

Now, some weeks after this discussion in Margaret's Bar, Lola practically staggers into the foyer of the Church of Saint Ann's. She lowers herself to the bench and leans back against the wall. Father Robert loosens his collar as he steps out of the office and joins her.

"Long day, huh?"

"Nobody wants me," she moans, referring to convents.

"Leo wants you," Robert reminds her, willfully redirecting the discussion.

But she won't let him and sits forward. "How can I give myself to this man I love when I suspect that if we… you know…" she falters and he comes to her rescue:

"'Intimate relations' is a sufficiently indirect and church-friendly euphemism."

"If we have 'intimate relations' I might kill him."

Robert reaches out and touches her arm. "Easy…" But he is at a loss for words and doesn't want to get preachy.

"I'm not insane," Lola insists with some heat.

"Right, "Robert nods, "you're emotionally challenged."

"Yeah," she confirms, "emotionally challenged."

Robert fishes around in the pockets of his jacket and finds a folded-up sheet of loose leaf. Tearing a section out of it, he hands the scrap of paper to her. "There is a convent not far from here that is in no position to reject a novitiate applicant."

Lola takes the piece of paper and reads: "Our Lady of the Highway."

"They can use a capable office manager too."

"What's wrong with them?"

"You'll find out."

She lowers the paper and looks at him without enthusiasm: "Wow. Thanks."

"There's always Buddhism," he suggests.

But she leans back on the bench, sighing, and apologizes: "No, thanks, really." Lifting the paper again, she repeats, "Our Lady of the Highway".

"They're good nuns," Robert insists, "but they're in trouble."

Resolved, decided, resigned—she can't tell—Lola folds up the scrap of paper and puts it in her purse. "I'll make the best of this," she proclaims. "I promise."

And so, finally, Lola is here at the convent of Our Lady of the Highway meeting the mother superior and the prioress. She sits patiently, increasingly intrigued and less worried, as Evelyn and Magdalena pace back and forth on their side of the gallery's partition.

"So, you can make things happen," Magdalena asks.

"When I feel really strongly about something," Lola clarifies.

"Like what," asks Evelyn.

"What do I feel strongly about?"

"No, what kinds of things happen."

"Things break. Or bend. Lights go out. My boyfriend…"

Magdalena stops and twists around on the heel of her boot: "Ah! There's a boyfriend."

"Yeah, I know that's sort of a problem for someone wanting to be a nun, huh?"

The mother superior corrects her: "You won't be a nun."

"You'll be, if we accept you, a novice," the prioress adds.

"A postulant," Magdalena continues.

"Though you'll have to obey the rules."

"And live here with us away from the world."

Lola catches her breath. But she feels she should finish what she is trying to say: "Well, this man, my boyfriend, Leo—he teaches junior high school math—he says I sometimes do—usually if I've been, well, drinking—strange things to the weather."

Evelyn, for one, is impressed. "Oh, well, that's new."

Lola is so accustomed to meeting ridicule and outrage at this point in her story that she's nearly speechless.

"Really," she asks.

"You seem surprised," Evelyn responds.

"If someone told me they could effect the weather just by feeling upset I, myself, would think they were crazy."

Magdalena drifts back towards the grille and suggests, airily, "Well, yes, of course, but, Lola, we're Catholic nuns and believe God was born as a human child in a barn somewhere in the Middle East two thousand years ago. It makes us more open-minded than most people."

Lola sits back in her seat, relieved.


A moment later, Magdalena steps into the convent's main hallway. She closes the door to the inner gallery after first casting a glance back across at Lola sitting there on the far side of the partition. She joins Evelyn who is pacing back and forth from the stairwell to the kitchen.

"What do you think, Sister Prioress?"

Evelyn stops, takes her fingers from her lips, and states flatly: "I think we have a live one here, Mother Superior."

"She seems sincere."

"She's got an honest-to-God conscience."

"And she likes beer."

Evelyn nods, affirming, but adds, "And she might be a good administrator."

For her part, Magdalena is intrigued by something else:

"And she has a boyfriend."

Evelyn is used to Magdalena's often radically unexpected logic. She steps back and watches the mother superior.

"And why, exactly, is that a good thing?"

"He must be terribly devoted if he's willing to part with her for three months as she completes her novitiate and sorts out her, you know, spiritual potential."

As always, Evelyn catches up with her sister's reasoning and agrees: "Yes, I see. We can use someone on the outside too."

"She said he's a teacher."

"Junior high school."

"That takes guts. I like these people, Sister Prioress."

"But what if she discovers she has what it takes?"

"To become a nun, you mean?"

"Yes."

"It would resound to the greater glory of our blessed father in heaven."

"And break the heart of a school teacher in Brooklyn."

"Sister Prioress," Magdalena reminds her, "you cannot make an omelet without breaking some eggs."

"Okay. Let's do it."

They head back into the gallery.


Outside the convent, on what he has learned is called Resurrection Avenue, Leo is standing on the hood of his rented car trying to get a better look in at the grounds. Jesus comes out from the little door, casts a glance at him, and freezes.

"Dude, chill."

Leo ignores him. But the groundskeeper has other things on his mind and continues up the street. He comes around the corner of the wall and finds the kid, Xavier, hanging back in the shadows, nervous, not sure where to be. He too freezes when he sees Jesus.

"What the hell you doing troubling the sisters, you little bastard?"

"Where's Vincent," the boy asks.

"How the fuck do I know! But if I get my hands on him, I'm gonna kick his fucking ass, that prick!"

"I think the cops got him," Xavier whispers, peeking past Jesus to Leo climbing down off the car.


And Vincent is, in fact, just arriving at the police precinct. Led in by two bored cops, he's cuffed to a chair.

Detective Pena, the poster child for dissatisfied civil servants everywhere, comes up the hall and tosses a half-eaten sandwich in someone else's wastepaper basket.

"Hey!" someone protests.

"Shut the fuck up," the detective replies, then, stopping and glaring down at Vincent, "What's this?"

"Stolen auto through the window of a Starbucks and resisting arrest," reports the arresting officer.

"That is my mother's car!" Vincent points out.

"Who gave you the black eye, kid," Pena asks, not really wanting an answer somehow.

As he unbuckles his holster, the arresting officer adds, "He might have a ruptured hernia or something too."

Vincent now sees there's a chance he can be the victim of all this: "She kicked me in the balls!"

"Your mother?"

"No! The nun!"

Confused, Pena looks at the cop. The cop looks at Vincent: "What nun?"

Vincent goes all defiant and aloof. "I don't have to talk to you."

They couldn't care less. Pena grabs the candlesticks off the desk. "Stolen goods?"

"Most likely," the cop replies before heading off to the men's room.

Pena studies the candlesticks and discovers they are inscribed. At the base of each are the initials OLHW. He looks at Vincent: "You were beat up by a nun?"

Vincent looks away, insulted, and refuses to discuss it. "I don't have to talk to you," he declares again.

Pena crosses to the desk of junior Detective Oscar. "Call over to Our Lady of the Highway and see if they've had any visitors recently."

Magdalena and Evelyn are back with Lola, sitting close to the partition:

"Now, Lola," begins the mother superior, "convent life isn't for everyone. Obedience, penance, community service, and prayer—I know, it sounds terribly exotic at first. But in practice, it's really quite a different thing."

"I'll try my best," Lola assures them. "But, Sisters, honestly, I'm not even sure I'm a Catholic."

"Were you baptized?"

"I think so," she says uncertainly. "I was very young. I can't remember. My parents lied to me about everything."

Evelyn asks: "Did you receive your confirmation?"

"Definitely. In the fourth grade." This she remembers clearly; it having been the day her father was arrested for embezzlement or tax evasion—she's not sure—fraud of one kind or another.

"And you can use Excel for Windows and the standard bookkeeping and tax preparation programs, right?" the prioress confirms.

"Oh, sure. That's easy," she assures them. "I already have all the necessary software."

"Okay, good," Magdalena decides, "I'll tutor you in the faith as we go."

Evelyn looks aside, planning the weeks ahead: "When can you start?"

"Anytime after tomorrow."

"Excellent," Magdalena announces, standing.

Veronica appears at the door from the main hall and whispers: "Sister Prioress, the police are on the phone."

Evelyn and Magdalena exchange glances. "Excuse me," the prioress murmurs, leaving the inner gallery.

She comes out into the main hall and approaches the wall-mounted rotary phone. "Our Lady of the Highway, Sister Prioress speaking. How may I help you?"

"Good afternoon, Sister Prioress," Oscar says familiarly, "this is Detective Oscar from the Thirteenth Precinct. We were just wondering if you've had any burglaries recently."

Evelyn feigns ignorance: "Burglaries?"

"We picked up some kid in possession of a couple of candlesticks with the cloister's initials on them."

Her hunch confirmed and not wanting further attention to be drawn to the convent, she nods and placates him: "Oh, thank you so much, Detective. But we've had no unwanted visitors," she lies. "Those old candlesticks might just have been put out with the garbage. We've been doing some cleaning."

Oscar studies the impressive pieces: "Oh yeah? They're real silver, you know."

"Are they? Well, good luck then to whoever keeps them. Bye!" And she hangs up without further ado.

Lola lets herself out of the cloister and reappears in the garden. She makes her way towards the exit while taking note of the various vegetables she passes. Reaching the door, she finds it locked. She looks around and sees Jesus' little home and workshop at the far end of the garden and heads towards it.

"Mister Jesus," she calls.

Jesus is at his all-purpose workbench, poring over the pages of a large ancient-looking book. He glances up, hearing Lola approach: "Hey, Miss Lola," he calls, "in here!"

She stops and looks in from the threshold.

"What'd they say," Jesus asks, "you in or not?"

"I'm in. I'll come to stay next Wednesday."

"Great," he says, relieved and eager. "Look, Lola, do you know foreign languages?"

"Some Spanish," she replies, coming a few steps into the room, "a little French from high school."

"No Dutch, huh? Or Latin?"

He points to a certain passage in the antique tome. Lola leans close and studies it.

"No, I'm afraid not. What is this?"

"It's the Rule," he announces proudly, showing her the cover, "The Rule of the Convent of Our Lady of the Highway. It was written by the sister who started this joint back in 1669."

"Wow. Shouldn't this be like in a museum or something?"

"No way! I use this thing all the time. Lots of useful stuff in here. The parts in English, anyway. There are good recipes and advice about planting vegetables and, look," he insists, turning to a marked page, "how to make beer."

Leo is still waiting out on Resurrection Avenue. The sun is going down. Finally, the little metal door opens and Lola steps out, excited. Jesus waves goodbye.

"How'd it go," Leo asks.

"I think I'm going to like it here, Leo."

"Yeah? Really?"

"The sisters rock!"

She climbs into the car and they drive off. As they do, they pass a high-end black SUV with *Magnificent Waste Management* printed proudly across its side. Hubert Jones, vice president of operations, is standing beside it, watching the convent through binoculars. A little further along, calmly surveying the landscape, is his boss, owner and CEO, Gordon Normal. He is in his fifties and wearing a sharp-looking expensive suit. He's used to being right, obeyed, and working hard to insure these things.

"It's the perfect location, sir," Hubert calls.

"Of course, it is," the waste management czar declares, grabbing the binoculars. "Now we just have to get rid of those goddamn nuns."

THREE

It's dawn. A bell tolls softly through the dim halls of Our Lady of the Highway. Magdalena, Evelyn, and Veronica emerge from their small bare rooms on the second floor—referred to as cells—and move silently downstairs.

Simultaneously, in a tiny apartment in New York City, a mobile device resting on a bedside table begins to chime. Lola wakes, grabs the phone, and reads the display: "*lauds*." She tumbles out of bed and heads for the bathroom.

The three nuns enter a small chapel off the main hallway on the convent's ground floor, halfway between the kitchen at one end and the vestry at the other. Seconds later, they are joined by the older nuns, Sisters Catherine and Agatha who have long since taken to sleeping on cots at the back of the kitchen pantry.

This little chapel is reputed to be the original enclosure made by the foundress before the rest of the convent was built. It's eighteen feet by twelve and sunk a few steps down from the level of the main hall. It has two rows of *prie-dieu* before a simple altar and one small window high up near the ceiling which brings in little light because someone, sixty years ago, had the good sense to install an electric ventilation fan.

The five sisters find their accustomed places, kneel, and pray the morning prayer, or *lauds*, as it is called in their tradition: "God," they whisper, "come to my assistance. Lord, make haste to help me."

Lola is in her shower reciting the same prayers: "My soul magnifies the Lord and my spirit rejoices in God my Savior for he has looked with favor on the lowliness of his servant." She leans out from under the hot water, dries her hand on a towel and consults her mobile device, reminding herself of the lines to follow. "He has scattered the proud in the thoughts of their hearts, he has brought down the powerful from their thrones, he has lifted up the lowly and has filled the hungry with good things."

The exhaust vent is not working and she opens the window to release some of the steam from the room. Across the back alley, though, directly opposite Lola's bathroom, a number of drunk young men are still up partying from the night before, sitting on the sill of their kitchen window, smoking. They notice Lola's bare shoulders and back. "Hey, beautiful," one of them calls, "need some help over there!"

Lola wipes soap from her face, opens an eye and turns. Seeing them, she slams the window shut.

Back at the convent, done with their morning prayers, the sisters enter the kitchen and get down to the business of breakfast. Their routine is simple, utilitarian, and perfectly silent. One gets the cereal, another gets the bowls and spoons, a third carves up an apple.

Lola, for her part, is in her tiny kitchenette waiting for the kettle to boil so as to make tea.

In Brooklyn, the sisters eat their cereal in silence.

Behind Lola's apartment, across the alley, the party of drunk young men clamber mischievously out onto a fire escape directly across from her kitchenette. Inside, she pours hot water over a tea bag and continues reading prayers from an app on her mobile device. "Give ear to my words, Oh Lord," she recites, "give heed to my sighing. Listen to the sound of my cry…"

Giggling childishly and gripping the last of their beers, eight or ten guys crowd out onto the tiny ancient fire escape. They turn their backs to Lola, undo their belts, and prepare to display their buttocks.

Done with their meager breakfast, the sisters of Our Lady of the Highway wash up and return to their places at the large table. They wait in silence. Sister Magdalena casts a glance at the wall clock.

It's 6:25.

Biting into a piece of toast and then setting it aside, Lola scrolls to the concluding prayer and reads it while making the sign of the cross: "May the Lord bless us, protect us from all evil, and bring us to everlasting life. Amen."

She then glances into the alley and falls back, startled.

Outside, a row of youthful male asses is arrayed for her consideration. The guys twist around from the waist and lift their beers in joyful salute: "Yeah!!!!"

Lola spins away and holds her head in her hands. A commotion is heard outside; crumbling brick, bending metal, surprised, horrified voices—

And then screaming.

Lola spins back around and sees the overloaded fire escape detach itself from the crumbling wall of the building and start to topple grotesquely into the depths of the alley. The terrified young men, their trousers around their ankles, are screaming for their lives and reaching desperately for something to grab hold of.

Lola falls back into the room and covers her face in her hands.

Days earlier, as we have seen, Lola visits the convent of Our Lady of the Highway and is interviewed by the mother superior and the prioress with the aim of determining whether she is suited to be a novice. Though she is nervous and skeptical, the sisters intrigue her. And she is particularly comforted by the lack of suspicion and ridicule with which they hear of her dangerous psychic abilities—or curse, as Lola herself tends to say.

Nevertheless, she decides there are conversations with the sisters that it will not be wise to share with Leo just yet. While her devoted boyfriend is outside worrying about her safety, Lola is being welcomed in past the gallery's partition and into the hallowed halls of the convent proper:

"You see, Lola," Magdalena begins while ushering the young woman down the main hall towards the kitchen, "we are in the world but not of it. Though we dedicate ourselves to a life of seclusion and contemplation, sometimes we need to poke our heads out into the world and see what's going on."

They stop at the entrance to the kitchen as Evelyn looks up: "In other words," the prioress summarizes, "the convent is starving to death and we have no way to support ourselves."

But Veronica chimes in happily: "So we have decided to make beer!"

Lola now sees a collection of two dozen different microbrew specialty beers lined up across the counter. Nearly blind old Agatha is studying one in particular. "What one is this," she asks.

"That's a good one," Lola says, coming closer. What's come to be called microbrew or craft beer is all the rage these days and she's sampled plenty.

"You know it," asks Magdalena, who doesn't strike Lola as a beer drinker. If anything, in a different life, she'd be a champagne and fine wines type woman.

"It's not my favorite," Lola adds, "but it's pretty good."

"I like the label," Veronica says.

Wasting no time, Evelyn grabs the bottle opener: "Let's try it." She opens the beer and pours a little into small plain glasses. The sisters sip cautiously. Lola tosses hers back, then, considering:

"It should probably be colder."

"Yeah," Evelyn concurs, nodding, "refrigeration is going to be an issue."

Magdalena lays a hand on Veronica's arm and commands gently: "Make a note of that, Sister: Beer should be cold."

Veronica leans down over her notepad and begins scribbling. But she looks up, pointing out: "In England they drink warm beer."

"This is not England," Evelyn says with easygoing authority. Before taking her vows, she was an ace bartender in Los Angeles. She's been operating a hastily assembled microbrewery of her own at the back of the convent's laundry room since arriving nine weeks ago.

Magdalena agrees about this not being England: "Yes, this is Brooklyn and we must make the kind of beer that the affluent and informed hipsters of Williamsburg will love to drink and be proud of."

"A humbly crafted beer brewed by cloistered nuns in the

heart of Brooklyn," Veronica rehearses, imagining a bill-board along a highway.

"Yes," concurs Magdalena, delighted, "something just like that."

"Do you know how to make beer," Lola asks, practically.

Magdalena tilts her head to the side. "A little."

"We're getting better," Evelyn adds, pouring Lola some of their own brew. "Try this."

Lola takes the glass and samples this beer made by nuns.

"What do you think?"

"Cool," Lola replies, smiling.

Evelyn opens a window, sits on the sill, and lights a ciga-rette. "Lola, who do you know? Anyone?"

"How do you mean?"

"Anyone with access to the things we need," Magdalena elaborates.

"We need a fully equipped multi-batch industrial brewery of a certain size and capacity," the prioress continues.

"And beer bottling equipment," Magdalena reminds them.

"Yeah," Evelyn says, "a semi-automatic bottling machine; up to three hundred bottles per hour."

Lola continues sampling their beer while she runs the numbers in her head: "That's, like, up to twenty-four hundred bottles per eight-hour working shift, considering you work pursuant to state labor laws."

Evelyn swings her booted feet down off the sill. "I think we can fit that in with our observance of the Hours and our perpetuation of the vigil," she says, encouragingly. "But we need more sisters." She clamps her cigarette between her teeth and pulls out a sheaf of papers from beneath her flowing habit. "Look, I've drawn up a schedule."

"The thing is, Lola," Magdalena decides it's time to explain, "we'll need you to sign for things, be our business manager, so to speak, our contact with the outside world."

Lola is already more than ready to help these sisters in any way she can. But she can't disguise the disappointment this causes her: "I was hoping to get away from the outside world."

The mother superior sees the young woman's romantic imaginings of cloistered life bruised and feels for her. She comes closer and takes Lola's hand, leading her to a bench running alongside the kitchen table. "Yes, of course," she begins, "I understand you have fears that must be overcome. But, Lola, there's no way to get out of the dark and scary forest except to walk through the…" But she forgets the point of the anecdote and just invents an end to fit the occasion: "…well, the dark and scary forest—or something like that. Anyway," she ends, standing, "you must see everything that you are asked to do here as a trial of your suitability for the hard way by which the journey to God is made."

Sister Agatha wakes up momentarily and pumps her fist, feebly: "Amen." She promptly falls back to sleep while Magdalena samples another of the beers.

"For us," the mother superior continues, "Sister Prioress and myself, the trial might have been to *enter* the cloister. Neither of us are born contemplatives. We like action; combat even."

"They have scars," Veronica adds, thrilled, "really."

Lola looks around from one to the other and starts to regard these women differently. Though, Magdalena is not yet finished:

"But for you, on the other hand, Lola, the trial might be to confront the outside world face-to-face simply because it does frighten you as much as it does."

Lola considers this. She blinks. "Mother Superior, may I ask a question?"

"Of course."

"Are you all wanted by the law?"

Magdalena is impressed. This young woman is perceptive. Still, she proceeds with caution, dragging her habit over her boot that still contains a handgun: "Interesting question. Why do you ask?"

"Just a feeling I have," Lola replies, shyly. But it's more than a feeling. Her parents were often in trouble with the law. She has an instinct for fugitives. And her hated work at Rutledge did bring her into contact with criminals.

Magdalena is sure she would have had to explain all this to the young woman eventually, so she crosses over and checks to make sure Agatha is asleep. Then, returning to Lola:

"Sister Veronica is wanted by the FBI for crimes against the US military-industrial complex, yes."

Veronica comes now to sit opposite Magdalena on Lola's right, adding, "And Mother Superior herself has a price on her head in most of South America for her excellent work disrupting the importation of weapons."

Lola takes this all in, then glances over at Evelyn. But the prioress just holds up her hands:

"I've done time but I'm square with the law," she assures Lola, adding, "for the time being—at least in the State of New York."

Magdalena opens a new beer and hands it to Lola. "You see, doing the Lord's work often gets us into hot water with the authorities. But holy mother Church has seen fit to harbor us here."

Evelyn smokes and reminds them, "As long as we can get

this busted up dump back on its feet again."

Lola drinks, sighs, and considers all she's heard. She likes these people. Finally, she stands: "Do I get to wear a uniform?"

"It's called a habit," Evelyn informs her.


So that was last Thursday afternoon. Now it's the following Wednesday morning. The sisters are still waiting silently at the kitchen table, patiently thinking their own thoughts, as Mother Superior glances up at the clock again.

It's 6:29 and 45 seconds.

As the second hand ticks its labored way to the half hour, Magdalena adjusts her wimple and gets ready.

6:30 on the dot, a bell tolls and they burst into action.

"Okay, sisters," Magdalena says softly but with command, "what's on the agenda?"

As Evelyn and Magdalena buckle themselves into work belts, don safety goggles, and grab power tools, Veronica reads from her notepad:

"At eight there is the visit by the water authority people."

"After we tear out the wall in the vestry," Evelyn adds, "there's the laundry to do."

"And at three o'clock," Veronica calls as Magdalena and Evelyn are halfway down the hall towards the vestry, "there is your meeting with Mister Gordon Normal of Magnificent Waste Management Corporation."

Magdalena stops and frowns. This scheduled part of their day troubles her more than most. "Oh, yes, that."

The phone in the hallway starts ringing and, as Evelyn goes to answer it, Magdalena wrenches her thoughts to more immediate concerns: "Who's turn is it to relieve Sister Bernadette at vigil?"

"It's my turn, Mother Superior," Catherine says as she passes by on her way to the stairwell.

"Okay, sister, go. Be brave."

Catherine descends the stairwell slowly, gripping the banister with both hands. Magdalena estimates it will take her ten minutes to reach the basilica.

Evelyn turns from the phone, holding out the receiver.

"Mother Superior, it's Lola."

Lola is curled up in ball in the corner of her kitchenette.

"Mother Superior," she whispers desperately.

"Lola, are you alright?"

"I did it again."

"You did what again," Magdalena asks, concerned.

"I made something happen."

Sister Magdalena flashes a look at Evelyn and gestures she should go on ahead without her. Then, taking a breath, she returns to their prospective new novice: "Easy, Lola. What happened?"

"I made this gang of gross young men fall off a fire escape."

"Where?"

"Outside my kitchen window. I made the whole fire escape fall. It came right off the building."

Magdalena is skeptical but compassionate. She sits.

"Lola, why were these young men on your fire escape?"

"No," Lola rushes to explain, "it was across the alley. They were partying all night. And they were, you know, flashing me."

"Flashing you?"

"Yeah, it's like they pull down their pants and…"

"Oh, of course. I see." This being clarified, Magdalena moves forward: "Lola, we must pray for these young men."

"Yes, I know, because they're all being taken away in ambulances now!"

Magdalena stands back up, concerned but determined. "Lola, you can not be certain you made this fire escape collapse."

"I'm sure I did."

"Why?"

"They're always tormenting me. They can see right into my bathroom sometimes because there's no ventilation and I have to keep the window open a little to let the steam out and…"

"But… Yes… Okay. I understand. How many of them were out there?"

"Eight, ten, a lot."

"And it's an old building, no?"

"Well, yeah," Lola is forced to admit.

"There were too many of them out there. It's as simple as that. The old fire escape could not support the weight."

Lola looks down to the alley where emergency rescue personnel are carrying away the traumatized young men. She leans back in, bites her lip, and reconsiders. "Yeah, I guess," she murmurs inconclusively.

But Magdalena hears in the young woman's tone that she herself has won this little battle of nerves: "So, we'll expect you at five this evening?"

"Yes," Lola responds, chastised. "Yes, Mother Superior."


It's a few minutes till eight o'clock in the morning now and Jesus is waiting outside the gallery's grille partition with Donna Brown and Jim Little from the New York City Water Authority. He checks the time as they cautiously glance around. He's seen this hundreds of times, people uninformed about the life cloistered nuns lead. It's always this mix of fascination and horror.

"Sister Magdalena will be along soon," he mumbles, feeling the need to stand up for the nuns. "These sisters, they're like clockwork. Every minute of the day is organized. Chop-chop, no goofing around. They're always on time."

"They're never allowed to come out," Donna asks.

"They don't wanna come out," Jesus clarifies.

Donna looks away and shakes her head. "Weird."

Jim, though, intrigued, comes closer to the grille. "What do they do with their time in there," he asks.

"Pray, mostly," Jesus explains. "But they grow vegetables too. And they're always cleaning. Cleaning like crazy. I ain't had a day off since—" But he remembers he has to close the blinds inside the grille so that visitors can't see the nuns. "Excuse me a minute. I gotta get these blinds closed."

He lets himself inside the partition and reaches for the ropes to draw the blinds just as Magdalena appears, busy and preoccupied. For a moment, Jim has a clear view of her profile. But the blinds are drawn and he loses sight of her. A moment later, he hears her come forward.

"Good morning," the mother superior calls, welcoming them cheerfully, "please have a seat."

"Are you… the…" checking her clipboard, Donna reads, "the mother superior?"

"Yes, I am."

Jesus whispers helpfully: "She's the one in charge."

"Well," Donna explains, hoping she is heard through the blinds, "we've inspected the grounds and it appears the convent violates a few city ordinances."

The mother superior's calm, musical voice filters back to them unseen, perfectly proactive and helpful: "And what can we do about this?

"First of all," Jim suggests, timidly, "we need to get the convent on the city grid."

"The grid?" the mother superior repeats, cautiously.

Jesus interprets for her: "The city water system, Sister."

"Ah," she responds, relieved, "I understand. Thank you. But you see we have our own well."

Donna rolls her eyes: "Yes, of course."

And Jim jumps in to prevent anything disrespectful:

"Sister… Mother… Superior…" he fumbles, then, "you might have noticed you are surrounded by miles of sewage treatment plants, chemical manufacturers, and waste treatment facilities. The water table in this area can be reasonably assumed to be, well, contaminated."

On Manhattan's Lower East Side, just on the edge of Chinatown, Leo places the last of Lola's belongings in a rented van and locks the door. It's been decided everything will be stored at his place in Brooklyn while she's in the convent. She'll be away three months and can't afford to keep paying the rent. When she returns to the real world, jobless, they'll decide whether to live together at his place or find a new apartment as a couple somewhere else.

After checking the parking regulations spelled out on a sign nearby, he pockets the keys and heads back inside. But he stops to watch the last of the many ambulances depart the scene of this morning's nearly tragic fire escape collapse. It'll be in all the papers this evening, he thinks. Word on the street, though, is that no one was killed. TV reporters are already referring to the outcome as a miracle.

Climbing the six flights of narrow and tilted stairwell, Leo wonders if he's ready to marry. He's made it this far, to forty, without feeling his life to be lonely and empty like some other men he's befriended. Sex has never been too hard to find, at least since late adolescence. Although, he does admit he has often wished for girlfriends he had more in common with outside the sheets.

Pausing for breath on the fourth-floor landing, he feels like it's he himself who has entered a convent. He has never gone further than kissing Lola. Often, he holds her close to himself and knows she, say, feels his erection pressing longingly against her. He can see the effect—her own natural desire fighting a willed resistance he at one time felt must be her own particular brand of volatile sexual madness. It would be breathtaking to indulge that. But what would that mean—forcing his way past her resistance, pretended or otherwise? They call that rape, he concludes, and continues his ascent.

No, he does not doubt she desires him. More than that: he's convinced she cares for him. And, for his part, as he recently told his new friend, Father Robert, he can no longer imagine a life without this troubled, kind, resourceful, and possibly delusional heart-stopping beauty by his side.

The apartment is now empty. Lola kneels on the floor, double-checking the few possessions she's about to leave with, placing them one by one in a small suitcase.

"That's all you're allowed to take?"

"They give me two habits to wear. I hope they provide shoes. And I'm bringing my own underwear because that would just be weird, right?"

Leo comes down beside her and she leans back against him. He puts his arms around her.

"Three months," he says more or less to himself.

"Yeah," Lola replies, trying to understand her own actions.

"It'll be summer by then."

"You can come visit on Saturdays," she says for the thousandth time. But hearing herself say it again, she writhes a little in frustration and manages to twist halfway around to face him, grinding her bottom into his crotch and complicating an already highly charged afternoon.

"Are you sure you want to do this," he asks by rote, trying to ignore the obvious.

"I'm not a good girlfriend to have."

"You're the only girlfriend I want."

"But I've got problems."

"So do I."

"No," she protests lovingly, "you're totally..." But then, thinking about it, she continues, deeply curious: "What kind of problems do you have?"

"Apart from being in love with a girl who's about to enter a convent and who refuses to have an orgasm in my presence?"

"Yeah, apart from that."

"I've got a bad temper."

"You seem very patient," she counters, looking at him sideways.

"I keep it bottled up," he admits. "Deep inside, I'm this totally irate, indignant, acrimonious fuckhead."

"You hide all this rage very well," she compliments him, grinning skeptically.

"I'm a math teacher."

"Kiss me."

Their mouths find one another and they spiral into passionate kissing. But then Lola's mobile device chimes.

"Oh, it's *none*."

"What," Leo asks, more than anything else amused by the constant torture he agrees to submit to for this beautiful creature.

"Midday prayer," Lola explains, slipping away. "It'll only take a couple of minutes."

She opens her prayer app and kneels. Leo watches her.

"How many times a day you have to do this?"

"Six times. I found this great app."

"Like Muslim people?"

"I think so. Maybe. I'm not sure they have an app, though."

"Do you have to face in any particular direction?"

This stops her just as she's about to begin praying. She's intrigued: "Oh, I don't know. I'll have to ask the sisters about that."

"I'll just wait over here."

And he leans back against the far wall as Lola makes the sign of the cross and whispers: "God, come to my assistance. Lord make haste to help me..." With head bowed and eyes closed, she prays silently, every now and then glancing at the app for reference.

Leo looks on and thinks he's got to be one of the luckiest guys in the world, all things considered. And he remembers—

A year earlier: Leo is having a drink with some friends at a fairly upscale bar in lower Manhattan. Lola and Richard Drake are to his immediate left and he only notices them because Lola bumps into him with her elbow as she tries to keep some distance between herself and her boss.

Leo's attention is split. One of his friends is describing the interesting work he's involved with creating algorithms for a software manufacturer and Lola is ordering her drinks:

"I want a frozen margarita," he overhears her say, "a pint of Stella Artois—draft—a glass of water with ice, a shot of

Jameson's and a hot chocolate. But if you don't have hot chocolate a cappuccino will be fine."

The bartender is a young woman of obvious competence, but she feels the need to clarify: "You mean, all at once?"

"Yes, please," Lola confirms. "And a straw, thanks."

Drake sips his martini, crowding Lola amorously: "I'm thinking of promoting you to claims adjuster."

Lola stares dead ahead and watches the bartender gracefully and efficiently conjure her strange order into existence. Leo is amazed, too, as much by the young woman's skill as by Lola's bizarre requirements. He watches out the corner of his eye as the drinks are arrayed before her. She sips from one beverage and another with a concentration itself bordering on instinct; unobtrusive, though determined. Leo also sees Drake's hand caress Lola's ass as the chief executive of Rutledge Insurance places his lips near to her ear:

"What do you think of that?"

Drake's martini glass explodes and the drink soaks his shirt.

"Fuck!" he exclaims, jumping back.

"Wow! Oh my god! Sir, are you okay" the bartender asks, flying in with a towel.

"Where's the men's room?"

"Back on the left."

Drake storms off.

Lola, though, hasn't reacted to any of this. She continues sipping her collection of drinks and glances at Leo, who has totally lost the thread of his friend's story of high-level programming.

"I made that happen," she says, not proudly.

Leo sees no reason to disbelieve her: "Good for you."

~

Sister Magdalena guides elderly Sister Agatha into the kitchen. Bernadette and Veronica are seated before bowls of thin soup and crusts of hard bread, waiting. Agatha is happy and childlike. Seating her before her meal, Magdalena sits and bows her head to say grace. But…

"Did the Dodgers win," Agatha asks.

The other sisters look up, perplexed.

"Sister, please, it's mealtime," Bernadette commands, "no talking."

"What?" the blind and nearly deaf old lady responds.

Magdalena abandons grace and fixes Agatha's napkin to her habit. She breaks the old woman a piece of bread, softening it in the soup. "Yes, Sister," she says, "the Dodgers won; they won excellently."

"Oh, good!"

Bernadette is furious. "Don't lie to her!"

Magdalena has a lot on her mind and, in any event, is not a big fan of the Order's rules and regulations: "Why not?"

"Who are the Dodgers," Veronica asks, curious, never a sports fan.

"A baseball team," Bernadette answers in spite of herself.

"They don't come here anymore," Agatha continues, wistfully.

Speaking over the elderly nun's head, Bernadette places down her spoon and addresses Magdalena: "You see, now she won't stop."

"They used to come and ask for our prayers," Agatha insists, "just before the playoffs."

Veronica figures it out: "Oh, you mean, the Los Angeles Dodgers!"

"I have no idea," Magdalena admits, leaning over her soup.

"No, the Brooklyn Dodgers," Bernadette finds herself

having to explain. Then, turning to Sister Agatha, "Sister, the Dodgers left Brooklyn in 1957."

Agatha is beyond recall now, cruising along on memories from over sixty years ago: "The shortstop and the catcher, mostly—nice young men. Oh, I do hope they win the pennant. They try so hard."

Standing, irate, Bernadette proclaims: "You see, this is what happens when the Rule is not observed. Why are we in a cloister at all if the Rule is not observed and frivolous chit chat is allowed to erode our souls!"

Though they were warned in advance, Magdalena and Evelyn are dumbfounded by the older sister's severe principles. They feel absolutely ashamed for disappointing her so thoroughly. They shut up and eat their soup.


Meanwhile, two limousines stop before the tiny service entrance of the convent. A gang of corporate mid-level executives get out, men and women, mumbling directives to one another as they clear a path for their boss.

Gordon Normal steps out of the second car, straightens his tie, and shoots his cuffs. "Okay, Jones, let them know we're here."

Hubert Jones points to a younger man, Connor, and indicates he should go ring the buzzer. Connor approaches, looks around, and finally spots the crappy little doorbell seven feet off the ground to the left of the dented metal entrance. He reaches up and presses.

Just inside the door, Jesus waits. The buzzer causes a small bell to chime quietly and a red light to flash above the door. Jesus doesn't answer. He makes them wait.

Connor presses the buzzer again.

"Seems mighty quiet," Gordon says, looking around,

assessing his future plans. "What do you think they do in there? Is that buzzer even working?"

Jones steps up, nudges Connor away, and wraps on the door with his knuckles. It opens immediately and they all fall back. Jesus pokes his head out, overprotective and unshaven.

"Yeah?"

"Oh, hello," Jones says, collecting himself. "You must be…" And here he consults his notes and reads, assuming, like most people, he is pronouncing a Spanish given name, "Hey-Zeus Ortiz, the superintendent."

"Just call me Jesus."

"Jesus?"

"I'm American," Jesus asserts as always, "born here and everything. I don't even speak Spanish. Call me Jesus."

Gordon Normal comes forward himself. Jones has his uses, he thinks, but the man tends to get tripped up by useless minutiae. "Thank you, Jesus," he says good naturedly. "I'm Gordon Normal and I have an appointment to speak with the mother superior."

Jesus nods, looks the man over from head to toe, then glances around at the five or six executives and their shining limousines. "Yeah, I know. You all coming in?"

"Well, yes, of course. This is my staff," Normal explains, gesturing to his underlings.

Jesus is honestly impressed: "All these people work for you?"

"They do," Normal confirms, smiling. He likes this guy, Jesus. He doesn't trust him for a second, but he appreciates how thoroughly he's caught his own staff off guard. Most of them, Normal remembers, have master's degrees. They've lost the common touch, so to speak, if they ever had it all.

"So, who's running the waste management facility," Jesus

asks, concerned.

"Oh, I have hundreds of employees, Mister Ortiz, hundreds of men and women working in all these buildings surrounding this… this…"

"Convent," Jesus states helpfully. Likewise, he doesn't trust Gordon Normal as far as he can throw him. The man has had his eye on Our Lady of the Highway for years and expects him, Jesus, to believe he's forgotten what it is? He's almost insulted. But he lets it go.

"Ah, yes, a convent," Normal acknowledges, "thank you."

"Our Lady of the Highway," Jesus adds as some sort of oblique challenge.

"Exactly."

"I could use a staff."

"Excuse me?"

"I do everything around here myself. The sisters, they try to help out but, you know, they've got to always be praying an' shit."

Normal is beginning to lose patience: "Oh, well, I guess everyone has their work to do, Mister Ortiz."

"Word."

"Excuse me?"

"You gonna leave these cars out here unattended?"

"The cars," Normal asks, incredulous. How long does this congenitally criminal groundskeeper intend to stall?

Jones steps forward: "The drivers will remain with them."

"This ain't, like, you know, the safest neighborhood in the world to bring a nice car an' all," Jesus tells them, as if they were little children.

Normal has had enough: "Thank you, thank you, but may we come in?"

Just then the tolling of a bell is heard. Jesus checks his

wristwatch and looks skyward. "There it is."

"There's what?" Normal stops, looking around.

"The bells."

"Ah, the bells."

"It's three."

"Yes, our appointment is at three."

"Right," Jesus agrees, "so now I can let you in."

Exhausted, Normal nods: "We'd appreciate that."

"No problem, sir."

Jesus stands back, opens the door wide, and allows the executives to enter. Upon entering, Normal's chief assistant, Elise, stops and admires the grounds. "Oh, how quaint," she exclaims.

"Quaint's good, though, right," Jesus worries.

"It's lovely," she assures him.

"Thanks."

Jones, in spite of himself, is curious too. "You take care of all this yourself?"

Jesus is glad for an opportunity to show off and, simultaneously, broadcast his daily woes: "Yeah. Mostly. Like I said, the sisters help out but they always gotta go back and pray right in the middle of doing something, losing my tools an' shit. Look at this!" He reaches down into the cabbages. "I've been looking for this rake for a week!" And he steps aside to return the rake to his toolshed.

"This is remarkable," Jones admits, having for months thought of the place as just another eyesore standing between his boss and his boss' commercial objectives.

Elise, whose job it is to be the most uptight person in the company, is herself experiencing an almost unrecognizable moment of calm. "So peaceful," she sighs, relaxing.

"Yeah, but it's the perfect place for a sewage treatment

plant," Normal reminds them. "Trust me."

Meanwhile, inside the convent, Sister Bernadette grabs the ropes and lowers the wood slat blinds inside the iron grille partition and shuts them completely. Magdalena is seated on a chair in the center of the inner gallery.

"He won't be able to see me," the mother superior points out, weakly.

"Exactly," her sister confirms, "and you won't be able to see him either. Why allow the possibility for temptation?"

"We have business to discuss," Magdalena insists, willing to risk some slight exposure for this potentially very helpful meeting.

Bernadette secures the blinds. The gallery is dark now, the sisters are mere silhouettes. "How will the imperatives of that business change if the man is unable to see your face?"

"Meetings are a way in which people take the measure of one another," the younger, more worldly nun maintains. "He might not be able to decide if I'm acting in good faith."

Bernadette sits on a chair a few yards away. "Sister, it is not for you to advertise your good faith. You're a cloistered nun who has renounced all worldly favor and gain. He's a real estate developer and corporate CEO. Let the man say what's on his mind. That is what he has asked for. That's what you agreed to—against my advice."

"He may be able to help us."

"Open a brewery?"

"Perhaps."

The older nun ignores this, stands, and prepares to leave. But she pauses in the doorway. "Speak and listen honestly. The rest, the handshakes, the interested smiles, the endearing levity, it's all facile posturing anyway; at best, manipulating, at worst, vain."

As Bernadette closes the door and returns to the main hall, Gordon Normal and his staff are shown into the outer gallery. Jesus ushers Normal to a chair beside the grille and gestures to the staff that they can sit on the bench along the far wall.
Normal is unsettled.
The staff grow quiet and apprehensive.
Jesus lingers just inside the door.
"I'm here," Magdalena's lucid, transparent voice announces from behind the partition.
Gordon Normal flinches. His chair skids back an inch. He's not a man who's easy to scare, but this is a little bit more otherworldly than he anticipated.
"Mother Superior," he asks.
"Yes. Good afternoon."
Normal looks back at his staff and they ever so slightly cringe. He reminds himself again that most of them will need to be replaced before the end of the next fiscal year. But then he clears his throat and gets to the matter at hand:
"Well, Sister, I'm here to talk as we discussed on the phone."
On her side of the partition, in the spare, darkened gallery, Magdalena clasps her hands together on her knees and hopes for the best: "Yes," she begins optimistically, "let's begin."
"Do I go inside or do you come out here," Normal asks, adding: "My staff is with me."
"We stay as we are, Mister Normal."
Normal is blank for a few seconds. He glances back at Elise, the most reliable of the bunch. She just shrugs. He's on his own and turns back to the grille:
"With all due respect, Mother Superior, in that case we

could have done this on the phone."

"I believe that is what I suggested."

"Well, yes, you did. But—I'm sorry, I didn't think this was done in real life."

Magdalena can barely believe it herself: "It is, I'm afraid."

Normal leans forward on the chair, his elbows on his knees and, lowering his voice, clears the air: "Sister, I am prepared to pay five hundred million dollars for the property the convent sits on."

Magdalena nearly faints. She's been expecting some sort of offer, but nothing this substantial. She's been up late for over a week arguing with Sister Bernadette about how much of the convent is actually needed by the Order. Would it be possible, for instance, to maintain the basilica and carry on the vigil but sell off the rest of the property? Bernadette wouldn't budge—the grounds in their entirety are holy, she said. The much more pliable Sister Catherine was terrified as well at the thought of abandoning the convent. And the Rule of the Order—as passed on from one generation to another— stipulated that a mother superior could not make such a decision herself. A unanimous decision would have to be reached by the existing community of sisters who had been cloistered for at least ten years. So, Magdalena is in no position to steer a new course.

"I understand," she replies weakly, "but we cannot sell it."

Normal is dumbstruck. This figure is even a hundred million dollars more than what he decided to offer for the convent when he left his office an hour ago. But this place has gotten under his skin; the tricky groundskeeper, this strange partition, and this lovely voice filtering through to him from inside—what? He's getting angry but he calms himself:

"Listen, Sister, we all know Our Lady of the Highway has seen better times."

If Gordon Normal could only see the mother superior now: a hand to her brow, eyes closed, her free hand clutching her rosary beads. She sighs, finally, and looks up into the shadows near the ceiling:

"How would you define better times," she asks, almost desperately, genuinely curious, because she really needs to discover some way to accept the position she is now forced to maintain. She needs the man to give her the ammunition she can use to convince her sisters.

"More prosperous times," Normal states, disappointingly.

No, she thinks, that's not good enough.

"Our work is to pray for world peace, Mister Normal. None of us sisters own anything and all the convent has is held in common."

"But, still, there must be practical everyday needs? Electricity, modern plumbing, heat!"

She would love these amenities to be more reliable. Certainly, the Order could accomplish so much more good with the use of them. But she's bound to adhere to the party line: "Our indoctrination has conditioned us to live with the bare minimum. Prosperity is something of a foreign notion to us, Mister Normal. But, please, do go on."

He's getting desperate. He was hoping it wouldn't have to come this: "What about your safety?"

Magdalena smiles, though she's almost in tears. She, too, was hoping Normal wouldn't have to play this card: "Ah, yes," she sighs, "that has become an issue lately."

The man feigns ignorance and concern. "Oh, really? I'm sorry to hear that."

"Yes," Magdalena plays along, "we are sometimes, recently, intruded upon by a few misguided boys with unloaded handguns."

And Gordon Normal looks down as she nudges Vincent's firearm slowly out from under the grill with the toe of her ankle boot. He's furious and glances at Jones.

Jones frowns and looks away.


As the reader will, no doubt, remember, Vincent was picked up by the cops shortly after his botched raid on the convent. After the kid's cuts and bruises have been tended to, he has to sit down with Detective Pena:

"So, you're telling me you got beat up by a nun," asks Pena with a grin.

"This was like no regular nun, officer. I got aunts back in PR who are nuns and I'm like, you know, all: RESPECT! But this bitch was mean!"

Pena sets down his pen, weary, and continues. How many little, naive, braggarts like this does he process each week? He moves ahead: "So was this before or after you drove the stolen Honda Civic though the window of the Starbucks?"

"That is my mother's car, I keep telling you!"

"Where did you encounter this nun, then?"

He's got the kid off balance now.

Vincent's not so concerned about the nuns. He's sure Jones at Magnificent Waste will cover for him come what may. But he's terrified of getting smacked with auto theft.

"That ain't important, man! I did not steal that car!"


Her meeting with Gordon Normal accomplished, Magdalena staggers out of the gallery and into the hall where Bernadette and Veronica are waiting to catch her as she falls into their arms in despair.

Bernadette nods, firm but fair:

"Good work, Sister."

"Five hundred million dollars," the dazed young mother superior moans deliriously.

"You showed him we can't be bought with money!"

They help her down the stairs to the basilica.

"Just think what we could do with five hundred million dollars," Magdalena sighs. "Family planning clinics throughout Central America; we could get the union for the workers; hospitals; legal aid for immigrant refugees…"

"Sister," Bernadette urges with evident tough love, "pull yourself together!"

"We could be fully independent, without the need to lobby politicians and special interest groups!"

Reaching the landing, the halfway mark down to the basilica, they stop and Bernadette tries to buck up her idealistic fellow believer. "Your job is to pray! The Lord will abide and help us if we remain steadfast!"


Gordon Normal storms out from the gallery and into the convent's garden, followed by his panicked entourage. Jesus is waiting for them:

"Who's her immediate superior," the CEO wants to know.

"She's the boss lady 'round here, sir," Jesus explains.

"No, I mean, the Catholic Church is a big organization. There must be someone reasonable I can talk to. A priest or a… I don't know. I need to talk to the head office."

"There's the bishop."

"The bishop?"

"He's the boss of the diocese."

Normal turns aside to Elise: "What's a diocese?"

She's already surfing the internet on her tablet and reads:

"A district under the pastoral care of a bishop in the Catholic Church."

"Ah! Okay, a regional corporate officer of some kind," Normal announces, encouraged. "Right, okay, excellent. Where can I find the bishop?"

Down in the basilica, Sister Evelyn is completing her vigil on the floor before the altar. "Turn then, most gracious advocate, your eyes of mercy toward us, and after this exile show to us the blessed fruit of your womb, Jesus. Oh clement, oh loving, oh sweet Virgin Mary…"

Staggering into the basilica, Magdalena falls to her knees and taps Evelyn on the shoulder. Wrenched back into mundane reality, the prioress gasps and stands while Magdalena takes her place on the floor. Evelyn watches her friend a moment, concerned, then backs away, weak from her prayerful labor. A moment later, the doors close with a resounding thud, Evelyn being the only one strong enough to move them.

"Dear God," Magdalena begins with effort, "forgive me for my presumption and ignorance of your ways which are not known, but help me to learn the patience to bear the burden of this submission. Guide me in the tricky ways of small-time crooks, entitled corporate manipulators, sleazy politicians, and shortsighted righteously indignant people like Sister Bernadette."

She pauses, raises her face from the floor and looks across the flagstones to the far wall, collecting her thoughts.

"I do, Father, learn from your example and see that the battle, though against us on all fronts, is fought one field at a time, no matter how small, and this convent here, a burden I receive gratefully to temper my pride and presumption, this convent is, as I say, the field I have to work with at present."

Only now does she turn her gaze to the altar.

"Please assist me in making of it a light to help find the lost and a haven for the just, the generous, the kind, and the…" She sighs and leans up on one elbow, continuing, "…well, actually, the just, the generous, the kind, and the crazy brave. Because, dear Father in heaven, we have to think on our feet and rub elbows with the world as we find it, no?"

She lets this sink in with God.

Satisfied with having said what she needs to say, she prostrates herself again, face to the floor, arms out at her side, making of her body a cross, and continues: "Our Father who art in heaven, hallowed be thy name, forgive us this day our trespasses as we forgive those who trespass against us."

A little earlier in the day, back at Lola's soon-to-be-vacated apartment, Leo waits as she finishes her midday prayers.

"Let us praise the Lord," Lola concludes, "and give him thanks. Amen."

Finished, she stands, clicks off her mobile device, and acclimates to the everyday again after ten minutes of buoyant mindfulness and pleasurable mental tension she's anxious to discuss with Sister Magdalena. But right now, she finds herself unprepared for the reality of leaving this handsome and kind man seated there on the floor in front of her.

"Time to go," Leo says, pensively.

"Is it?"

"Well, the sisters are expecting you at five, right," he calculates, standing. "There's bound to be traffic on the bridge."

She moves into his arms. "Yes," she whispers, holding him close before adding, "but first."

And she leaves it at that.

Leo looks down at her.

They kiss.

The lights in the stairwell start to flicker.

Lola closes the apartment door and tears off her shirt. Leo stumbles out of his trousers.

"You sure?"

She rushes back across the room. "Not all the way," she demands eagerly.

"Part of the way?" And he falls over on the floor as he kicks away his jeans. She lowers herself down to him.

"Most of the way."

"Lola, you're killing me."

"I know."

And as the unmistakable sounds of love are heard up above, the bare bulbs lighting the stairwell explode one by one. The fire alarm sounds. The sprinklers are set off. Tenants come running from their homes, annoyed, and scramble down to the sidewalk.

FOUR

Firefighter First Class Burke is stomping up the stairwell of Lola's dilapidated building, extinguishing small flames issuing from the electrical outlets and lighting fixtures. He smashes a hole in the flaking old plaster and shoots a burst of fire retardant in at the sparking wiring. He kicks open doors to look for more trouble. Finding none, he calls further down the stairwell. "Top floor, last apartment. You down there?"

"Yeah," his partner, Flynn, replies from below, double-checking the various apartments. "Casualties?"

"No," Burke calls, then, making sure: "Electrical, right?"

"Yeah. Just the stairwell."

"Hold on," Burke calls as he reaches the top landing and kicks open the last door.

Lola jumps back, half into her underwear, and stifles a scream. Burke looks from her to Leo passed out on the floor, naked.

"I didn't mean it," Lola confesses, "honestly."

Disregarding her, Burke comes down over Leo as Flynn arrives in the doorway. "Whoa," the younger firefighter lets out, seeing Lola shimmy into her jeans. But he rights his priorities immediately and, of Leo, asks: "He okay?"

"He's breathing," Burke ascertains. Then, keeping his gaze averted, addresses Lola: "What happened?"

"We had sex," she admits.

"Too much information," the firefighter cautions as he stands and looks around. "Anything," he asks Flynn.

Flynn is at the kitchenette's gas range. "No gas leak. You smell anything? Fumes?"

"No," Burke answers, stooping back down to Leo, "I think he's just passed out."

Flynn fumbles with his walkie and allows his attention to stray over to Lola again. She's reaching back to secure her bra.

"Damn," the young man barely whispers.

"Flynn, focus," Burke states plainly.

Flynn speaks into the walkie: "Hey, we need a stretcher up top on six. Unconscious Caucasian male no injuries." Then, pausing to think, he adds: "Conscious Caucasian female no injuries, code eleven."

Down in the street, the probationary paramedic, Edson, looks aside to his older partner, Arsham. "What's a code eleven," he asks. The seasoned veteran is already climbing from the truck.

"R-rated."

"Let's go!"

Upstairs, Leo comes to.

"Hey, fella, you okay," Burke asks.

Leo's not sure what happened, but he feels fine. "Yeah. I just…" But he really can't say what happened.

Lola throws his jeans at him: "Here, Leo, get dressed."

Burke holds up his finger and passes it back and forth before Leo's face. "You see my finger?"

"Yeah," he answers, distracted, trying to stand.

"Don't exert yourself," Flynn cautions, "they're coming up with a stretcher."

But Leo climbs into his jeans and shakes his head: "It's okay, really. I'm fine."

"We seriously have to go," Lola insists, helping Leo on with his shirt.

Edson and Arsham arrive, winded, on the landing.

"Yeah, look, thanks," Leo manages, embarrassed, "but I really have to get her back to the convent."

The firefighters pause. They look from one to the other and then back at the couple. Burke points at Leo:

"Too much information."

And they all thunder down the stairwell in search of other fires to put out. Lola and Leo wait, watching them go, then hustle to get out of the building themselves.


About this same time, Gordon Normal is in the garden at the convent and he wants to know where he can find the bishop of the diocese.

"Downtown Brooklyn," Jesus informs him.

"Elise, organize that," Normal calls back over his shoulder.

"On it," Elise replies and has already got phone numbers and contact information to hand. She's dialing her mobile phone as they head for the exit. Jesus opens the door for them but Normal slows and glares at Jones, whispering:

"Who the hell are these nincompoop punks you sent over to frighten the nuns?"

"They came highly recommended," Jones lies.

"I mean, what's it take to terrorize a few old maids who pray all the time?" But then he stops, hearing Elise interrogating one of the drivers.

"Where are the cars?" she asks.

Normal steps out through the little door and finds the executives standing around in the muddy street looking for their limousines. The drivers look guilty as sin, staring at their shoes. "We—I—went around the corner to—relieve myself and—well, but." The first driver leaves it at that. His associate does no better: "And I went—to the—you know, bodega over there to get—something to—and."

Normal wonders once again why he second-guesses his immediate impressions. For months he's sensed incompetence pervading his operation like a bad smell emanating from a clogged toilet way down the hall. "Who hired these guys," he asks, not wasting time.

"That would be me, sir," Connor offers bravely.

"Okay, you're fired," the boss decides. "Scram." Then, turning to Elise: "Call a car service."

But she's already on that too.

The remaining executives have already forgotten Connor who is wandering away, his career in waste management finished, trying to locate a subway station or a bus stop.


By now, Leo is driving Lola from Manhattan to Brooklyn in the rented van packed with all her belongings. From the passenger seat, she watches him. He's strangely calm, at peace.

"You okay?"

"Yeah," he says, changing lanes.

"You sure?"

He glances over at her. Has he been missing something? It's sometimes hard to tell with Lola. "Are *you* okay," he asks in return.

"No," she says with some urgency, "I'm freaked out."

"Why," he ventures, though he's already afraid to hear the answer.

"Well because I had an orgasm and it started an electrical fire in my apartment building."

Leo pulls over to the curb on Delancey Street at Essex and stops the van. "No, it didn't."

"And it made you have some kind of a seizure!"

"All those buildings in your neighborhood are dangerous wrecks, built a hundred years ago to stand for maybe ten or twenty years. It's a wonder they don't all topple over into the street—sometimes they do."

Lola looks away and out at the passing traffic. She reminds herself not to sulk. "So, you don't believe me."

"About what, exactly," Leo feels it necessary to confirm.

She dies a little every time she has to address this out loud, sounding like a maniac even to herself: "About my, you know, unwonted psychic powers."

But, once again, Leo surprises her. "No, I believe you."

She looks across at him and says nothing her expression can't say better. But he's gazing out at the trash tumbling by in the wind and she needs to poke him with her finger.

"Really?"

"But not because I think you set the building aflame by making love to me," he answers, thoughtfully.

"Oh. Well, then, why?"

"Because that was the best sex I have ever had."

And then, after another long moment, he turns and looks at her too. Lola hesitates before leaning close and placing her hand on his chest. "You didn't die temporarily or anything, did you?"

"What?"

"Or have some kind of out-of-body experience?"

"No," he assures her, shaking his head.

"Leo, you passed out!"

"I was satiated," he exclaims, "exhausted, and in love! I fell asleep! Sue me!"

She climbs over into his lap and kisses him passionately. He smells good this time of day, she notices, ten or twelve hours since his last shower, having sweated a little lugging her stuff down to the van, the tang of sex still clinging.

"Wow, Leo, we're good together," she decides.

"We are."

"But I have to enter this convent."

"For three months."

"Yeah," she confirms, experiencing the force of her decision to do so in a whole new way.

"Okay."

"You're not angry?"

"No."

She returns to the passenger seat. Leo starts the van and pulls back out into traffic. "It's okay if you want to see other women," she suggests.

Leo won't even go there. He reaches out with his right hand while driving and places a finger to her lips. She grasps his hand lightly and kisses his palm.

"Really," she continues.

"Stop talking."

"Because I know a man has, you know, needs."

Now Leo thinks he might be a little offended. He is certain he's getting a little fed up. "What, and, like, you don't have needs too?"

She just shrugs and looks out at the East River as they proceed up onto the Williamsburg Bridge. "Yeah, but I can handle it. My self-discipline is very highly developed because of my situation."

Her situation. More psychobabble from the therapist or self-help verbiage she's come across online somewhere. Or did she get this from the nuns?

"Well, if you can handle it then I can handle it too," he declares, driving on in silence.

She thinks she's hurt his feelings. "I just feel guilty for making you have to do that."

"Lola, I'm a grown man," he explodes in a small way. "In my life, on occasion, I've gone without so much as a kiss for three months."

They drive on. She stares at her knees. He already regrets having raised his voice.

"Is that true," Lola finally asks.

He glances over at her, then back at the bridge ahead. There's always more to learn about someone, he thinks, no matter how much the center of your life they might be. "You find that hard to believe?"

"You're not bad looking," she admits, tilting her head to one side.

"Thanks."

"And you're sweet."

This is all very much appreciated, but he's really dying to know: "You've never had a dry spell, then, huh?"

Lola looks away and sighs, shrugs like it's all so unremarkable: "Oh, sometimes. Maybe. It's different for girls."

He tries his best to catch a glimpse of her face as he drives. "How do you mean," he asks carefully.

"From about the age of twelve or thirteen on there's always someone who wants to kiss you."

Leo pulls over, right there on the bridge, and stops. Horns

are honking immediately. "Like who?"

"Boys, men, neighbors, other girls, strangers in cars, teachers. You know, there's always someone. Leo, I think we better not stop here."

"Whoa," he half gasps and holds his hand to his brow.

"It wasn't like I was abused or anything. That's just how it is."

He puts the van back in gear and moves on. Gradually, casting tentative glances at her as he drives, he manages to ask:

"How do you deal with that?"

"With being a girl?"

"With all this unasked-for sexual attention."

"I don't know. I just sort of imagine I'm a small round unseen object with no feelings. That usually works. I don't know how other girls deal with it."

Leo wishes he hadn't asked. He drives on.


Sister Evelyn is checking in on the progress of a fairly substantial, though jury-rigged, microbrewing operation in what was once the convent's vestry. Bernadette and Catherine follow her into a large enclosure formed by four sheets of massive heavy gauge plastic. They look on in a mixture of curiosity and disapproval as the prioress checks thermometers and tubing.

"The temperature in the germinating room should remain at sixty degrees Fahrenheit," she explains as they approach the edge of a large table in the center of the space. It is, in fact, a six-inch-deep basin filled with raw barley soaking in water.

"How long do we soak the barley," asks Catherine, her otherwise traditionalist sensibilities not so bruised by innovation.

Bernadette, however, just frowns.

"About forty hours," Evelyn answers, "and the water needs to be changed pretty regularly. I've modified this old industrial basin Jesus found and rigged it up so I can release the old water and let that out..." She twists the tap of a faucet down below, demonstrating. Then, straightening up and reaching for another up above, she continues, "...while letting the fresh water in."

Bernadette is shaking her head in dismay. "That the Lord's work on earth has come to this! God have mercy on us sinners!"

"Amen, Sister," Evelyn concurs, getting a little desperate for a cigarette.

"But won't we need something to put the beer in, Sister Prioress," Catherine inquires.

"Oh yeah. We're working on that."


Gordon Normal and his staff are still waiting for the car service to arrive out on Resurrection Avenue. Jesus gestures for Gordon to step aside and talk privately.

Gordon does.

Jesus is scrolling through his mobile phone contacts:

"I can get your limos back for you," he whispers out the side of his mouth.

"Is that so," Normal asks, not surprised.

Speed dialing, Jesus explains: "Only one dude around here stupid enough to do this in broad daylight."

Normal happily recognizes extortion and smiles.

"Thanks. I won't press charges if the cars are back here, intact, in ten minutes."

"Sure. But, listen," Jesus takes the opportunity to point out, "the sisters need bottles."

"Excuse me," Normal asks, genuinely lost.

"Beer bottles. Lots of 'em. And seeing as how you got this gigantic recycling business—"

Normal is by now perfectly fascinated by this scheming, double-crossing con man: "Mister Ortiz," he begins.

"You can call me Jesus."

"Jesus," the gentleman obliges, "are you trying to shake me down?"

"Oh," Jesus protests, "I wouldn't think of doing anything like that. Honest. It's just, you know, the sisters: they're starting a brewery."

"A brewery!"

But now Jesus' phone vibrates. "Hold on." He steps aside and answers, barking into the phone, "Xavier?"

Directly across the street, in an abandoned parking garage, Xavier is standing near a window opaque with grime, gazing, terrified, at the two limousines. "Yeah," he squeaks.

"Listen, you bastard, we know you got those limousines!"

"What the fuck am I supposed to do with them now, though, Jesus!"

"Oh, you think you can play tough, huh, wise guy!"

Confused, Xavier just looks at his phone.

Jesus glances aside at Normal who is not fooled by any of this. "He's trying to negotiate."

"What size bottles, Jesus?"

"Twelve-ounce longnecks, preferably green, if you got 'em. Hold on." And he steps away, whispering loudly into the phone for Gordon Normal's benefit: "Of course, I won't tell your mother! Just tell me where those stolen limos are!"

A few hours later, at the Brooklyn diocese building, Father

Robert is shown into the bishop's office by Sister Ellen. The bishop is glad to see him but is busy with aggravating paperwork. Robert is happy to announce: "Mother Superior thinks she's found a few more sisters for Our Lady of the Highway."

"Where?"

"Honduras."

The bishop drops his pen and frowns: "Damn it, Father! You telling me we gotta go all the way to Central America to find a few good nuns these days!"

"Sorry, your reverence. It's the best we could do."

Frank stands and moves to the minibar. "Ah, it's not your fault. They speak any English?"

"Two of them do."

"Criminal records?"

"Nothing to speak of," the priest assures him. "They come from parishes that have been forced to flee the violent gangs that more or less run the city of San Pedro Sula after the recent *coup d'etat*."

"There will be more of that before the year's out, come the bad weather and the food shortages. How many?"

"Three. Making it nine sisters in the convent and bringing the vigil down to about two and half hours for each nun."

"How old are they?"

Robert reads from a brief he's prepared: "In order of seniority: fifty-four, thirty-seven, and… sixteen."

"Sixteen!"

"I know. But…"

"Yeah, we can't be choosy," Frank admits. "I suppose the immigration authorities will raise a stink."

"Mother Superior believes she can make use of the network she and Sister Evelyn put together to reach these shores themselves."

"The less said about that the better, Father," the bishop reminds the younger man as he sits back behind his desk.

"Agreed."

"And who the hell is this man, Gordon Normal, who's called here three times in the last half hour?"

"Gordon Normal is the CEO of Magnificent Waste Management Corporation. He and his various subsidiaries own and control almost all the property surrounding Our Lady of the Highway for two miles. He wants to buy the land the convent is on."

"Interesting. I suppose he's offering a significant amount of money."

"In the many millions, I'm sure."

Frank stands up again, startled: "Jesus, Mary and Joseph," he shouts loud enough to cause Sister Ellen to look up from her own paperwork outside.

"But the sisters have refused to sell," Robert continues.

"My God! With that amount of money, they could relocate anywhere they wanted! Somewhere nicer, quieter, safer!"

"I'm afraid it's not as simple as that, your reverence—"


The night after Sister Dominique died, back behind the tool shed on the premises of Our Lady of the Highway, Jesus is using a small motorized backhoe to dig a grave. Troubled, Father Robert is keeping lookout. Jesus finishes with the grave and shuts off the engine.

"You know this is against the law, right," argues the priest.

"Father, you don't know the half of it," Jesus mutters as he climbs off the backhoe and makes his way across the garden to the convent. "Come on," he calls back over his shoulder.

"Half of what," Robert wants to know.

"The sisters think this place is holy. They have to be buried here. It's in the book."

"The book? What book?"

"The Rule," Jesus says. "The Rule of the Convent." And when he reaches the coffin, he gestures to the priest, "Here, help me with this."

Robert sets aside his bible, comes over, and lifts one end of Sister Dominique's tiny coffin. They carry it back across the garden to the grave site. "Where did you find the Rule of the Convent?"

"In the vestry, in the room where they keep all the records and stuff, when I was a kid."

They reach the grave and set the coffin down into it. Father Robert is as curious as he is anxious. "What do you mean, as a kid?"

"I was born here, Father," Jesus tells him, climbing back onto the backhoe, "I never knew who my mom was. One of the nuns, maybe. Or some girl on the run from the law. Those were bad times around here; race riots, drugs, juvenile delinquents, car bombs." He starts up the engine and shifts into gear. "The sisters took in lots of us kids. I had the run of the place till I was ten or eleven."

As Robert goes back for his bible, Jesus lifts a pile of soil and starts covering the coffin. By the time the priest returns, he's ready to climb off and finish the job with a shovel.

"There's all kinds of useful stuff in that book, Father," he sums up. "So, I stole it for safe keeping like."


Meanwhile, Gordon Normal, Hubert Jones, and Elise are observing this late-night activity at Our Lady of the Highway from high up in their corporate HQ.

"What the hell are they up to now, Jones," Normal asks as he puts on his jacket to leave.

Jones peers through binoculars: "I think they're burying a body."

Elise shivers: "These religious fanatics are a menace to the community!"

"Now that's got to be against city and state ordinances, right," Jones asks, lowering the binoculars and turning away from the window.

Normal takes the binoculars and looks for himself. "Not enough to shut them down, though. They'd probably just get a summons or something. We need to discredit them entirely." Then, handing the binoculars back to Jones, he adds: "We've got to get in there and have a look around."

"Rumor has it there's a new mother superior on the way," Jones informs him.

"Elise, let's make an appointment to meet this new mother superior—whatever that is."

"Will do."

"I'll make an offer they'll probably refuse. But we'll get a better idea of who we're dealing with."

He starts from the office, but turns back when he reaches the doorway. "And, Jones, in the meantime, send some teenage punks over there to scare them a little; help convince the sisters this is no neighborhood for such well-meaning and devoted religious ladies like themselves."

Jones lowers the binoculars and blinks, worried, before turning back around to his boss. "Sure. I'll get right on it."


So, that was all a few months ago. And we know what's gone down since then. Right now, though, Normal and his staff are still waiting out on Resurrection Avenue for the limos to be returned when Leo and Lola arrive in the rental van. The lovely couple stop and get out across the street from the executives who, simultaneously bored and scared for their jobs, can't help but look on as the lovers embrace tenderly. Still holding her to himself, Leo glances at the convent.

"Are you sure you want to do this?"

"Not really."

"There's still time to change your mind."

"I promised the sisters."

"Like you said, we're good together."

"We'll be even better if I go through with this thing—I think."

"I'll be waiting."

They kiss once more and then Lola carries her suitcase to the entrance.

Elise falls back, crushed. "Oh, no!"

Another of her female associates, Debbie, shakes her head in despair. Even Hubert Jones has an opinion on this: "Now, that's a waste," he declares.

"Miss, please, don't do it," calls Debbie.

Lola is confused by this small crowd of corporate executives and looks to Jesus who stands waiting in the doorway, smiling his busted-up grin.

"Hey, Miss Lola!"

"Don't throw your life away," Debbie pleads.

"Um, sorry, I have to, you know…"

"The world has so much to give," Elise insists.

"Yeah, I guess. But, well, sorry. Bye."

And Lola enters.

Jesus is about to close the door, but then leans back out and calls to Gordon Normal. "The limos are in that garage right there. The door is unlocked. Bye. I'll come get those bottles whenever you say. Thanks."

The door is pulled shut and they all listen as bolts are

thrown and locks are made fast.

"That's really heartbreaking," Elise sighs.

Shaking his head, Normal makes for the garage. His staff, he decides, are emotional slobs. "Come on."

The executive staff of Magnificent Waste Management follow their boss but, passing Leo, slow down and can't help themselves:

"What did you do to her?" accuses Elise.

"Or what did you *not* do to her," Debbie hisses, raising the stakes.

Jones, more reasonably, inquires: "Why don't you save her from this?"

Leo is overwhelmed. He defends himself before he even decides he has to: "It's only for three months."

"Consider the damage that can happen in three months in a place like that," Debbie nearly screams.

"They'll warp her mind," Elise adds, searching for some Kleenex.

"They'll turn her into a cold and unfeeling zombie," says Jones, man to man.

Still caught off guard, Leo tries to explain: "The idea is that quiet meditation and service to others will have a healing effect."

Gordon Normal stops, intrigued. He hasn't been interested in this little drama. But now he comes closer. "So, there is something wrong with her?"

Leo has had enough. "Who are you people?"

Normal offers his hand, but Leo's not sure he wants to take it. "Gordon Normal, CEO, Magnificent Waste Management Corporation. Forgive our interference, but we're all a bit shook up."

Now Leo sees an opportunity. He needs to know more

about the convent. "You've been inside," he asks.

"Well, inside the foyer or the vestibule or the porch or whatever."

"Is it, you know—safe?"

Normal needs to stigmatize this convent, so, glancing at Jones, he hands the show off to him: "Safe," he asks, begging elaboration.

Jones plays along, heavy on the melodrama. "Not safe," he announces. "Those helpless brides of Christ in there are at the mercy of any godless criminal with an eye to easy gain."

Leo looks to Normal for an interpretation.

"Apparently," the boss explains, dialing it down a notch, "our fair ladies of the turnpike have had armed intruders recently."

Off to the side, the corporate females are a cloud of anxiety: "I shudder to think what goes on in there anyway, much less… much less…" Elise refuses to imagine. Debbie shakes her head: "Poor misguided unprotected women…"

Sensing they've got Leo on the ropes, Normal comes in for the knockout punch: "It's practically our civic duty to close this place down!"

Upstairs in the convent, Lola is shown to her tiny cell by Veronica, who indicates a small parcel of clothing neatly placed on the narrow and hard bed. "This is your habit," she says, fidgety. "I hope it fits. We can make alterations tomorrow."

"Thank you."

"Soon it will be *vespers*. You'll hear the bell. Afterward there's the evening meal."

Lola wants to help the girl relax and wishes she knew how. "Okay," she replies and smiles.

Veronica knows she ought to leave but lingers, excited, shy, embarrassed. Keeping her eyes lowered to the floor, she finally manages to pour forth a small torrent of explanation. "It's nice to have someone kind of around my own age here, though we're not supposed to be friends and have favorites."

Lola is moved and steps forward to reassure her. "We'll all be friends."

Veronica looks up, shyly. "I really do like your shoes."

Lola compares her sensible but attractive footwear to Veronica's well-worn pair of heavy-soled boots. "Would you like to try them on," she suggests, thinking this is a convenient way to get past the clumsy preliminaries of friendship.

Veronica is breathless. "Can I?"

"They'll fit, I think," and Lola starts undoing the clasps.


Jesus is carrying cardboard boxes piled high with empty green bottles into the garden and stacking them outside his toolshed. He is assisted by Xavier, who is, as always, terrified.

"I'm afraid of those nuns, Jesus."

"Good, you dumb fuck."

"They beat the piss out of Vincent and I ain't seen him in days."

"What the hell were you scumbags doing breaking into the convent! That's a sin, man. Those sisters is holy!"

"They paid us to."

"Who did?"

"That guy from Magnificent Waste Management, Jones."

Jesus' outrage implodes. He can hardly form the words:

"God damn! You mean you working for the enemy!"

"They just wanted us to scare 'em and shit. We didn't mean nothin'."

"Go get the rest of those bottles and stack 'em here."

The kid takes off and Jesus crosses to a barred window looking out from what is now the brewery.

"Sister Evelyn," Jesus calls. "Hey, Sister!"

Evelyn appears, obscured behind the pebbled glass and cast-iron bars.

"Oh, Jesus, have you got the bottles already?"

"Yeah. Two hundred or so. I'll get more later."

"Excellent. God bless you. What about a refrigerator?"

"No luck. But I'll talk to this guy I know tomorrow. In the meantime, put the bottled beer in the basement below the basilica."

"The basement?"

"Yeah. It's always cold down there."

"I don't recall there being a basement below the basilica."

"There is. I used to play there as a kid."

Sitting chastely on the edge of her cot, Lola is enjoying the feel of her new habit. Meanwhile, Veronica is admiring her ankles as she paces back and forth in Lola's pumps. They're both startled when Evelyn appears. She's in a hurry and wants not to be seen.

"You two. Follow me. Come on."

Intrigued, Lola and Veronica exchange excited glances and follow.

Coming down the stairs from the dormitory, Evelyn grabs a flashlight from beside the wall phone. She hands it to Veronica.

"Take this," she commands, "downstairs."

Evelyn pauses and casts a glance down the hall to make sure Sister Bernadette is preoccupied in the brewery. Lola trails a little behind, not knowing her way around. But

Veronica calls girlishly from below:

"Lola, this way!"

Evelyn whips around, scolding her with a glance, and Veronica claps her hand over her mouth. Lola catches up and they descend.

Evelyn silently pushes in through the large doors and steps into the basilica, followed by the younger nun and the new novice. Magdalena, stirred from her vigil, lifts her forehead off the floor and looks back at them without stopping her prayers. Evelyn gestures to her that all is okay and continues quietly along the edge of the large space towards the altar.

Lola is astounded by what she sees here: the bright and forceful mother superior lying face down on the stone floor in abject submission! What has she done to deserve this?

Magdalena, of course, has no idea what is going on but dares not interrupt her prayers. Nevertheless, she leans up on one elbow to observe—or, at least, listen.

Evelyn is studying the floor behind the altar, kicking at the edges of the flagstones. Veronica is preoccupied with her new borrowed shoes but Lola catches on.

"What are we looking for, Sister Prioress?"

"A trapdoor or something," Evelyn replies. "Jesus said he used to play down here and…"

But now Lola spots cobwebs under the altar being stirred by a small steady draft. "Here, Sister, look!"

They come over and huddle under the altar. Brushing away decades of dust, they find a latch. They grasp it and wrench it back.

Below is darkness and the sound of lapping water. Evelyn peers down through the hatch and hesitates: "Sister Veronica, hand me that flashlight."

Switching it on, the prioress casts its beam down onto a

rotting wood staircase leading to a small stone pier above dark, oily water. Not the basement she was looking for but maybe something better. She leads the way, testing the rotting stairs step by step. Lola follows. Veronica watches from up top.

Fifteen feet out from the pier is a large rusted corrugated piece of sheet metal hung on casters. "This is the canal, I guess," the prioress says, casting the flashlight's beam along the far edge of the ceiling. "That's a door."

Lola follows Evelyn's thinking. She locates a chain hanging down against the far end of the mysterious little grotto, steps over and tugs on it, tentatively, and nothing much happens except the sheet metal rattles. Evelyn comes over and takes hold of the chain herself. She gives a more forceful tug and causes the door to slide open a few feet, revealing the wide, polluted industrial canal outside.

Up top, hanging in through the trap door, Veronica is delighted. "Wow! Who knew!"

Evelyn is having ideas.

Lola is having ideas, too, and she innocently suggests: "With a little work, this could be an excellent shipping and receiving depot."

Evelyn nods, agreeing, though her ideas take her further afield.

"Sister Veronica."

"Yes, Sister Prioress?"

"Please relieve Mother Superior at vigil."

"Now? But…"

"Please."

"Okay." The girl complies and vanishes.

Magdalena dutifully, expertly, professionally, keeps up her prayers as Veronica kneels, taps her on the shoulder, and prostrates herself as expected. Only then does the mother superior jump up and run for the altar.

Down below, Lola is studying the area behind the pier, a low ceilinged twenty-foot-square space carved out of the rock. "And, you know, this is a good place to store the bottled beer. It's cold enough and will save on electricity needed for refrigeration."

"Yes, of course," Evelyn agrees, preoccupied.

Magdalena comes carefully down the steps to join them, amazed, and immediately enthusiastic about this new find, as if it were the answer to her prayers. "Oh! Sister Prioress, this is perfect!"

"That's the canal," Evelyn explains, "which leads to the East River, which leads to…"

"New York Harbor."

Lola watches, realizing, finally, that the sisters have some previously discussed project on their minds.

And they do—

A few days earlier, Magdalena is on the phone in the main hall. Evelyn stands aside and keeps lookout.

"Enrique," she asks cautiously into the receiver.

Their friend Enrique is on the docks in Honduras with five nuns he's trying to smuggle out of the country. He's anxious. He hesitates. But when he sees the coast is clear, he gestures for the nuns to hurry up a gangplank onto the waiting ship. Only then does he reply to Magdalena on his cell phone: "*Sí*. Yes, Sister, it is me."

"How is it going?"

"It goes well. Our friends should be in New York Harbor by Thursday."

"Good. Are they okay? Are you safe?"

"The sisters are a little shaken up. Some are hurt. Things are bad in the town." He steps back into a recessed doorway from where he can watch the ship and not be seen himself. "There are two more of them than we planned on."

"That's fine. And what about you? You have to get out of there too, Enrique."

"Soon. But right now, no. You will have someone at the same place in the harbor?"

"Of course. We still need to find a way to get them to the convent unseen. But we will. Soon. In time. I promise."

"God bless you, Sister."

"Peace be with you always, Enrique."

So now, while Magdalena and Evelyn are whispering in the convent's kitchen about how they will smuggle five refugee nuns into the country, Leo enters Margaret's Bar and discovers the ever-cranky detective Pena nursing his third can of beer—cold, domestic, and cheap.

"Professor!" the edgy cop calls brightly, though it always sounds like a threat.

"Hey, Detective," Leo responds. Pena is not his favorite guy in the world. "How's everything?"

"How's my boy doing in school?"

"Ben? He's great. He's a gifted mathematician," Leo tells the man for the tenth or eleventh time.

But Pena is afraid of talk like this: "And that's what— good, right?"

"Yeah. Of course, it's good. He's a bright kid."

"Because sometimes I think that kid is fucking retarded."

Leo doesn't hate anybody but he really wishes this man would find another bar to frequent. "Ben? No. Ben is very bright. He's just shy." Then, to Chastity: "Whisky and a beer chaser, thanks."

"Tough day at the junior high school, huh, professor," Pena teases him.

"No," Chastity interjects good-naturedly, "his girlfriend just entered a convent."

But the humor falls flat. Chastity sees immediately that Leo is unhappy to be discussing this and feels horrible to have blurted it out. Leo lays his hand on hers and communicates, wordlessly, that it's alright but let's move on.

Chastity slinks off.

"Whoa! Enough said," Pena concedes. "Chicks are weird about religion man." He drinks, burps, and blows his nose into his handkerchief. Finally: "She'll get over it, though." Then, curious, the detective asks: "What convent?"

Doing his best to remain civil, Leo confesses: "Our Lady of the Highway."

Pena goes all serious and grim. He puts down his beer and stands up off his barstool: "Oh man! No. That place ain't safe!" And he goes on to regale Leo with tales of his own pain-in-the-ass workweek.

Days ago, of course, Vincent is still handcuffed to a chair beside Pena's desk and the detective repeats his questions till the kid is worn out:

"So, you're telling me you got beat up by a nun?"

"That is my mother's car," Vincent insists, petulantly. "I keep telling you."

"Where did you encounter this nun?"

"That ain't important, man! I did not steal that car!"

"No, it is important because someone or other has been breaking into Our Lady of the Highway on a fairly regular basis."

Suddenly Vincent wonders if they give a shit about the car at all. It is, as he says, his mom's. But technically he did take it without permission. And crashing it through the window of the Starbucks could've happened to anybody. About the nuns, though, he choses to lie outrageously:

"Officer, I did not see her inside the convent! What are you nuts?! It's a whatever the fuck—a cloister. Girls only. No, she was like just prowling the street."

"Prowling," Pena repeats, tired.

"Yeah, like she's this wilding nun an' shit, attacking young men at random."

Pena has had enough. He walks outside to the hallway and closes the door, crossing to Detective Oscar's desk: "Lock him up."

"The sisters don't want to press charges."

Pena goes to the watercooler and gets a drink. "Lock him up anyway. Just for the night." He drinks and tosses away the cup. "And throw someone we know in the cell with him. This little prick is bound to brag his ass off and we might learn something." He throws on his jacket, getting ready to leave, but stops: "You reach his mother?"

"Yeah."

"Is it her car?"

"Yeah," Oscar chuckles, "but she says he stole it and she'd be happy to press charges."

FIVE

Dawn arrives again at Our Lady of the Highway. It's Sister Catherine's turn to be up early and ring the bells at precisely six o'clock. She sits upright on the steps leading into the bell tower, nodding off now and again. But years of habit have made it impossible for her not to be awake for *lauds*. She blinks her eyes awake, checks her old wristwatch, and enters the tower.

The bell tolls softly.

Magdalena, Evelyn, and Veronica each emerge from their cells and move silently down the long hallway towards the stairwell.

In her own cell, dressed in the white habit of a novice, Lola sits on the edge of her narrow bed and fortifies herself. She takes a deep breath, stands, and goes out.

Sisters Bernadette and Agatha are already approaching the chapel off the main hall when the others appear descending the stairs, Lola at the rear. They all enter the small chapel and lower themselves to their knees. Bernadette pulls the string that turns on the electric ventilator up in the window and takes her place.

They pray.

"Come to my assistance, Lord, make haste to help me. My soul magnifies the Lord and my spirit rejoices in God my Savior for he has looked with favor on the lowliness of his servant…"

Leo comes through the subway turnstiles and waits on the platform, choosing not to read the newspaper he has tucked up under his arm. Anyone noticing him would think he has something fairly heavy on his mind.

And, in fact, someone has noticed. Father Robert is on the opposite platform, on his way to his own early appointments around the parish. He waves to get his friend's attention. It works and Leo snaps out of his reverie. "Good morning," he calls.

"Yankees and Red Sox tonight at seven?"

"Where?"

"Where else—Margaret's! Meet me at the rectory!" the priest yells just as their respective trains barrel into the station.

The sisters finish their small breakfast and silently wash up. This is accomplished almost immediately and they sit in silence around the table. Lola is taking everything in, learning the ropes. She looks to the wall clock.

It's 6:27 a.m.

Sister Veronica looks particularly happy and peaceful and this makes elderly, cranky, Bernadette suspicious. Lola notices the older nun lean aside and glance beneath the table to see Veronica's feet, prettily clad in Lola's own pumps. She herself looks aside at some cutlery on the nearby counter and hopes not to be scolded. She glances up at the clock again.

It's 6:29 and 54 seconds.

She waits as the seconds tick slowly by. Finally, 6:30 strikes and the sisters are bustling immediately:

"Okay, sisters," Magdalena begins, "a lot to get done today. Who's next up at the high altar for vigil?"

"That would be me, Mother Superior," Veronica says dreamily, "at seven."

"Good. Till then, please help Sister Lola get started with the accounting." Turning to Evelyn, Magdalena continues, "Sister, what can we expect in the brewery?"

"Another batch ought to be ready by early afternoon, Mother Superior. I can use a hand with the new bottling machinery."

"Yes," Magdalena nods, understanding, "we'll do our best in shifts throughout the day." Calling across the room, she asks: "Sister Bernadette, have the bottles arrived?"

Bernadette frowns. "Yes, Jesus arrived mysteriously in the middle of the night with another truckload of them."

They both know what this means: with the breakdown of negotiations with Normal, Jesus has simply resorted to robbing the recycling plant. But Magdalena puts a positive spin on it:

"God bless the man. He is resourceful, isn't he?"

Lola and Veronica move off to start their day's work and as Veronica goes on ahead, Bernadette grabs Lola's elbow.

"Where did she get those shoes?"

Terrified, Lola hesitates. "They're mine."

"They're shameful."

"She likes them," Lola rejoins pathetically.

Just then, passing the counter, Magdalena notices the cutlery and stops. "Now, how do all the spoons get bent like this?"

Not needing this explained, Lola hurries out of the kitchen. She moves up the main hall, close to the wall, like a fugitive, and turns into an office with a few desks and outdated office equipment. Sitting, she tries to wake up the computer by tapping the keyboard.

"This computer is…" But then she has graver doubts. "Where's the mouse? There's no trackpad." She stands back away from the desk to take in the whole picture: "Is this a computer?"

Veronica points to the serial number on the back and reads: "Computing Device."

Lola joins her and reads as well: "Patented 1987."

They stand back, skeptical. "There must be a power switch."

"Here it is," Veronica discovers.

Lola flicks the switch. The young women fall back as the machine kicks into gear like an old lawn mower. Veronica looks on as Lola tries to use this ancient computing device:

"Okay, let's see," she says, typing, "one hundred minus ten equals—"

They wait.

They continue to wait.

"It's working," Veronica suggests optimistically.

Lola bites her lip. Then they both fall back, happily, reading the display: "Ninety!"

Still, Lola is concerned.

Veronica, however, is at peace with the world in a whole new way: "I'm so glad. I have to go do vigil now."

"Vigil," Lola asks. She's heard this referred to already.

"Five hours. Lying flat on the floor. Uninterrupted prayer. In the basilica."

Lola recalls Magdalena doing such a thing yesterday evening and assumes it's a punishment. "Did you do something wrong?"

"Of course," Veronica sighs, "I'm wearing these shoes. And that's vanity, pure and simple. So, I'll have to pay for it. See you this afternoon."

As Veronica drifts out, holier somehow than she has ever been in her life, Magdalena appears. "So, Sister Lola, what is the nature of the current crisis?"

"Mother Superior, I think I made a mistake."

"With the accounting? Already?"

"No. I mean I let Sister Veronica wear the shoes I arrived in. They're really just a simple low-heeled pump but…"

"I thought she was a little whimsical at breakfast."

"She's really into shoes."

"I know. She's a fetishist. It's her particular weakness."

"Does she really have to lie face down on the floor of the basilica for five hours just for wearing flattering footwear?"

"Of course not."

"But she is. She just left."

"No, Lola, you're mistaken. She is just participating in the Rule of our Order," the mother superior explains. "The sisters of this convent have been praying for world peace without interruption for nearly three hundred and fifty years. It was considerably easier when there were twenty-four nuns, a relay every hour. But now, with so few of us—well, you see the situation. My job, quite specifically dictated by the bishop, is to recruit more nuns for the vigil and, by any means necessary, make the convent… oh, what's the word?" She consults a scrap of paper she draws from beneath her habit:

"Ah! 'Sustainable.' That's it: sustainable."

"Mother Superior, may I make a suggestion?"

"Of course."

"We need a modern computer."

"I was afraid of that."

"And the internet. Wifi."

"Our resources are limited."

"Can I use my mobile device here?"

"Certainly."

Magdalena moves off and Lola whips out her mobile device, speed dialing Leo.

Leo is in the middle of a lesson. His class of bright thirteen-year-old kids are crowded casually around his desk as he works at the blackboard.

"Okay, right. Suppose we decide we want all polynomial equations to have roots. But we have no numbers in our possession except the natural numbers. Then a simple linear equation like…" he writes across the board, "$2x = 3$ has?" He points to Ben, Detective Pena's shy but talented son. "Ben?"

"Um…" is about all the boy wants to venture until his arrogant and unpopular classmate, Chris, steals the show:

"No root."

Leo hates when kids do this. He was asking Ben a question he knows Ben can answer just to get Ben more comfortable talking aloud in class. "Good," he's forced to say. "Thank you, Chris." Then, opening it up to the whole group again: "Now, in order to remedy this condition, we invent—what?"

"Fractions," Sasha tosses out, hiding her face in the collar of her sweater just in case shame is about to crush her to pieces.

"Exactly!" Leo exclaims. Sasha, too, is smarter than she suspects. "But a simple linear equation like, say…" and he writes out on the board, "$X + 5 = 2$ has no root even among the fractions. And, so, we invent—what?"

"Negative numbers."

Leo's day brightens. It's Ben. He knew this kid would reach these conclusions on his own with just a little encouragement. "Negative numbers!" Leo shouts, triumphantly. "Outstanding!"

Everyone cheers like they're a football team.

But a mobile phone is heard ringing and they all stop, mortified. Chris is excitedly looking around to pin the blame on someone.

"Mobile phone! Mobile phone in class! Grounds for suspension!"

"It ain't mine, promise," pleads Sasha.

Leo, though, is amazed to recognize the ring tone. "Chris, knock it off," he scolds lightly, then reaches for his briefcase. "Wow, that's mine." He scrambles through his briefcase as the kids have fun at his expense:

"Oh! Major bad," Derek giggles.

"Probation," Sasha announces mock solemnly.

Even Ben joins in with: "Double-Whammy Probation!"

Derek makes himself sound like a busted PA system: "Will Mister Haroldson please report to the penalty box!"

"I know, I know," Leo grins, amused. "I'm breaking the rules but, then, it's got to be…" Reading the name on the display, he answers: "Lola?"

Now the kids are delighted—their teacher has a girlfriend!

He gestures for them to disburse and amuse themselves elsewhere, though Chris hangs back.

"Sorry to bother you," Lola says.

"You alright?"

"Yeah, but I need my laptop."

Leo grabs a pen and starts to make notes on a scrap of paper he finds on his desk. "Okay. Sure."

"It's in one of the boxes at your place."

"Got it."

"Thanks."

"I thought you had to stay apart from secular society and abstain from technological culture and so on?"

"I know, that's crazy," she admits. "What was I thinking? It was something I read online, I think."

"You need anything else?"

"Oh, yeah," she remembers and turns away to whisper. "Underwear." Leo writes this down as she continues: "We can only do laundry once a week here till they hook the place up to the city water system or something. There's some in the small, red leather, designer suitcase with the funny handle. You know the one—the handle looks like a dog collar."

Leo scribbles all this down and turns away, listening while he paces the classroom, reluctant to sign off.

Chris, meanwhile, leans in and reads the note: laptop + underwear + red leather + dog collar.


Gordon Normal strides up one of the corridors down on the administrative floor of Magnificent Waste Management Corporation's massive complex. He enters a conference room where Elise is seated with Donna and Jim from the Water Authority. Elise stands:

"Mister Normal, this is Miss Brown and Mister Little from the City of New York Water Authority."

"Hello, how are you?" Normal smiles, coming forward to shake hands. "Nice to meet you."

"Likewise," replies Jim, fascinated to meet the man fashionable magazines are always writing about.

"Thanks for taking the time" Donna adds, less awestruck.

"Not at all," Normal says, making a small show of his magnanimousness. "I understand we might be in violation of certain city ordinances."

"That's right, Mister Normal," Donna says with relaxed, smiling certainty, indicating there is no room for discussion. Normal nearly flinches, so unaccustomed is he to being told, even obliquely, what to do.

Elise is better informed and, at a glance from Normal, she rushes to extinguish possible ill will: "Going forward, it will be necessary for Magnificent Waste Management to forgo disposing of drainage runoff directly into the canal."

"I see," Normal nods, trusting Elise to have run interference already. He's prepared to acquiesce and somehow still retain the upper hand. He just needs a minute. Happily, Jim buys him that time with further niceties:

"And we understand that connecting the facility's massive drainage to the city's sewage and water pollution control infrastructure represents a substantial investment."

"Well, but we've got to do it," the CEO announces with exaggerated humility, seeing the bigger picture.

"I'm glad you understand," Donna smiles, pleased.

"It's got to be done. Being careful about the environment is just good business, is it not?"

"Of course," Donna nods and closes the folder before her, standing, anxious to be done with this.

"I'm going to be mayor one day," Normal pontificates, "and I want this to be a shining example of government and commerce working together to make things right."

Donna doesn't respond as expected and simply allows Elise to usher her out of the room. Normal is stunned. Jim hangs back, though, eager for more time with the king of garbage.

"Careless planning and irregular development over the years has led to a situation in which, now, we're discovering unforeseen infractions almost every day in this area."

Normal is silently irate, but, nevertheless: "Is that so?"

Donna, however, has stopped at the window in the hall and juts her chin down towards Our Lady of the Highway: "Even that convent out there."

Normal is very interested all of a sudden: "Oh, you've met the sisters, have you?"

"Well, at least one," clarifies Jim, joining them.

"The mother superior," says Donna, "Sister Magdalena."

Normal's eyes widen, "Sister Magdalena? I see she has a name!"

"You've met, then," Donna asks.

"If you can call it that," he replies. "Blocked by bars and blinds. Couldn't even see her face."

"We weren't allowed inside, but we did see her through the bars for a moment," explains Jim.

"Is that so?"

"An attractive women."

"And very well-spoken, I thought," adds Elise. "Much more sophisticated than you'd expect."

Donna buttons her coat and nods: "It's just so strange she'd want to be locked away and hidden from the world like that."

"As if imprisoned," Elise agrees.

Normal lets the others walk on ahead and pauses, running that phrase back and forth through his head: *as if imprisoned.*

Over at the junior high school, it's lunch recess and Leo is alone in his classroom searching for something on and around his desk. The principal, a frigid middle-aged disciplinarian named Missus MacGillicuddy, appears in the doorway with the scrap of paper he's misplaced.

"Are you looking for this, Mister Haroldson?"

Leo glances over, sighs, and approaches, relieved. "Ah! Thank you, Missus MacGillicuddy. A breeze must have swept it off my desk."

She doesn't offer it to him. She holds it back. "No, it was brought to me by one of your students."

Leo stops, thinks, then ventures, "Chris?"

"He's still very upset with having been given detention for using his mobile device in class last month."

Leo sighs and looks away. "Oh, man. Listen, I forgot to turn my phone off. It was an emergency."

"Your student claims his own infraction of the rules was an emergency too."

"No, he was, in fact, texting Ben threatening demands for the answers to a pop quiz."

"Be that as it may, you've set a very bad example here."

"Look, it's Lola's first day in the convent. I felt I needed to be on call."

"Lola?"

"My girlfriend."

"Has entered a convent?"

"Temporarily," he explains. Then: "it's like a therapeutic type thing."

"She's ill?"

"Not really. Maybe."

"And she called you at work."

"She needs some things she left at my apartment."

MacGillicuddy reads from the hastily scribbled note:

"Such as her laptop, underwear, red leather, and dog collar?"

It sounds kinky even to Leo. He coughs and tries to repair the damage. "Out of context that might appear…"

But she hands back the list. "Your private life is your own

affair, Mister Haroldson. But our students ought to be safe-guarded from the sordid details of it."

Suitably chastised, grateful, and frustrated all at once, he just wants this to be over. "Of course. Understood. Thank you."

MacGillicuddy stops and turns back in the doorway. "This incident with the phone call in class will have to go into your file."

"Of course."


Gordon Normal stands at the window of his office looking down at Our Lady of the Highway when Jones arrives with a tablet, sorting web pages.

"What'd you find," Normal asks.

"The nearest matches I've found are with a radical activist nun operating in various Central American countries. Originally a citizen of Argentina, studied in Paris and London. Sister Tatiana-Magdalena dos Santos e Ramirez, commonly referred to as Sister Tatiana-Magdalena. Wanted in seven countries and, due to treaty alignments, not a welcome visitor to the United States either."

Normal considers this and returns to the window. He asks himself again: what manner of lunatic would refuse five hundred million dollars for an apparently valueless plot of dumping ground beside a polluted canal? And the answer keeps coming back the same way: a radical activist nun with a price on her head.


Jesus answers the street door and is disappointed when he finds Leo standing there. "Can I help you?"

"I have some things for my girlfriend."

"You mean Sister Lola?"

This stings. But Leo bounces back: "Well, yeah. Tell her Leo's here."

"I'll take it," Jesus offers.

But Leo hangs on to the stuff and backs away. "She's expecting me."

Jesus waits, thinks, then steps aside and let's Leo enter.

"Listen, man, I'm just saying it's been less than twenty-four hours." Then, as Leo enters and he redoes the locks, he adds: "You gotta get distracted with something and let her do her thing."

Moments later, Leo sits waiting in the outer gallery as Jesus sweeps the floor far across the room. They both look over as they hear someone approaching. Lola appears inside, behind the grille, and comes forward, smiling. Leo stands and drifts toward her.

"Hi," Lola says softly, seeing Leo is taken off guard by her habit.

"Hey," he finally replies. "Wow. I didn't expect... well..."

"What?"

"You look really pretty in that."

"Thanks," she smiles, flattered, "but I think it's supposed to, like, disguise my feminine individuality and stuff."

"Whatever," Leo sighs, never having been too up-to-date about fashion anyway.

"Thanks for coming and sorry for calling you at the school."

Leo snaps out of it and lies: "Oh, it was nothing." He passes her laptop in through the bars of the grille, then the power adaptor and, finally, a plastic bag. "Underwear," he whispers.

"Thanks."

"So, are you okay in there?"

"Leo, it's only been one day."

"I heard it's dangerous."

"The convent?"

"They say criminals have been breaking in."

"Oh, that's just these idiots the waste management company hire to scare the sisters. They want to buy the land and build a toxic waste dump or something. But Sister Evelyn beat them up and they ran away."

Leo's trying to look in past the inner gallery and into the hallway beyond. "What goes on all day?"

"We make beer!"

"Really?"

"The sisters built a microbrewery with all this equipment Jesus found around town." She hands him two bottles of their brew, excited. "Here, take some."

Leo takes the two unlabeled bottles as she passes them through the grille. "For real?"

"We bottled a hundred and twenty today."

"Is it any good?"

"I think so. But we need feedback."

Leo slips one bottle into each of his coat pockets. "How's everything else?"

"I think I bent some spoons at breakfast but I'm not sure. We're expecting the arrival of some new sisters tonight."

A bell tolls. Lola looks up and back over her shoulder:

"That's the call to *vespers*. I have to go."

They press close to the grill and interlock their fingers.

"I love you," Leo whispers.

"I know."

But she has to go. She steps back, turns slowly, and leaves. Leo sighs and looks at Jesus who is still standing just inside the door with his broom.

"It's better cold," Jesus advises.

As Leo rides the subway back from OLHW, at Saint Ann's Father Robert is juggling two phones while throwing on his coat to leave the rectory. Patsy is placing letters before him on the desk for signing.

"Listen, Father," he calls respectfully into one phone, "if you can get a subway over to Jackson Heights and do the 5:30 mass at Our Lady of Grace on Saturday I can get Father Joseph from Seton Hall to do those funerals in Hoboken tomorrow morning." He hangs on while his associate checks his calendar, then, "Right, uh-huh." Turning to the other receiver, he proceeds, "Father Joseph, you drive, correct?"

Meanwhile, Patsy puts another call on hold: "Father, it's Sister Maria Theresa in Yonkers."

"What now?"

"The girls volleyball team. Their bus broke down and they have no way to get to the county playoffs in the morning."

Father Robert just stares into the middle distance, mentally triangulating schedules, distances, and resources. Then: "Hold on, Fathers." Placing down the two receivers, he grabs his forehead and addresses Patsy: "Call that priest, what's his name, the Armenian guy in Washington Heights."

"Father Vladimir?"

"Yeah, him," he says, slapping the desk, "he's got three buses and a volleyball team so bad they're never likely to go anywhere."

"But Father, they're Eastern Orthodox."

"Don't be so factional, Patsy. We're all in this Christianity thing together. Sink or swim." Returning to his previous calls, he adds: "And get Sister Maria Theresa that bus. I owe her one." Then, lifting the receivers, "Sorry Fathers, I gotta go. We'll continue this later. Peace be with you."

He hangs up and sees Leo in the doorway holding aloft the two bottles of beer.

In the cloister's rusted and dented pickup, Jesus skids to a stop out on Resurrection Avenue and jumps out. Moments later, he comes rushing into the gallery from the garden carrying a length of heavy-duty rope coiled over his shoulder, two life preservers, and a large, powerful flashlight.

Lola is waiting for him at the gate in the partition. "What took you so long? Everything okay?"

"Some religious fanatic stopped traffic on the BQE, threatening to blow himself up with all of Exit 32A. Here," he says, placing the coil of rope carefully over her shoulder.

"Oh, wait," she says, buckling at the knees.

"It's heavy," Jesus cautions, "careful."

Robert and Leo enter Margaret's Bar and Leo places the beers before Chastity.

"What's this," she wonders, amused.

"The sisters of Our Lady of the Highway are making their own beer, Leo explains. "They need feedback."

Chastity gets three glasses and hands Robert a bottle opener. He goes to work on the bottle caps as the skeptical bartender studies Leo:

"You visited her already?"

"It's not like how it…" he begins, but then admits: "She needed her laptop and stuff."

Chastity tastes the beer. The guys do too. Then she pours some for Chet, a retired plumber who more or less lives at the far end of the bar near the window.

"Not bad," Chet says.

"Refreshing," Leo admits.

"Funky," is Chastity's professional opinion.

Father Robert muses, "Mysterious."

Nodding, Leo sips again and qualifies, "But uncomplicated."

"Suffused with the odor of holiness," the grizzled plumber declares loftily and Chastity reminds herself to learn more about this most regular of her customers; wordless for hours at a time, he'll say the most beautiful things on occasion.

"Amen," the priest agrees. "What channel's the game on?"

Chastity tosses him the remote and tastes the beer again, savors it a moment, and then asks no one in particular: "You think the sisters themselves drink this stuff?"

Sisters Bernadette and Catherine are industriously bottling beer. Their old, confiscated, second or thirdhand bottling machine makes a lot of noise and threatens to fall apart from its own mechanical spasms. But for the time being it's functioning dependably.

Bernadette pauses and steps aside. Waiting to make sure Catherine's not looking, she takes a sip of a beer she has stashed on a nearby shelf.

Down the hall, Lola steps in from the inner gallery lugging the rope and life preservers. She sees Sister Agatha slowly climbing the stairs from the basilica and ducks into a doorway to hide. Sister Evelyn intercepts the elderly nun.

"Good evening, Sister," she calls softly. "How are you feeling?"

"Thank you, Sister Prioress, I'm fine. Just a little stiff. It's such a help to have you all with us now."

"Get some rest. I'll see you at *compline*."

"Bless you, Sister," Agatha replies as she moves off

slowly, blindly, and nearly deaf to her cell behind the kitchen.

Evelyn gestures to Lola that all is clear and takes the rope from the girl as they hustle downstairs.

Below, Magdalena is standing outside the doors of the basilica, pacing, checking her wristwatch, tense. "They must be out of the harbor by now," she says uselessly to Evelyn as the prioress descends towards her.

"They'll wait till darkness," Evelyn assures her, "we still have time."

They push in through the heavy doors to the basilica.

Conveniently, Veronica is on duty at vigil. She continues praying as she glances at the conspirators passing quietly by. She nods obediently to Magdalena and smiles mischievously at Lola. But as Evelyn and Lola pull back the trapdoor and descend to the pier, Magdalena hears Jesus whispering loudly at one of the windows.

"Mother Superior! Sisters! What can I do?"

Magdalena comes over and calls quietly up to the window. "You have been a great help already, Jesus. It's best you not be here. Go hang those flyers you made. Peace be with you and we'll talk in the morning."

By now, Evelyn and Lola are down on the pier and the prioress is showing the novice how to work with the rope. "We want to tie this off to..." she looks around. "What is this?"

"I think it's the pump for the well."

Evelyn climbs in over the bedrock and checks its strength. "That'll do." She fastens the rope to the pump as Lola climbs down to the lowest bit of the ancient pier, still two or three feet above the waterline.

Magdalena arrives, her nerves taut, and, seeing Lola, cries:

"My God! Sister Lola, please, wear the life preserver!"

Meanwhile, Jesus comes out to the street from the little door with his old pit bull, Desmond. He's got a stack of flyers under his arm which he places on the ground and steps on while he wrestles the door closed and slips a beefy combination lock into place on the outside. The dog looks around for a good place to piss.

"I like these new sisters, Desmond, but I worry about 'em."

Desmond grunts, uncertain. He pisses briefly and trots back to the truck. Jesus opens the passenger side door and helps the dog climb clumsily up into the cab.

Night begins to fall on the canal behind the convent. A long, low-slung motorboat moves slowly forward into the deep watery industrial murk. As it comes closer, five nuns can dimly be seen huddled in the bow. A man is at the stern, his hand on the tiller. He watches the canal ahead of them, on the lookout for a known and expected signal but careful, too, to spot the dreaded giveaways of surveillance.

Gordon Normal is at work late, poring over documents at his desk. He's distracted, though, and reaches for the intercom.

"Elise? You still there?"

"Yes, Gordon. I'm here."

"Try again and see if you can get the convent on the line."

"Okay," she replies dutifully.

"Be sure to ask for 'Sister Magdalena'," he adds.

"Right." She doesn't need to be reminded. He's been obsessing about this for days.

Meanwhile, the helmsman stops the boat in the canal and waits. The five nuns wait too, exhausted and anxious. Some of them are obviously ill. One is passed out. In the gloaming, one can make out bloodstained bandages, bruises, and cuts.

One nun, Jeanne, seems to be the one in charge or, more likely, just the one who's the least tired and infirm. She keeps her eye on the helmsman so as to move quickly when he sees the signal he's looking for.

Lola, wearing the life preserver, is stationed down on the lower edge of the pier with the flashlight as Evelyn pulls the chain that opens the corrugated metal door.

The helmsman and Jeanne cock their heads, alerted by this distant noise.

The door hasn't been opened in decades and the noise it makes as it slowly slides open is excruciating. When it's finally pulled aside, though, and things quiet down, the sisters hear the phone ringing far away in the main hall upstairs.

Elise is at her desk at Magnificent Waste waiting for someone to pick up.

Down on the pier, the conspirators are worried.

"Who would be calling us now," Magdalena gasps.

"Who's upstairs," Evelyn asks Lola.

"Just Sisters Bernadette and Catherine working in the brewery."

This is unfortunate and Evelyn frowns. They want to keep this little operation a secret from the older sisters. "They'll be wondering where we are," she says.

"We can't let them know about this," Magdalena insists.

"I'll go and answer it," Lola volunteers and starts climbing up onto the pier. But Magdalena stops her:

"No. It's too late. Stay where you are. I'll see to it."

Bernadette has stepped outside the brewery to have another few sips of beer while the bottling machine clanks and rattles away inside. She, too, hears the phone. Aggravated, she sets down her brew and goes to answer it. But Magdalena is rushing madly up the stairs from the basilica.

On the other end, Elise is losing patience and is about to hang up when Magdalena reaches the phone just a few steps ahead of Bernadette. "Our Lady of the Highway," she says, winded. "How may we help you?"

"Oh, hello. I'd like to speak with Sister Magdalena."

Magdalena knows immediately that this is a setup. A bad sign. She covers the receiver with her hand and addresses Bernadette, spotting the bottle of beer at the far end of the hall. "All is well," she smiles. "Please, Sister, return to your work. Thank you."

Suspicious, Bernadette trundles away as Magdalena considers how to respond on the phone. Finally: "May I ask who is calling, please."

"This is the office of Mister Gordon Normal of Magnificent Waste Management Corporation."

"Ah, I see. Hello," Magdalena dissembles artfully, "this is the mother superior. You must be Elise. We've spoken before."

Elise frowns, her ruse undone.

"Yes, Mother Superior, that's right." Then, giving up, she concludes: "In fact, I'm sorry, I see Mister Normal has left for the day after all. Sorry for troubling you."

"Not at all," Magdalena replies warily.

Down in the canal, the helmsman tilts the outboard motor up out of the water, grabs the oars, and glides slowly a few yards, never taking his eyes from the dark recesses up ahead.

Evelyn is crouched down on the pier, trying to see through the low door and out into the canal. Lola, being lower, has a better view. "You see anything," Evelyn asks.

"Nothing yet."

Evelyn checks her wristwatch. "Make the signal: one long, two short."

Lola lifts the heavy lamp and prepares to signal.

The helmsman, waiting, sees the signal—one long and two short flashes of light. He looks to Sister Jeanne who leans out over the bow, low, right down over the water's surface. She has a heavy-duty flashlight herself and returns the same signal—one long, two short.

Lola's jaw drops, excited. "Oh my god. It works! They're out there."

"They signaled back?"

"Yeah."

"Signal again. The same way."

Lola signals.

The signal confirmed, the helmsman nods to Jeanne. She and another, very young, nun, Marie, grab oars as well and all three of them start to row; quietly, steady, but swift.

Elise leans into Gordon's office. "No luck. 'Mother Superior' answered the phone."

But Gordon, standing at the window, is too preoccupied to be riled up by this. "Did you see that?"

"What," Elise asks, joining him.

"Flashing lights out on the canal. Like, you know, signals."

What with his increasingly paranoid certainty of a vast liberal elite conspiracy aimed at destabilizing him and his aims—just him, they have no other targets, it's all about him—Elise half expects Gordon to start spotting UFOs pretty soon. She checks the time and decides: "Your car is waiting downstairs."

The refugees sweep silently over the calm dark surface of the water, making for the dim glow of the grotto, lit now by candles Evelyn and Lola are lighting.

Upstairs, Magdalena slowly replaces the phone's receiver. That was a disturbing call. No one should know the mother superior's name but her sisters, Father Robert, and the bishop. That was decided weeks ago before she even arrived. How did Magnificent Waste Management come to ask for her by name?

But she has work to do now. This will be dealt with tomorrow. She runs back down to the basilica, bolts the door, and hurries to the altar. The fugitives pull in their oars and silently coast the rest of the way in towards the pier. Magdalena comes down the stairs just as the boat glides in and fills the small grotto. The helmsman stands and tosses a line to Evelyn who ties off. Magdalena grabs the chain and pulls the door shut. Evelyn then grabs hold of her own secured rope and hangs down off the pier, hoisting the immigrant sisters up and depositing them beside the mother superior.


Over at Margaret's, Leo and Robert are concerned about a possible double play by the Yankees. Further along the bar, Charles and his friends are busy at their mobile devices. Jesus comes in with Desmond and the stack of flyers under his arm. He's also got a few bottles of OLHW Beer.

"Jesus," Father Robert exclaims, surprised.

The busy, preoccupied youth look up from their devices.

Jesus, spotting Leo, comes forward and mumbles with concern: "Hey, you gonna be okay?"

Leo sighs with relief as the failed double play at least brings up the opposing team's best hitter. Then, glancing at Jesus: "I'll do my best, thanks."

The groundskeeper turns to Chastity, handing her a flyer:

"Can I hang up some of these?"

She takes one and reads it aloud as Jesus hands more out to everyone else: "Prayers of Intercession by the sisters of

Our Lady of the Highway."

Charles' friend, Jenny, looks up from her tablet, intrigued: "Our Lady of the Highway?"

Charles hands her the copy he's just been handed: "Yeah, look, old school: scotch-tape, glue, Xeroxing. So eighties."

"My great-grandmother had a sister who was a nun there," she says, perusing the flyer. "I didn't think it still existed."

"Oh yeah," Jesus assures her, "they been there forever and unless they get people to visit and ask them for their prayers they might have to go out of business."

Charles has been an intern at a publicity agency for two and a half years and is determined to break out on his own. He's skeptical, but sees everything that happens as a possible opportunity: "But how will people asking for prayers of intercession, or whatever, from the nuns help the convent stay open?"

"Decent beer," Jesus declares simply.

The roomful of youthful beer lovers pay heed. "Now that's an angle," Charles concedes.

"These holy sisters themselves have their very own micro-brewery."

"That's awesome," says Jeff, a thirty-two-year-old aspiring cinematographer.

The Yankees not only blow another double play but allow a run. Leo breathes a little easier and, as a relief pitcher is brought in, he turns away and is entertained by the sudden mobility of Charles and his crowd. They're up and walking around, handling the flyers like some brand-new invention they can't see the use of—turning them over, studying the edges.

"Do I need to be Catholic," Charles asks at length.

Jesus gets a can of beer from Chastity and cocks his head

sideways, stumped: "Father?"

"Not technically," Robert allows, preoccupied with the relief pitcher's stats against lefties.

"What do they pray for," Jeff thinks to ask.

"Anything you want, I guess," Jesus decides, pouring beer into Desmond's bowl. "Your family's health. Your brother in the Army. Your kid's homework."

Jenny's friend, Elaine, is a party planner of some notoriety on the Williamsburg social scene. "Quaint," she announces sagely.

"Antique," suggests Jeff.

"Primitive," Charles determines, assuming his is the last word.

"The beer any good," asks Jenny.

Robert pours her some. "Here, see what you think."

Jenny tries it. It appeals to her. She passes it on to Elaine who has no opinion about beer. Still, she is curious: "Um, like, okay, where is this place?"

"Just eight blocks away," says Leo.

"Near the waste management facility," Robert adds.

"They do brunch," asks Jeff.


Back at the convent, Bernadette is passed out in a chair behind the bottling machine in the brewery, a half-empty bottle gripped loosely in her hand. Catherine is too timid to wake her by main force, so stands a few yards off and ventures: "Sister Bernadette, dear? Sister, it's time for evening prayer."

Unconscious, Bernadette just grumbles and shifts in her seat.

Catherine now steps aside and stops, alarmed, seeing Magdalena, Evelyn, and Lola leading the five new, unknown nuns up from downstairs and towards the chapel. Magdalena sees her, hangs back and, glancing in, registers the situation with Bernadette. She suspected this—something about Bernadette's livid insistence on the evils of beer sounded a little like a personal problem.

"Come, Sister," Magdalena implores Catherine, "it's *compline*. Let Sister Bernadette sleep for now. She's worked hard."

"But who are…" Catherine begins, gesturing timidly towards the strangers before she is hushed by the mother superior.

"I'll explain in the morning."

She starts to lead Catherine away to the chapel but stops and turns to Lola. "Sister Lola, keep an eye on Sister Bernadette, will you?" They both glance in at Bernadette snoring, the bottle of beer threatening to slip from her hand. "None of us are angels, of course," Magdalena adds kindly. "We're just nuns."

"Yes, Mother Superior," Lola replies timidly.

"You're not afraid, are you?"

Lola is absolutely afraid. But assuming this delicate little obstacle is a test of her dedication and faith, the young woman lies flagrantly: "No."

"It's okay to be afraid," Magdalena reminds her.

"I'm not, really," the novice insists, then adds, "I think."

"Very well. Help her to bed. I'll see you in the morning."

Lola watches as Magdalena leads Catherine down the hall and into the chapel where the elderly nun will no doubt be introduced to her new sisters. Then, pausing for strength, she approaches Bernadette, anxious to get that bottle before it falls. Tiptoeing towards the sleeping nun, she accidentally kicks a discarded bottle lying on the floor. She freezes and winces, agonized, as it rolls noisily away.

The half empty beer in Bernadette's loosening grip slips a little more.

Lola comes closer, reaches out, and almost gets it. But within inches of her charitable fingers the bottle falls and shatters on the concrete floor. Bernadette jumps up out of her seat, furious, startled, and unsteady.

Kneeling, Lola cowers back.

Bernadette glares down at her like an avenging angel on crack:

"And what mischief are you up to, girl!"

POP!!!

Startled, they both look aside to the packing table where dozens of capped bottles of beer stand. One of them has exploded and is foaming over.

POP!!!—another one explodes as they're watching.

Lola stands up and takes a step back, guilty, convinced she's causing all this.

POP!!! POP!!!—a few more explode.

Bernadette drags her bleary and astonished eyes from the bottles to the new novice. "God save us all," she declares, "you little witch!"

Lola trips and falls, terrified, and the bottles on the packing table start going off like a round of machine gun fire.

# SIX

Father Robert dodges traffic, leaps over a puddle, and disappears down the stairs to the subway. Hearing the train pulling into the station, he weaves through a clot of malingering tourists blocking the turnstiles, just manages to swipe his MetroCard, push through onto the platform, and stumble into the train as the doors bang shut.

Moments later, as the train barrels through the tunnel, he makes his way to a seat further up the car where he finds Leo seated with his briefcase on his knees, brooding. Robert sits opposite his friend and needles him jocularly. "How's it going?"

Leo sees no reason to bluff. "I'm lonely."

"Yeah, and?" Robert urges, grinning excitedly.

Leo has come to wonder if the priest is living some sort of adventure vicariously through his struggles to be alone without Lola. "What do you mean, 'yeah and…' what?"

"You love Lola more than ever now, right?"

Leo sits back and sighs. Once again, just as he'd like to punch the priest in the arm and tell him to shut up, he finds his friend is on to something. He glances to the middle-aged

Hindi woman seated beside him. She has stopped flipping through the pages of a fashion magazine to hear his answer. But now she looks away.

Leo stands his briefcase on the floor between his feet and leans back in, elbows on his knees. "Of course, but I have no idea what kind of changes Lola's going through living in a convent trying to focus on the spiritual life and to forget all about the body and…" he's at a loss for words, "…well, and so on."

The Hindi lady and some Wall Street guy directly across from her exchange glances, raise eyebrows, and pivot away from this overheard conversation.

"I'll be seeing her today," Robert continues.

"Oh yeah," Leo asks, eager for news.

"I'm on my way out to hear their confessions."

"Can you take her something for me," Leo asks, already lifting his briefcase.

Robert scowls, tortured. "Oh, wow, in fact, no, I can't. It's…"

"No," Leo asks, disappointed. He knows by now all these Catholic sacramental procedures are rife with detailed exclusions and amendments.

The Hindi woman will not hear of this, though. "Oh, you have to," she insists to the priest.

"It's totally against church policy," Robert explains to her, "it's a violation of the sacrament of confession. There can't be…"

And now the Wall Street guy folds up his paper and leans forward in his seat, addressing Leo. "Are we to understand your girlfriend has entered a convent?"

"Well, yeah," Leo admits, aware of becoming the focal point of attention in the rattling subway car.

"Temporarily, as a test," Robert adds.

"For what," the man wants to know.

"Well…" Robert begins, holding a hand up to silence Leo, whom he thinks could mislead their new friends by virtue of his lack of objectivity. But the Hindi woman brushes him aside and addresses Leo:

"She's holy, isn't she?"

Now everyone in the subway car is listening. Teenagers remove their earbuds and try to hear. A homeless guy stops rearranging the empty bottles he's collected and looks on. Robert sighs and scratches his head; this is out of control. But Leo is struck by the freshness of his neighbor's question.

"Well, I'm not religious. But since I met this girl…"

"Lola," the Wall Street guy confirms.

"Right, Lola. And since I've met Lola…"

Father Robert grabs Leo by his coat and drags him out of the car as they pull into the next station. Moments later, the train pulls out, banging and scraping its way off into the tunnel again, and Leo is left alone on the platform with Father Robert.

"Sorry," the priest calls over the racket. "I know this isn't your stop. But this is where I get off."

Leo shrugs. "No problem. Thanks." He stands at the edge of the platform and gazes down at some rats foraging for breakfast amongst the garbage on the tracks. "Once I get thinking about it, I start asking questions I don't understand myself."

"Understand this: you're being tested. Bear with it. You'll be happier in the end. Stronger. Lola will come back to you."

"You think so, huh?"

"Yes, I think so. Now wish me luck."

"For what?"

"Hearing confession."

"Is it really that difficult?"

"It can be hairy."

Leo imagines it: a bunch of nuns who believe praying affects reality, who never mix with the outside world, talking to a man once a month about the state of their souls. "Yeah, I guess having to hear everyone's innermost fears, regrets, and guilt feelings must be kind of, well, messy."

Robert sighs, nods, and pulls is coat tighter around himself: "Yeah, well, that too." And with a shrug, he sets off up the steps to the street.

Jesus enters the convent's outer gallery from the garden with two guys from the cable company. He rings the silent buzzer beside the gate in the grille. The cable installation service employees, Gus and Bruce, look around, intrigued.

In her office, Lola is busy at her laptop when she hears a little chime and sees the red light beside the wall clock flash. She gets up and goes out.

Jesus turns back to the cable guys. "Sister Lola will come out and tell you what to do. You can't see the other sisters, but Sister Lola is only a novice so you're allowed to see her."

"Why are they in there," Gus asks, the older of the two.

"Yeah, what'd they do," the youthful Bruce wants to know.

"They didn't do anything," Jesus points out, "they pray and do good deeds and stuff."

Lola arrives at the gated door. "Yes, Jesus?"

"Oh, hey, Sister Lola," he says, removing his cap, "these guys are installing the cable for the internet."

"Oh, hi," she says, smiling, stepping out through the gate.

Bruce is immediately struck by her prettiness. "Oh, my

my," he lets slip a little too loudly. Gus, too, removes his baseball cap, hoping to deflect attention from his ill-mannered partner: "Good morning, Sister."

"Good morning."

"So, we're not allowed to go inside?"

"That's right. Can you bring the cable in at this part of the building?"

"Sure," Gus declares, studying the walls. "We can come in there over the door and run the cable to just upside of these—ah, bars here."

"We call it a grille," Lola says, seeing he's a little troubled by them. "Sounds less like prison."

Gus is reassured. "Okay. Done. How far away from the grille will you need the router?"

Lola looks back at the grille and calculates the distance to her office. "Oh, through the gallery, across the hall…" then, turning back, she concludes, "I think about thirty or forty feet."

"Okay, we'll install a junction box right up there and leave you with fifty feet of extension cable and the router."

"That would be great."

They hear someone banging on the door out beyond the garden.

"Jesus," Lola proposes, "that must be Father Robert at the street door."

Jesus snaps to attention. "Oh, okay! On my way, Sister. On my way!"

Gus is already planning the work ahead, talking out loud to himself as he figures: "That's brick and plaster up there, maybe eight or ten inches. Okay, I need to get the medium drill outta the truck." Then, as he is on his way out: "Bruce, set up the tall ladder over here. I'll be back."

The dashing young Bruce is alone with Lola. He grins handsomely and winks at her. She pretends she didn't see that and turns back to the gate: "I'm going to go back inside now," she says.

"Your loss, Sister."

Lola steps back inside, closes the door, and latches it decisively. "I guess so."

Meanwhile, Father Robert is banging on the street door with a big piece of lumber he's found by the curb. Tossing the wood aside, he waits. The door is opened and Jesus appears.

"Good morning, Father. Come on in."

"Jesus, why'd you put the doorbell way up where almost no one can reach it?"

"I ran out of wire. That's as far as it'd go after I almost killed myself on the ladder going up the other side. And I ain't got the proper tools anyway. And besides..."

"Never mind. Never mind..." Robert gives in, stepping aside to let Gus get past on his way out to his truck.

Leo leans against the chalkboard, listening, as the thirteen-year-old Ben struggles to explain himself.

"I just don't—I guess, sir—what's the point in studying algebra when—you know, what everyone says."

"Go on, Ben," Leo encourages him, "it's a good question. What does everyone say?"

"Well, it's like..."

Sasha stands, impatient, and clarifies: "The world's gonna end."

Leo hesitates. He wasn't expecting this. "Is it?"

"Yeah, like she says," Ben adds, relieved, and sits back down.

"When," Leo asks Sasha.

The girl is not certain but, willing to estimate, she looks at the ceiling and cocks her hip, arms folded. Finally, she decides: "Like before we're even able to get jobs and stuff."

Concerned, Leo comes down amongst the kids and sits in a vacant seat. "Now, just—" But he already thinks he needs to rephrase this. He adjusts. "Wait a minute, who have you guys been talking to?"

"It was all over the internet," Sasha says with certainty.

"There's a hole in the ozone," Ben adds.

"And terrorists with atomic bombs," Chris mumbles.

Then Derek waves his arms towards points east: "And this nuclear reactor in Japan that's poisoning the Pacific Ocean and this epidemic of killer jellyfish that keep on living even when you cut 'em in half!"

In the quiet that follows this, while Leo is trying to get his bearings, a timid girl near the back row, Lily, adds: "And God."

This stops everyone. They look back at Lily.

"God," Leo asks, urging Lily to elaborate.

"He's going to judge the living and the… well, the dead, I guess. But I don't understand that part."

Derek, standing, sees the whole conspiracy as clear as day: "You see, and so he created these killer jellyfish!"

"Derek, easy," Leo commands, "sit down."

Derek sits back down. But Sasha just shakes her head, convinced. "And there are meteors. A meteor hit the earth and killed all the dinosaurs. And they were, like, a lot bigger and tougher than we are."

Lily is on her own wave length, hardly aware she's talking out loud: "But some people will be saved."

Sasha turns around and asks plainly, "Who?"

"How many," asks some new kid from across the room.

Lily scrunches up her face in frustration and shrugs: "I don't know. One hundred and fourteen, maybe? I'm not sure. Going to church confuses me." Then the girl stands so as to be better seen by her teacher and asks, "Mister Haroldson, can you write a letter to my parents excusing me from church on Sunday?"

Derek drops his head to his desk in despair. "Man, I won't live long enough to get my driver's license even."

Leo has heard enough. He stands. He's not exactly sure how to deal with this or, even, what the meaning of it all is. But he feels strongly about first principles: "All right! Hold on. Enough. Close your books. Let's go for a walk."

"Field trip!" the kids all shout, perfectly and immediately just hyperactive adolescents again.


Father Robert enters the outer gallery from the garden and nearly collides with the ladder Bruce is setting up. He checks his step, apologizes silently, and crosses to a small door in the far wall. He has a key for it. He unlocks the door, pauses for strength, and enters.

Inside is a closet-sized room with a chair. Robert sits in it and closes the door, shutting himself in. He loosens his collar and takes a moment to compose himself, doing his best to pretend he's not claustrophobic.

In the wall on his left there is a sort of small window communicating to another tiny room. But one can't see through this aperture as it frames a dense wooden screen, not unlike the iron grille outside.

A door is heard to open and close in the adjoining closet and a shadow crosses the screen; one of the nuns is there, kneeling at the window less than a foot away from Father

Robert's ear.

"Bless me Father for I have sinned. My last confession was one month ago."

It's Sister Evelyn.

"What is the nature of your transgression, Sister?"

Evelyn hardly knows where to start. "Bodily, emotional, intellectual, spiritual," she ventures. Then, giving up, she admits, "Honestly, Father, I'm a train wreck."

"This is about the smoking," Robert understands.

"I try my best. But I forget myself. I know it's bad for me. It's even bad for others. And then I say it's of no consequence as long as I'm doing the Lord's work and, besides, what is this bodily existence anyway but an illusion and so on. And the whole slippery slope ensues: blackmailing Jesus into buying me a carton at the liquor store because he knows I know he's fencing stolen bicycles for his friend in Long Island City. And then, Father, honestly, stuff I don't want to even tell you about for your own good!"

Meanwhile, Lola, returning to her desk, stops in the doorway as she sees Sister Bernadette walking shakily up the hall. She waits for the older nun to reach her.

"Sister Lola," the ex-mother superior asks, "do you have an aspirin? I've a got a wicked hangover."

"I know. Here, sit down. I've made you some coffee."

Bernadette enters the office and sits as Lola organizes the needed beverage. "I haven't had coffee in years," the sister says.

"It'll help you feel better," Lola assures her cheerfully as she pours. She hands Bernadette the cup and watches as she drinks a bit, then some more. Finally, fortified, Bernadette comes clean:

"I said some stupid things last night, Sister. Forgive me."

Lola is relieved. She knocks a couple of aspirin out of a bottle and places them on the desk beside Bernadette's elbow. "Of course, I forgive you."

"Did I call you a witch?"

"Yes, I'm afraid you did."

Bernadette shakes her head slowly, tosses back the aspirin, washes them down with coffee, and stares down into her lap.

"I was drunk."

"I know," Lola agrees, smiling uncertainly. "But maybe also poisoned."

Bernadette lifts an eyebrow and waits.

"We're afraid," Lola continues, "the water we're using to make the beer is contaminated."

Bernadette considers this, but then shrugs it off: "We've known the well water we use here has been contaminated for forty years. If it hasn't killed us yet…" but then, she sets down her coffee and admits: "There are all kinds of poisons."

Lola feels immeasurably closer to the stern old woman now that they've endured some hijinks together. Because the night before, of course—

Bernadette drags her bleary and astonished eyes from the exploding bottles on the packing table to the new novice and, "God save us all," she declares, "you little witch!"

Lola backs away, terrified, and the bottles starts exploding like machine gun fire.

The other sisters, including the new arrivals, are reciting their prayers in the chapel. They thank heaven for their deliverance, despite the fact that some of them are seriously wounded. Magdalena, though, hears the commotion outside and is knocked out of her meditations. She looks back over her shoulder just as Lola runs past the chapel door.

Seconds later, the terrified novice scrambles up the stairs and reaches the dormitories. Bernadette is heard advancing not far behind. Lola runs down the hall, looking for her cell, desperate to elude Bernadette who has just reached the landing, missed the top step, and fallen flat on her face.

Lola jumps into a cell and slams the door, desperate not to witness the old woman's humiliation.


This morning, though, Bernadette sips her coffee and shakes her head in dismay. "Alcohol is my weakness. Always has been."

Lola places down her paperwork and lets the woman speak.

"I ran a convent in Indochina for ten years that was pretty much in the middle of a swamp running for twenty miles in any direction. Drinking the water was instant cholera." Bernadette sips her coffee. "It was safer to drink alcohol we received as charity from the military. The whole convent was soused for a decade. We built three schools, though. I hope they're still standing."

Lola takes advantage of this heart-to-heart to address her own concerns. "Sister Bernadette, I really do want to work hard to perfect myself and find peace and do good."

"I don't doubt that, Sister Lola."

"You don't really think I have some kind of evil in me, do you," the novice asks hopefully. But these hopes are gently undone when Bernadette replies kindly:

"I think we all have some kind of evil inside us."

Not comforted, Lola sits back. "Oh," she sighs feebly.

"That's where I part ways with our new mother superior," Bernadette is happy to expound. "She thinks everyone is naturally good and are corrupted merely by environment and circumstance which is, I think, just some kind of airy-fairy post-Enlightenment behaviorist mumbo jumbo." Setting down her coffee cup, she leans in close to make her point: "If everyone was naturally good, God the Father would not have needed to sacrifice his own son to expiate our sins in advance, now, would he?"

Lola blinks. This is a lot to digest. "Well, Sister, I'll have to think that over."

"Do so," Bernadette advises, sagely. "Food for thought," she adds, standing. She feels renewed, even magnanimous. "Thanks for the coffee." But as she turns away, she meets the mother superior in the doorway.

Magdalena is pale, preoccupied and anxious. "Oh, Sister Bernadette. How are you feeling?"

"I'm better. Sister Lola made me some coffee. Please forgive me for my outrageous behavior last night."

"Of course, Sister. But I expect you'll want to spend some extra time in private prayer today."

"Yes."

"And, of course, our confessor, Father Robert, is here. I encourage you to make your confession to him."

Bernadette scowls, aggravated: "The man is a mere child."

"He's a good priest," Magdalena insists.

"I was being shot at by Chinese Communists for the word of God before he was even born!"

"And I'm sure he appreciates that. Sister Prioress is just finishing. Please, go. Now. Thank you."

Bernadette grumbles but obeys.

Stressed out, Magdalena sits beside Lola's desk. "How are our new sisters getting on?"

"Resting in the small chapel," Lola reports in a whisper. "Sister Joan's wound is infected. I think we need a doctor."

"Does Sister Bernadette suspect anything yet?"

"Not yet. She slept late."

"I just can't get used to being the boss around here," Magdalena confesses. "Sister Bernadette has run convents for over thirty years and me—never." She slumps back in the seat and sees the big picture. "Just because I've been given responsibility everyone has to obey me—even sisters with greater experience!"

Lola reaches over and holds Magdalena's hand. "You're doing pretty good, I think, Mother Superior."

Bernadette and Veronica sit in the hall waiting near the door to the confessional. Sister Evelyn emerges, sighs, refreshed, and wanders off. Veronica offers Bernadette the chance to go first, even though she herself is pretty anxious to get in there. Bernadette is not eager and so gestures for the younger nun to go on in before her.

Inside, Veronica closes the door after herself and kneels, hands clasped. Robert is bravely battling his claustrophobia.

"Forgive me, Father, for I have sinned."

"How long has it been since your last confession, Sister?"

"One month."

"And what is the nature of your transgression?"

"I gave into my vain and depraved desire for pretty shoes again, Father, and, in doing so, I got Sister Lola in trouble with Sister Bernadette and…"

"Whoa! Hold on. Slow down!"

"I know this is my first confession with you and you don't know anything about me yet, but I try to be good, really, and…"

Robert is perspiring, struggling to breathe. He loosens his collar even more and consults a note pad. "Sister…

Veronica?" he confirms.

"Yes," the girl replies.

"How long has it been since your last confession?"

"You asked me that already."

"Oh. Um, well…" He wipes his brow with a handkerchief. "So, what is it that troubles you?"

"Father, I'm… I'm… sensual."

This is big. A priest can't screw up here. Robert pauses but then continues carefully, by the book: when in tricky situations don't say anything important: "I see."

"I deprive myself of everything and try to concentrate on the spirit but I can't help myself."

"Help yourself from what?"

"Shoes."

"Shoes," he repeats, truly lost.

"They make me crazy just looking at them and, and…"

"And what, Sister?"

"Sister Lola had such nice shoes. And she's so pretty. And we're practically the same age and…" She can hardly bring herself to say it. "And she performs miracles!"

Now Robert really needs air. He's hyperventilating. "What! Wait—hold on a minute." He bursts out the door into the gallery and directly into the ladder Bruce is using to install the junction box. The ladder falls away with a clatter and Bruce, desperately grabbing hold of the partition way up high, drops his power drill on Father Robert's head and the priest falls to the floor.

Gus is outside drilling a hole in the building while Jesus and Xavier lug a large first aid kit towards the entrance.

"Where'd you get this," Jesus wants to know.

"Stole it off an EMS truck near the hospital."

"Goddamn it! How many times I got to tell you: we don't

rob hospitals!"

Back inside, Bruce is kneeling over Father Robert who is just regaining consciousness.

"Jesus Christ Almighty," the handsome cable installation guy swears and is immediately panicked by an unearthly reply:

"*Benedictus qui venit.*"

Bruce jumps up and turns to see Agatha, this spooky, old, blind nun behind bars, and nearly screams.

"*Christi crux est mea lux,*" the apparition intones.

Veronica leans closer to the screen in the confessional, angling herself to maybe get a better glimpse of something outside and, worried, calls, "Father?"

Jesus comes bounding through the door into the gallery with the first aid kit and sees the situation. "Hey! You fucking degenerate, what'd you do to Father Robert!"

"He just… I was…" Bruce stammers, but then just wants to know: "Is he alright?"

Jesus slams down the stolen first aid kit and rushes to the priest. "Sister Agatha," he yells, approaching the fallen man, "pull the blinds for crying out loud! You're breaking the rules!"

"Oh my, yes!" Agatha realizes, "Okay. Thank you, Jesus."

Bruce is totally freaked out and flees.

Deep in the quiet of the confessional, Veronica hears the commotion outside, assumes it's a response to her confession and, panicked, makes a run for it. Banging out into the hall, trying to find somewhere to hide, she comes face to face with Bernadette.

"What," Bernadette asks blankly, seeing the expression on the young nun's face.

Veronica, tears welling, runs away and disappears into the

depths of the cloister.

Knowing it's her turn, Bernadette heaves a sigh, stands, and steps on into the dark little room.

Outside in the garden, Gus is feeding cable into the hole he's drilled in the wall when Bruce storms out, throws down his work gloves, and gives notice: "Gus, I quit!"

"What the fuck is it now?"

"I can't work under these conditions."

"Are you shittin' me?"

"They keep foreign old ladies locked up behind bars in there, man!"

Inside, Jesus helps Father Robert to his feet. "Father, you okay?"

"What happened?"

"Here," Jesus insists, "get back in here and sit down." And he helps the young man back into the closet. He closes the door. Jesus, too, hates confession days. The sisters get all emotional and weird. He just wants to get it over with.

Finding himself back inside the close, dark room, Robert assumes he's still addressing Veronica. However, it is Bernadette who looks up, groggy, and hears what she doesn't want to hear:

"Okay, Sister, look, this is very serious," the priest begins. "You're not a novice and you should know the modern church's attitude about miracles."

Bernadette is speechless. But she figures out the mistake and is about to speak up when Father Robert continues: "Now, though I commend you for using the privacy of this sacrament of confession to talk about this, I must ask you to recant. Sister Lola does not perform miracles!" Bernadette's mouth falls open and she makes the sign of the cross. "This is a very dangerous thing for you to say," Father Robert continues and, as he daubs at his cut lip with a handkerchief, Bernadette quietly steps out from her side of the confessional.

Back out in the hall, she silently closes the door. Convinced her worst fears about Lola are confirmed, she turns and jumps when she discovers the new novice standing there in the hallway.

"What's going on," Lola asks, concerned Bernadette might still be ill despite the wake-up coffee and aspirin.

Bernadette is nothing if not brave. She clears her head, straightens her back, and moves on: "I'm needed in the brewery."

Lola watches her go. Then she steps into the gallery and sees the stolen first aid kit just outside the gate. Passing Sister Agatha, who is seated calmly just inside the grille, seemingly waiting for someone, she heads for the gate. "Sister Agatha, what are you doing down here in the gallery?"

"Where are the people who need our prayers?"

Lola turns the latch and lets herself out. She drags the first aid kit in, closes the gate, and replies: "Oh, they'll be along. We've put ads in the paper. Don't worry."

Meanwhile, in the confessional, Father Robert leans towards the screen, afraid he's chased Veronica away. "Sister Veronica? You there?"

But she is not.

Bernadette joins Evelyn in the brewery. The prioress places a set of empty bottles in the bottling machine, throws the switch, and allows the device to do its thing. She notices Bernadette spying Lola as the young woman drags the first aid kit across the hall and into her office.

"What do we know about this new novice of ours," Bernadette asks.

Evelyn grins mischievously. "She has magic powers."

Bernadette frowns and Evelyn's smile vanishes.

Just then they both see Lola cross back and head for the confessional. She glances in at them and waves before disappearing from view.

Bernadette gets down to work and carries a crate of bottles to the packing table. "This is not something to joke about, Sister Prioress."

Evelyn dummies up and keeps working. But then she stops and asks, curiously: "Why? Have you seen something supernatural happen?"

Bernadette pauses and looks across at the prioress, uncertain if she's being teased. She might not be. She considers responding, but then lets it go and continues with her work.


Robert is standing in the door to the confessional, leaning against the jamb, taking in the air of the gallery, eyes closed. Behind him, Lola enters on her side and kneels. She makes the sign of the cross and initiates the sacrament softly.

"Forgive me Father for I have sinned."

Father Robert jolts into consciousness and gathers his wits. He closes the door and sits. "Lola?"

"Yes, Father."

"I'm sorry," he corrects himself. "Sister, forgive me."

"No problem," she replies, hopefully.

He rubs his sore head and wriggles his banged-up jaw. "How long has it been since your last confession?"

"Twenty-three years, I think."

"Oh, right," he remembers. "Okay. Listen, Sister, who in this convent knows about your... your, well, supposed psychic talents?"

"Mother Superior and Sister Prioress."

"That's all?"

"They're the only ones I told. None of the other sisters were around."

Robert thinks a bit and Lola, on her side of the screen, waits in curiosity. Finally, Robert just gets on with it:

"What is the nature of your transgression, Sister?"

Lola has been doing some reading and is eager to deal with the situation: "I committed one mortal sin."

Father Robert smiles. Newcomers to the faith are often a bit too literal. "I doubt that," he replies kindly.

But Lola has done the research: "It's true, Father. I knowingly and intentionally lent my shoes to Sister Veronica."

"Sister Veronica," he asks with trepidation.

"Yes, and I did so knowing she's, like, way into shoes and considers it her weakness."

"She's a shoe fetishist."

"Yeah. Well. I mean, lots of girls are, Father."

"Yes, but… nuns are not intended to be girls in that sense."

"I know. But she was so… she seemed so sad. And…"

"Go on."

"I wanted her to be my friend because I was so afraid once I arrived here."

The priest considers all this and, finally: "Okay, yes, technically this is a mortal sin. Motivated by your own fears, you jeopardized the spiritual progress of your sister who, of her own free will, has renounced most of the amusements of this world, including pretty shoes."

Lola hangs her head and clasps her hands tighter. "Oh, man! I'm dangerous for people, Father."

"Hey, cut it out! That's not useful at all."

"Sister Bernadette saw it right away. She thinks I'm a witch."

This new information infuriates the priest. "Lola," he begins, jumping up, bumping his head. "Ow!" Dropping back down, he pauses. "Sister, hold on. Excuse me a moment." He steps out carefully from the confessional, catches his breath, removes his collar entirely, and looks over to see Jesus and the remaining cable guy, Gus, watching him with concern.

"Hey, Father, you okay?"

Robert nods, works out a kink in his shoulder, and goes back inside, closing the door behind him.

"What goes on in there," Gus asks.

"The sisters all confess their sins to Father Robert," Jesus explains, coiling up excess cable, "one at a time, though, like—in private. And him with his claustrophobia and all. It's wild."

But Gus is wrestling with a simpler issue: "Their sins?"

"Yeah."

"But they're nuns!"

"Nuns sin too," Jesus assures the man.

"No, no way," Gus stutters in disbelief, "really?"

"Oh yeah. Totally."

Inside the confessional, Father Robert returns to business: "Lola—Sister Lola—this is a little… I mean, I'm not supposed to do this, but… I need to share with you something I heard in Sister Veronica's confession."

"Oh," Lola says, worried.

"Sister Veronica thinks you perform miracles."

"You see!"

"Keep cool! What is she talking about?"

"I can't help it."

"You can't help what?"

It's the night before. Lola runs down the hall looking for her cell, desperate to elude Bernadette who is stomping drunkenly up the stairs, wagging her finger, and spewing forth Latin curses of exorcism. But just as the nun misses the top step of the stairs and falls flat on her face, Lola jumps into her cell and slams the door shut.

It's dark in the cell, of course. She presses herself against the inside of the door until she hears Bernadette staggering back downstairs. Exhausted and afraid, Lola finally sits on the bed. But as she lays back, she encounters another body and jumps up, shrieking, to her feet.

Veronica, equally startled, lifts her head from the pillow as the extinguished flame of the candle on the bedside table flickers into life. In its dim glow, she and Lola look from it to one another.

"I'm sorry," Lola apologizes, mortified, "I thought it was my cell. I'm sorry. Good night." And she runs out.

Veronica, though, still breathless, turns her attention to the miraculously lit candle.


Father Robert trudges along the sidewalks of Brooklyn. It's been a rough day. He's got dried blood in his hair and a bandage on his jaw. He stops at the corner to let traffic pass and looks around. This is a new neighborhood for him.

Leo is at the bar of a place called Teachers grading papers. The game is on. He looks over as Robert enters and stops in the doorway. "Wow," he exclaims, "you weren't kidding: hearing confession really is rough work."

Robert joins him, throws his bag down at the foot of a barstool, and focuses his attention on practical concerns: "And we're losing by what?"

"Two," Leo confirms, gesturing for the bartender. "Kansas City's on fire but the Sox are threatening."

"And how was your day," Robert asks defiantly, as if he had no obvious wounds.

"My thirteen-year-olds are afraid the world's going to end before they graduate high school."

"Jameson's neat and a Budweiser, thanks," Robert orders, then, to Leo: "What the hell kind of math are you teaching them anyway?"

Leo's attention, however, is distracted by a pretty woman whom he has seen sometimes on the subway. She's at a table with friends. She glances over at him, makes eye contact, looks away, and then returns. They both grin sheepishly—caught looking.

On the television above the bar there's the crack of a bat and Robert is on his feet. "Yes!" And as the priest's team strikes back with a stand-up double, the pretty woman approaches to order another round. Leo makes room for her so she can reach the bar with the empty mugs.

"Hi," she says, shyly.

"Evening."

"I see you on the subway sometimes."

"I think so," Leo confirms.

"Another round, thanks," she calls to the bartender past Leo's head. Then, returning to him, "I haven't seen you around here before."

"It's not my regular," Leo admits, though he seems to like the place.

"You're not a priest too, are you," she asks, gesturing to his friend.

"No. I'm a school teacher."

"Of course, you are," she laughs, "that's why they call this place Teachers. They have union meetings here, you know."

They shake hands.

"Leo," he says.

"Bethany," she reciprocates.

"What grade?"

"Second. You?"

"Seventh Grade. Math."

Bethany is impressed. "Oh boy," she says, "that can't be easy."

Leo closes his folder of half-graded tests and shrugs. "Just when I think I can't go on, I go on."

They like each other. This is easy and good. Her round of drinks arrives. "You want to join me and my friends? They're all teachers too."

Leo is tempted. He hems and haws but then demurs. "I'm sorry, no. I've got to find my way back home as soon as my team loses this game."

Disappointed but graceful, Bethany bows out. "Okay. Maybe next time."

"Yeah," he nods, sincerely, "I think so. Next time, definitely."

Leo discreetly checks out her figure as she walks away and Robert sees this. Leo sees him see this.


Bernadette's been in a daze all day, her conscience in an uproar. She's allowed herself to start drinking again after so many years. That, she knows, is just part of her transgression. She really needs to apologize to the mother superior for putting up such resistance to this otherwise practical plan of starting a brewery only because she herself was afraid of temptation.

But then this pretty new novice, Lola, is complicating her peace of mind as well. Sure, the exploding bottles of last night might be explained by Sister Evelyn's discovery that the yeast content of the last batch was too high and the beer bottled too early. The prioress will be working on that. But Bernadette has had experience with nuns granted graces before.

Granted graces—from whom?

That's always been a mother superior's toughest job; sorting out who's mistaking heavenly intervention out of vanity and pride. Of course, every nun worth her salt wants to be spoken to directly by God—worked upon by God. But in reality, God doesn't make himself known to you except through the miracles of endurance and selflessness. Few sisters have been able to endure such a distant and stern father. So, in their desperation and weakness, they make the contact happen; they manifest the touch of God through the nurturing of sickness, for instance. How many young nuns has she seen pass out while raking leaves only to wake an hour later claiming to have been touched by the Lord himself?

Too many. They tend to believe themselves to be seers, receiving coded info from the divine realms. Though usually run-of-the-mill hysterics, they're a real threat to the sanity of a religious community. And if Bernadette has any opinion about the existence of evil spirits and demons and so on, she locates their sphere of influence in the pride and vanity of overly zealous nuns.

A good mother superior sends them elsewhere.

But then there are the sisters who make things happen. She's seen it before—only once—and it was enough for a lifetime. It was during her tenure as mother superior (her first such placement) of a hastily founded convent in Cambodia. A certain nun under her jurisdiction hailing from the Philippines, Sister Justine-Marie, was as devout and hardworking as any sister alive. But she could kill reptiles just by looking at them. And when she got into one of her *states*—convulsing and swearing like a sailor—there would be snakes falling dead from the trees for ten yards in any direction.

Bernadette was sure this was not the heavenly Father sending her sister graces. It looked more like some evil magic sprung up from the depths of the mud and fungus. And Sister Justine-Marie became a star with the locals, barbarians as far from the one true faith as anyone could get.

Weird shrines in the jungle—

Crazy chanting through the night—

Sister Justine-Marie succumbed, believed herself divine, walked naked out into the swamps and died immediately of snake bite.

That's when Bernadette started accepting liquor from the army, clean water being too rare to find and the fructifying evils of the natural world too much to contemplate. The soil, the vegetation, the body, blossoming, decay, some primal, godless force behind it all—

Bernadette opens another bottle, sits, and takes a swig of the ever-improving OLHW brew. Lowering it from her lips, she sighs, relieved, and sees what she imagines must be an alcohol-induced vision: a small dark-skinned nun in an unknown habit standing over there in the entrance, lost, holding a medical tray with bloodied bandages.

"*Donde esta la basura*," the apparition seems to ask.

Bernadette is speechless. She blinks, rubs her eyes, mutters an oath, and looks again.

There's nothing there. The child-nun has vanished.

Bernadette steps out from the brewery and into the main hall, looking around, listening. There's some activity to be heard down in the chapel. "What's going on in my beloved convent?" she growls, her territorial mojo returning. Stealthily, she heads towards the chapel.

In the chapel, Magdalena is ministering to Sister Joan's wounds. The other sisters are holding the patient down. Though the patient doesn't want to resist, they're afraid Joan will not be prepared for the pain.

"Sister," Magdalena explains, "I have to reset your arm."

"I know."

"It's going to hurt terribly."

"I know, Sister. Do it."

Magdalena wishes she didn't have to but grits her teeth and, without giving the brave nun time to prepare, yanks the broken arm straight.

A heart-wrenching cry cuts through the convent. But it's done. Joan passes out. The others begin setting and bandaging the broken arm while Magdalena, exhausted, turns away and discovers Bernadette in the door.

"What in the name of God..." Bernadette begins. But Magdalena's tortured and remorseful countenance shuts her up.

"I'll explain later."

Stepping down into the chapel, Bernadette looks around at all the new faces. "Of course, you will," she replies, resigned.

Magdalena steps out into the hall and gestures for her to follow. "A bullet wound," she explains, "there's infection."

Bernadette is sober now. She looks from the crowd of unknown nuns to Magdalena, back to problem-solving mode.

"We must consult Mister Ortiz," she declares without ceremony and walks away.

Leo steps out of Teacher's and onto the sidewalk, heaving a labored sigh as he pretends to study the stars. Father Robert follows him out while waving to a woman—a friend of Bethany's—who leans out the door.

"Goodnight, Father," she calls, eyes moist with curiosity.

"Goodnight, Chelsea," Robert replies as polite and disinterested as possible.

The men look up and down the street for a cab.

"Father, me and you have to discuss celibacy."

"What, you mean now?"

Leo glances back in through the window and sees Bethany. She smiles and waves goodbye. Leo nods and smiles, waving back.

And Robert sees all this.

"No, not now," Leo decides, "but soon. The full, uncensored, ecclesiastical dope on the spiritually toughening benefits of sexual abstinence." He turns back to the sidewalk and starts walking. "But not now."

Father Robert watches him move off towards home before glancing back inside and seeing Chelsea wink at him, provocatively. He grins, less troubled than confused, and flags down a cab.

Dropping himself down into the backseat of the cab, he removes the bandage from his jaw. "Saint Ann's Church on Metropolitan Boulevard at Sixteenth Street, please."

But the driver hesitates, watching Robert suspiciously through the rearview mirror. So Robert inches forward and speaks past the Plexiglas divide: "Something wrong?

"You a priest," the young man wants to know.

"Well, yeah. So?"

"I can't drive you."

"What?"

"I don't drive priests."

Robert checks his wristwatch. Normally he would just get

out. But it's late. "Well, in fact, I'm also a citizen and a customer and by the laws of the city, printed here on the back of the seat, you are not allowed to decide not to drive me unless I've violated other city ordinances in your presence. In which case—"

"No, really, dude," the driver cuts him off, "this is not personal. I'm a Satanist. Totally can't drive priests. It's like, you know, not done."

It takes a moment for Robert to process this little tumble of information. Then, sincerely intrigued, he slides even further up the backseat. "Really? You worship Satan?"

"Swear to god, man. Look, see my tattoos." He rolls up his sleeve and displays for Robert tattoos that, apparently, explain everything.

Robert leans forward and looks them over. "Wow."

"I got some self-inflicted scars and shit too on my chest that make everything true and permanent. I mean, I'm sincere an' shit."

"Okay," Robert says, sitting back, conceding.

"Hope you understand, man" the worshipper of Satan adds graciously.

"I'd love to talk to you about this. Are you sure you don't want to just drive me home and we can talk? Really, I'm curious."

"No, dude. Totally not done."

Robert acquiesces, holding up his hands, "Okay, okay, enough said." And, stepping from the cab he calls lightly, "Go in peace, my friend."

"Yeah, fuck that shit," the driver replies.

He drives off and there are no more cabs on the street. Robert glances at the bar and sees Chelsea still watching him with renewed, more serious, interest. He goes back inside.

SEVEN

It's six twenty-eight and a half and Sister Bernadette is angry. She wants to throw a tantrum about these four unknown nuns sitting with them in the kitchen but she's incapable of breaking the Rule. She glowers at the weary mother superior. Magdalena gestures for patience. Bernadette looks, instead, to Evelyn who just returns her gaze impassively, resolute.

Further along the kitchen table, Veronica stares at her hands folded in her lap, crazily smiling at thoughts of her own. The new recruits, these bewildered and battered foreign nuns, look on, trying to figure out what's happening and who to be more afraid of just as Bernadette finally glances at Lola. The novice is like a deer caught in the headlights and a pane in the window across the room cracks, falls out in pieces, and splinters on the floor.

Magdalena looks from it to Lola and glares. The young woman lowers her head to the table, mortified. Then the mother superior flashes a warning at Bernadette, silently demanding order be restored.

The seconds tick by. Six twenty-nine and thirty seconds.

Lola elbows Veronica in the arm and indicates they should

clear away the dishes. Magdalena slowly stands, tired and stressed, girding herself for confrontation.

At six-thirty the bell rings and all hell breaks loose:

"Where did these nuns come from!" Bernadette shouts, standing.

"Sister Bernadette, please," Magdalena demands.

"Who are they! What are you up to! What's going on around here!"

"Sister, I must remind you I am the mother superior!"

Silence.

The new nuns are afraid to move.

Bernadette sits back down. Evelyn stands and comes over behind the four new sisters. The fifth, the wounded Sister Joan, is in a bed upstairs.

"Sister Bernadette, Sister Catherine, Sister Agatha," the prioress begins, "please meet and welcome Sisters Jeanne, Therese, Lucia, and Marie."

Catherine is immediately gracious and welcoming. She stands from the table, smiling, and ceremoniously moves from each new nun to the next, taking their hands in hers and bowing her head in humility: "Peace be with you Sister and forgive me my failures and weaknesses."

Jeanne is deeply moved and relieved as she returns the traditional salutation: "And peace be with you Sister, my life is nothing without your love and patience."

Catherine now moves to the next, Sister Therese, and repeats the formula: "Peace be with you Sister and forgive me my failures and weaknesses."

"And peace be with you Sister, my life is nothing without your love and patience."

Observing this, Bernadette, chastened, glances away and cries. Magdalena sinks back into her seat and holds her head in her hands. Meanwhile, the ceremonial welcoming bubbles over into a soft murmuring amongst all the sisters present. Finally, they turn to Bernadette, expecting her to extend the same ritual of welcome. But she is unable even to look at them and, drawing a handkerchief out from somewhere beneath her habit, blows her nose.

The others look to Magdalena who sighs and gestures for them all to leave. They do. Hearing a scrape on the floor, Magdalena looks back over her shoulder at Lola who is sweeping up the broken window pane. Seeing the mother superior's expression, the novice leaves the broom and dust pan where they are and vacates the kitchen immediately.

Alone now, Magdalena and Bernadette slowly pull themselves together. The mother superior gets up and comes closer. She reaches out and places her hand on Bernadette's where it lies on the table clutching the handkerchief. "How far we've come from these simple pleas."

"Forgive me, Mother Superior."

Magdalena winces at this and leans closer, desperately:

"Sister Bernadette, may I ask you a favor?"

"Yes," the older nun whispers, still keeping her eyes on the floor.

"Can you never call me mother superior again?"

Now Bernadette looks up, her old regular self: aggravated.

"But you are the mother superior!"

"I am nobody's mother!" the younger nun lets loose like a curse. "And I am not superior! I am a sister!" And, clasping both her hands onto Bernadette's, she concludes: "And I need my sisters with me."

Though appreciating the younger nun's evident goodwill, Bernadette bristles and falls back on dogma, reciting the obvious: "The bishop appointed you mother superior. The cardinal appointed him bishop. The pope appointed the cardinal to be cardinal. The church elected the pope and the church is God's body, his mind, on earth…"

"Of course," Magdalena sighs, standing and turning away.

"You can not change the rules just to fit your personality!"

Magdalena can't argue with this. Exhausted, though, she closes her eyes and indulges in a moment of self-pity she knows she'll have to do penance for later: "It's hard to be the boss."

Bernadette nods, agreeing; at least they're talking the same language now. She sniffles and blows her nose. Tucking her handkerchief back inside her habit, she dishes out a little sisterly tough love: "It is a burden. And burdens are all we ask the Lord to send us. Listen, Mother…" but then, starting again: "Sister—tell me about these new nuns."

"I wanted to keep you and Sisters Catherine and Agatha uninformed about this because… because…"

"Because you have broken the law," Bernadette surmises.

"Yes," Magdalena admits, but then, turning around, qualifies, "…of the United States of America."

Bernadette has heard this reasoning before and has little patience for it. "But the United States of America is where we live."

"And the United States of America sometimes operates in ways for its own interests which hurt the lives of people in other places."

"That's called politics. Sit down."

The mother superior obeys like she is, in fact, being scolded by her natural born mom. Nevertheless, once seated, she continues: "I have to find sisters wherever I can. Beatrice, Therese, Lucia: they've escaped from the midst of violence, looting, rape, and murder—the only surviving sisters of a convent that once held thirty-two."

"So, they're illegal immigrants."

"Refugees," Magdalena qualifies again, adding, "Sister Agatha has not long to live. Sister Catherine is eighty-five, we think, and has been doing penance on behalf of the whole world for over forty years. You yourself need rest. We need more nuns."

"Sister, you're reckless," Bernadette admits, "but you are God's daughter for sure." She blows her nose one last time, then: "But what now?"

"I've never been a mother superior," Magdalena begs, "tell me, please."

Bernadette hesitates. She begins to pace, her hands knotted behind her back: "Sister, a convent can become a mess in no time. Some of these girls here ought not even to be nuns. This one, the child, Marie—there may be extenuating, desperate circumstances in a war-torn place like you describe—a mercy, really... But it will be tough. Still: Veronica! She's unhinged."

Magdalena nods in agreement. "Yes, she was an emergency rescue situation too. But she loves God."

"Not everyone who loves God needs to become a nun. That girl begins to tremble when you simply speak the word shoe. Her sensuality was not indoctrinated out of her. That's bad training. What careless people—who were they!—that allowed her to take her vows in the first place? I don't know! She will fall in love with Lola, that is almost for certain. I've seen it dozens of times before. I'm telling you now what I'm sure you know already: this is a lonely life. A vocation like this is, well, unnatural. That's the point. A lonely naturally sensual young woman in a place like this will find comfort where she can. And then!" Bernadette can barely bring herself to describe it: "And then, God help us, Sister—then you've got jealousy! Favoritism! Not long after that: factionalism. Before you know it, you're no longer in charge of a spiritual community, but the warden of a prison camp or like the leader of a political party! The truth can't survive, much less flourish, in a place like that. A strict rule, yes, an authoritarian discipline, is needed."

All she says might be true enough but Magdalena can't argue with it. "I'll try to be more severe with her."

"And what about Sister Lola?"

"Lola," the mother superior asks, disingenuously, hoping to shield the new novice from controversy until she's found her feet here in the convent.

"You saw her break that window just now," Bernadette demands.

"I saw nothing of the kind."

"I saw you look right at her."

"Because I knew she would think she made it happen and I wanted to tell her to knock it off."

"Then how did it happen?"

"I don't know!"

"It's a perfectly fine day. No one outside throwing rocks or anything. No birds flying around. But I look at her, she's startled, and a window pane shatters."

"It's odd, I admit."

"It's not the first time either."

Magdalena knows this—


It's the previous Thursday morning. Veronica's feet are tucked in beneath the kitchen bench. Wearing Lola's pumps, she is twisting her ankles deliciously. Bernadette leans back and to the side to observe this under the table. Six-thirty strikes

and the sisters are up from the table and bustling immediately. Sister Evelyn takes the cereal bowls off the table and
Bernadette gathers up the spoons and places them on the
counter as Magdalena begins the day:

"Okay, Sisters! A lot to do today. Who's next up at the
high altar for vigil?"

Dawdling weirdly in the entranceway, Veronica replies,
"That would be me, Mother Superior, at seven."

"Okay, till then, please help Sister Lola get started with the
accounting," the mother superior gently instructs. Then, turning to Evelyn, she continues, "Sister Prioress, what can we
expect in the brewery today?"

Bernadette almost turns away just then to go refresh the
water on the barley but catches a glimpse of Veronica's hand
reaching for Lola's. Lola snatches hers away and, Veronica,
seeing Bernadette watching her, averts her gaze and continues out into the main hall. Bernadette grabs Lola by the
elbow.

"Where'd she get those shoes?"

"They're mine," Lola answers in a small, frightened voice.

"They're shameful."

"She likes them."

Just then, passing the counter, Magdalena notices the cutlery. Lifting a spoon from the small pile, she wonders aloud:
"Now, how do all the spoons get bent like this?"

As Bernadette turns and stares in amazement at the man-
gled silverware, Lola flees.


A week before the new sisters arrive from Honduras, Señora
Diaz comes out of early morning Mass at Saint Ann's with a
small flock of parishioners. Seeing Patsy mounting a colorful
new announcement on the bulletin board in the lobby, she

comes forward and studies it. Though she can make out something about the sisters of Our Lady of the Highway, Señora Diaz does not trust her English. As always, she looks around for her granddaughter, Inez, for translation. But the little girl is already running around out on the sidewalk. Instead, the old woman tugs at Patsy's sleeve. "The sisters! Ah, of the Highway! What says it, Señorita Patsy?"

A few other parishioners listen in as Patsy explains: "The sisters of the convent of Our Lady of the Highway are offering prayers of intercession for anyone who needs them."

"Intercession," Señora Diaz repeats. She thinks she recognizes this word but it's been a long time. "It is like they talk to Jesus for me, no?"

"Exactly. And all the other saints too."

A young father holding an infant and waiting for his wife to find her car keys is curious: "Why?"

Señora Diaz glares impatiently. These new middle-class white people from God knows where are bad Catholics, she can tell from a mile away. "Because they are sisters," the harassed matriarch explains. "It is what sisters do!"

"No," he clarifies diplomatically, "let me rephrase that." He's an efficiency expert for Federal Express. "I mean, can't a person pray for himself directly to God?"

Patsy begins to reply sensibly but Señora Diaz is all fired up and impatient: "No work like the sisters, *señor*," she insists. "They are the brides of Jesus Christ himself. When they pray it is like sticks of dynamite in the ears of the Lord!" She moves off, eager. "I go right now. My grandson Vincent, he is in jail again."

"No, Missus Diaz, wait," Patsy calls, alarmed by the old lady's fierce resolve, "it's a week from this Saturday, from ten till four."

This stops the sturdy grandma and she looks at the floor, disappointed. "Saturday," she sighs, "ten days from now."

"Yes. I'm sorry."

The old woman sits on the bench in the lobby and prepares to endure the next week and a half without divine assistance. She glances up at the young dad and repeats, pointing her finger at him: "Like dynamite in the ears of the Lord."

The days pass. Jesus enters the Bodega Pankaj, the only semblance of a grocery store within a mile of the convent. He carries a stack of flyers and waves to Pankaj, the owner, an Indian Sikh man nodding off behind the register. "Hey, Pankaj, can I post a couple a flyers up on the window here?"

Pankaj jolts awake and automatically shouts: "No credit!" But then, getting his bearings, he takes a flyer. "What is this?"

"The sisters will say prayers for you, me, anyone if we just come by and visit 'em on Saturday and ask."

Reading, Pankaj makes out, "'Prayers of Intercession by the sisters of Our Lady of the Highway'." Lowering the sheet, he looks to Jesus who has already made his way in behind the counter. "What is it, 'intercession'?"

"How long you been in this country, Pankaj! It's English! Use your goddamn translation app! Gimme' some tape."

Pankaj hands him the tape dispenser and lifts his mobile device as Jesus starts posting flyers. "'To intervene on someone else's behalf,'" he learns.

"That's right. It's like the sisters negotiate with God."

"For us?"

"Yeah."

"That's very generous."

"Well, you know, they're holy and everything and we're

just a bunch 'a bums. We need their help in a bad way."

"But I'm not a Catholic."

"Come anyway," Jesus decides, returning the tape dispenser, "there's cheap beer."

"At the convent?"

"Yeah. The sisters, they're making their own brew." Then, leaning back in from the sidewalk, he adds, "Saturday, from ten in the morning till four. See you later. Bring people!"

Saturday morning, our young hipster friends from Margaret's Bar are looking for the convent. They're lost. Jenny is consulting her tablet.

"This whole area is not even on the map!"

"Truly the land that time forgot," Charles declares, looking around, "but I sense potential."

Jeff studies the environment through an antique contrast filter held up to one eye. "Those burnt-out buildings would make great loft apartments."

"Quell your entrepreneurial whims, Jeff," Charles cautions paternally, "the whole district is owned by the notoriously ambitious Gordon Normal."

Charles now notices Señora Diaz passing by with the baby Joseph in his stroller. Inez is skipping along behind her, deadly serious, absorbed in some mysterious and important pattern in her own hopscotch footwork. But Charles wonders if maybe she's just dancing.

"Excuse me," he attempts.

"*Sí,*" the lady obliges, stopping.

"We're looking for the convent of Our Lady of the Highway."

Señora Diaz is pleased that young people such as these—mostly white (though Jeff looks mixed) and probably from atheistic suburban college educated families—are drawn to the deity. But they better not be here to make fun. The boys look gay, Elaine dresses like a slut, but Jenny seems earnest and sincere. "Is in this way, here, *ven, sigueme*," she advises, leading the way.

The hipsters hesitate.

"What's she…" Elaine begins, but Charles is already on the move.

"She wants us to follow her."


Xavier rolls crates of bottled beer on a hand truck through the garden to a table beside which Lola is packing a few coolers with ice.

"Thank you, Xavier. Pack those in these two coolers here."

"Yes, Sister."

Lola hustles on into the gallery.

Moments later, at another table of beer set up just inside the door, she's teaching Jesus how to use a credit card scanner. "Like this. See?"

"With the magnetic strip down?"

"Right."

He swipes the card and waits.

"You wait a second," she says, then…

"Okay," Jesus nods, seeing the transaction accomplished.

"See," Lola points out, "approved."

Pankaj steps hesitantly, respectfully, into the gallery.

"Sister Lola," Jesus announces, "this is Pankaj from over at the bodega."

"Hello, Pankaj," Lola welcomes him.

"Good morning, Sister," he replies, taking the beer Jesus hands him.

"Pankaj's brother-in-law, Rashid," Jesus interjects, "he's

the beverage distributor I told you about."

"Can you introduce us to Rashid, Pankaj, when the time comes," Lola wastes no time asking.

"Of course. His business is expanding rapidly," Pankaj assures her, sampling the beverage, "and I think the time will come soon. The beer is excellent."

"Oh! I'm glad. We had to tone it down a little."

"The flavor?"

"No, the strength."

Jesus huffs and puffs and shakes his head. "The water was… The contaminated water—"


Many weeks earlier, Jesus bangs in from the garden to the outer gallery and rings the buzzer beside the gate. He hangs on the grille, waiting for Lola to appear.

"Sister? Hey, Sister Lola! You in there?"

Lola is down the hall watching as the nuns are stumbling around with bottles of their own beer, giggling foolishly, wandering off in all directions, wide-eyed, hallucinating. She just looks on in alarm, helpless, as a few of the newer sisters surround her, reaching out tentatively to try and touch some kind of unseen aura surrounding the novice.

Lola hears Jesus calling and hurries away to the gallery for help.

"Hey, Sister Lola," he greets her when she enters, "the water authority is outside and they're ready to start work. But they need to make sure all the faucets inside here are turned off and closed."

"Jesus, something is wrong with the nuns."

"Yeah, well," he misunderstands, "that's why a lotta these dames enter a cloister in the first place."

"No, I mean, they're high."

"Come again?"

"They're stoned out of their minds, Jesus!"

Just then, some of the latest recruits drift into the gallery like happy child zombies and fan out across the dim space, fascinated by the high ceiling, the blinds, the texture of their own habits. One of them crouches down and traces the pattern of the floorboards with her fingertip, weeping."

"Holy shit," Jesus is forced to admit, turning away out of respect for the vows the nuns have taken.

"Sister Prioress let everyone taste the latest batch and…"

"Well, there's something wrong with that batch, Lola. Where's the older nuns?"

"They can't even stand."

Back in the brewery, Evelyn is crawling along the concrete floor trying to make her way to Magdalena, who is flat on her back, looking around in concentrated wonder. The prioress passes Catherine and Agatha under a table, whispering baby talk and cracking each other up.

"Mother Superior," Evelyn manages to call with difficulty—forming words seems to be a problem for her just now. "Are you… okay?"

"Sister Prioress," Magdalena replies breathlessly. "Is that you?"

Though she's already on her hands and knees, Evelyn is hit with a dizzy spell and falls over onto her side. She reaches forward, though, and grabs hold of Magdalena's ankle.

"Hold on, Sister," Magdalena whispers. "The world will go right side up again soon. Breath…"

"It's the water," Evelyn declares, grabbing hold of the edge of the sink and pulling herself up again. "Nothing else has changed in the… in the recipe." With her face inches from the faucet, she watches drops of water form, slowly hang, and then fall with a splash into the basin.

Meanwhile, Sister Bernadette, down on the floor of the basilica, wonders where her replacement is…

Now, back on the big day, Jesus places a ladder against the convent wall as he continues explaining to Pankaj. "Since then, of course, they been making beer with water on the city grid system because fermenting oats and barley in that *contaminated* water creates some kind of psychedelic narcotic or some shit." He starts his ascent, but turns back, and assures his friend: "Don't worry, we got some left." Climbing the ladder, Jesus peeks out over the top of the wall:

"Holy shit!"

"What?"

He ducks out of sight as Pankaj climbs up to see as well.

Outside on Resurrection Avenue there are hundreds of people awaiting entry.

"Damn," Jesus mutters, terrified, wondering if this is all worth it or not.

Leo and Robert, deep in conversation, come up the street and approach the crowd outside the convent without seeing it.

"You don't think it's odd my seventh-graders are all convinced the world's about to end?"

The priest shrugs. "You don't have to be religious to admit that, probably, everything has a beginning and an end; people's lives, baseball games, the world as we know it."

"The kids," Leo continues, "are bright enough to know a lot, I think, but still too young to understand any of it."

"That's why God invented grown-ups."

"But the grown-ups have decided sixty percent of the curriculum should now be taught online. And I worry the kids spend too much time alone as it is trying to understand things on their own without, you know, conversation. I took them for an impromptu field trip the other day, just to calm them down, and now I'm in trouble with the school and the Parent-Teacher Association…"

They slow down and stop, seeing the crowd up ahead.

"Wow. Quite a turn out," Leo admits.

Robert, too, has just now realized the scope of the event. "I hope they have enough beer," he worries as he watches Señora Diaz march right up to the door, cutting ahead of everyone, knocking people aside with the baby's stroller. Charles, Jenny, and the hipsters following in her wake.

Charles, especially, is taking it all in. "This is promising."

Jenny concurs, adjusting her glasses. "These nuns need a website."

Unknown to the world at large, though, mighty changes are occurring deep inside the convent walls—


Sisters Bernadette and Magdalena come walking up from the kitchen to the main hall. The other sisters are apprehensive but obedient, and the new ones are hiding behind Evelyn and Veronica. But Sister Bernadette wastes no time. She approaches Jeanne, clearly the newcomers' superior, takes her hands, and kneels.

"Peace be with you Sister and forgive me my failures and weaknesses."

"And peace be with you Sister, my life is nothing without your love and patience," Jeanne replies.

Bernadette struggles to her feet, approaches Therese and, taking her hands, sinks to her knees again. "Peace be with you Sister and forgive me my failures and weaknesses."

Likewise, Therese recites the formula: "And peace be with

you Sister, my life is nothing without your love and patience."

It's tough for the seventy-year-old Bernadette to get up again and Evelyn steps in to help her to her feet. Bernadette then limps to the adolescent, Marie. She starts to kneel again but the girl stops her, imploringly, by gripping her hands in her own.

Grudgingly, Bernadette gives in: "Okay." And, looking the sixteen-year-old in the eyes, hard, she continues, "Peace be with you Sister and forgive me my failures and weaknesses."

Marie replies in her broken English: "And peace to be with you Sister my life, as nothing is, with your love and patience, thank you."

Bernadette nods and studies this child. Teenage nuns are the worst headache imaginable. But this girl seems simple. Maybe there's hope. After similarly welcoming Sister Lucia, the veteran nun looks around at the others and sizes them up. She glances at Evelyn:

"Sister Prioress, you've done this before, right?"

"Yeah," Evelyn says, straightening her back and preparing herself for work.

Bernadette then looks across at Magdalena as if to say she can still back off, retreat, forego the path she's decided to take: "Mother Superior?"

But Magdalena is encouraged by the older sister's confidence in her and, in turn, nods to Evelyn.

The prioress receives the signal and takes charge.

"Okay, listen up," Evelyn begins: "Outside these doors, in the gallery, for the next six hours, will be a regular flow of people from miles around, asking for our prayers of intercession."

She lets this sink in.

"Sisters, if you thought chastity was tough, if you thought renouncing the company of your family and friends cruel, if you found the observance of the rule of our Order sometimes inhumane… Then, if you are still here with us, it is because you sense there is something valuable in this sacrifice, no?"

She steps aside, taking the measure of the women she is commanding.

"Sisters, you are about to confront the pain, the suffering, the fear, the sheer stupidity, the baseness, cheapness, greediness and, yes, also the helplessness and naivety, the innocence, even the saintliness of—the population at large. And if it does not destroy you, it will become clear at once that only your chastity, only your renunciation, and only your observance, only your submission to the Rule has made it possible for you to endure this descent into hell."

Less than forty yards away, out in the garden, Jesus opens the door to Resurrection Avenue and a hush falls over the crowd. He stands aside as Lola is revealed looking meek and pretty. The crowd is moved, they murmur, they jostle quietly for a better view of the saintly virgin in the doorway.

Lola takes a step forward and addresses those nearest her in the tones of a stewardess: "Good morning and welcome to Our Lady of the Highway. My name is Sister Lola, a novice of the Order of Clementine, and I'm here to assist you should you need anything whatsoever. Please keep conversation to a minimum while inside, be careful of our vegetables here in the garden, refrain from using mobile devices, and under no circumstances is photography permitted. Enjoy our fresh homemade beer and go in peace. Credit cards accepted."

Señora Diaz is pale. She might faint. She's staring at Lola, recognizing the saint with magic powers she encountered in the lobby of the church. She makes the sign of the cross, kneels at the young novice's feet, and kisses the hem of her habit.

Looking on, like everyone else—touched, shocked, or scandalized—Charles is impressed. "This is already definitely worth the trip," he confides to Jenny.

Jeff drops his contrast filter, immediately and dangerously in love. "Wow," he utters, weak in the knees, "I wasn't really expecting this."

"Easy, Jeff," Jenny advises. They all know their friend falls fast and hard for a pretty face.

To the continued amazement of the onlookers, Señora Diaz rises to her feet, turns to her adopted hipster acquaintances, and points out sternly: "She is a saint. Be good."

Meanwhile, Evelyn paces back and forth through the main hall: "Do you have a heart? Harden it, but allow yourself to feel. Do you have a mind—ideas? Quiet them, but listen. Think. Do you have a body, a flesh and blood self that can be threatened, attacked, abused? Set it aside. Forget it. It was never yours to begin with. And don't judge, lest you yourself be judged." She waits, watches, then: "Let us pray."

The assembled sisters kneel as one, Lola running in to join them at the last minute. They clasp their hands before them and pray in unison: "Dear God in heaven, and Jesus, Mary, his mother, and all the saints, come to our assistance, make haste to help us. Our souls magnify the Lord and our spirits rejoice in our Savior for he has looked with favor on the lowliness of his servants. He has scattered the proud in the thoughts of their hearts, he has brought down the powerful from their thrones, he has lifted up the lowly and has filled the hungry with good things. Give ear to our words, oh heavenly Father; give heed to our sighing. Listen to the sound of our cry. May the Lord bless us, protect us from all evil, and bring us to everlasting life. Amen."

At a sign from Evelyn, they rise. As the sisters approach the door to the gallery and prepare to enter, the prioress moves amongst them, straightening habits, improving posture. "There will be evil out there as well as good. Protect yourself from flattery. Don't be dragged into their fantasies. Stay hydrated."

Lola is handing out bottles of water.

All set, Evelyn pauses and studies her troops one last time. Then, satisfied, she leads the way in. "Okay. Let's do this." She steps forward and throws wide the double doors to the inner gallery. A subdued hubbub is heard outside, beyond the partition. The ten sisters move directly to seats aligned regularly the length of the grille. Evelyn pauses and calls back softly over her shoulder: "Sister Lola, watch our backs."


Dozens of people are on line in the outer gallery, waiting, as others kneel before the partition. Though obscured by the grille and blinds, Sister Bernadette addresses a haggard and prematurely aged man.

"And for what would you ask us to pray, my friend?"

"Well, Sister, I'd like, if you would, can you pray for my wife, and my daughter, and my son."

"What is your name?"

"Harry."

"Harry, is your family in trouble?"

"I don't know."

"How is that?"

"Well, you see, Sister, I... I've been a mess. A bad

husband definitely. And I, well… Phoebe, my wife, she took the kids and left me years ago. I was a drunk. Still am. I don't know where they are or if they're okay and… I just feel worse and worse about it year after year."

Meanwhile, further along the line, a plain and shy woman kneels opposite Magdalena:

"And for what would you ask us to pray?"

"For my parents, Sister, please. Mister and Missus Robert DeRoche."

Magdalena writes this down in the little chapbook the sisters have all been provided. "Are they deceased, child?"

"Yes. Killed in a car crash when I was ten."

"And you're alone now, aren't you?" the mother superior senses.

"Yeah, well, there's a man who works with me at the supermarket. He likes me, I think. He came to Mass with me last week. He's older. And he has only one arm."

Further along, Evelyn endures a preening young man. "I want so badly to be famous," Chad makes known.

Evelyn pauses first, considering, then asks sensibly: "For what?"

"I don't know. But I think I'm special. And I just keep missing all the opportunities other people get. I mean, like, Sister, do you watch television?"

"No."

"Well," he explains, "there are just like all these people my age who are rich and famous and really cool and just like me. But they hang out together and get their pictures taken and say fun stuff on late night TV and everything." He's visibly upset. "I just want to be part of that world."

Evelyn holds her forehead. "And for what would you ask us to pray?"

Chad has to think a moment. "Just pray for me: Chad. Chad who will be famous."

"That will cost you twelve bottles of beer," the prioress informs him without apology.

Chad looks back over his shoulder to the little concession stand Jesus is managing. On the wall is a sign reading: Suggested Donation: $1.00 per bottle. He turns back and checks his wallet. "Sure. Thanks, Sister!"

Further along, Veronica administers to Señora Diaz:

"Sister, please pray for my grandson, Vincent, who is good but not so smart."

"Vincent," Veronica confirms as she writes in her chapbook.

"*Sí*. Vincent Diaz. He is in the jail again."

Curious now, Veronica tilts up one of the blinds just a touch and sneaks a peek out at the woman. She wonders if she's the grandmother of the boy who stole their candlesticks. It's likely, she thinks. But what Veronica and the other sisters can't possibly know just yet is all that has been developing as a result of that small and fairly harmless burglary—

"So was this before or after you drove the stolen Honda Civic though the window of the Starbucks," the cranky, long-suffering Detective Pena demands to know.

"That is my mother's car, I keep telling you," Vincent insists.

"Where did you encounter this nun?"

"That ain't important, man! I did not steal that car!"

"No, it is important because someone or other has been breaking into Our Lady of the Highway on a regular basis, even though they refuse to report it for some reason."

Vincent decides to lie outrageously. It's worked before.

"Officer, I did not see her inside the convent! What are you nuts?! It's a whatever the fuck—a cloister. Girls only. No, she was like just prowling the street."

Pena is almost entertained. "Prowling?"

"Yeah, like she's this wilding nun and shit, attacking young men at random."

It's getting late. Pena gets up and steps outside into the hall, closing the door behind him. Crossing to the watercooler he gives instructions to junior Detective Oscar. "Lock him up."

"The sisters don't want to press charges."

"Lock him up anyway. Just for the night." He tosses back the ice-cold water and throws away the paper cup. "Someone's trying to terrorize these nuns. And I think I know who it is."

Gordon Normal, as it turns out, is at the diocesan offices seated across from Bishop Frank's desk.

"I want to build the world's first viable industrial-strength biogas energy facility right out here in Brooklyn."

"Biogas," asks the bishop.

"That's right. Methane gas extracted from human excrement."

"Innovative," the bishop is forced to admit.

"Someone's gotta be first."

"On the spot where the convent of Our Lady of the Highway now stands?"

"Exactly."

"But why there?"

"It's the perfect location. So much of the city's raw sewage already gets dumped into the canal just behind the convent anyway. The infrastructure overhaul can be hugely minimized. Of course, this won't happen overnight. But by the time I'm elected mayor, forty percent of every home in the five boroughs will have dedicated solid waste toilets connected to a revamped sewage grid channeling all this human shit into the central digestion center to be broken down and turned into cheap energy we'll then sell back to the consumer. It'll be hugely profitable."

"Forgive me, Mister Normal, I'm no technologist. But this seems a little, well—ambitious."

"Yeah, that's what they said about solar energy! Electric cars! Recycling laws! Bike lanes too! Remember that? I've got the city's Department of Sewage on my side. And contractors are strangling one another to get in on this first. I'm sure I'll be able to lobby for state and federal subsidies too. Especially once I'm mayor."

"You're pretty confident about all this, I see—getting elected."

"It's in the bag, Bishop. Just a matter of time. Not this next go-round but the one after."

"The convent is not, technically, under my jurisdiction, Mister Normal. The Clementine Order is an independently organized community. It's up to the sisters themselves to decide if they want to sell the land."

"But they listen to you, right?"

"Sometimes."

"To be perfectly honest," Normal begins, leaning forward with a cough, uncertain about the required etiquette, "your, ah... bishop-ness, I don't think these ladies of the underpass or whatever know the first thing about money."

"That's probably true."

"I'm offering five hundred million dollars, for crying out loud! They could open a brand-new convent in Connecticut or Barbados or Monte Carlo—you know, somewhere more upmarket!"

"I know. I know. But you have to understand their commitment to that location."

"What is it? What is so special about that little piece of polluted land in Brooklyn?"

"Sisters of the Clementine Order have been praying for world peace there, on that spot, nonstop, for three hundred and forty-odd years."

Normal leans back, huffs, sniffs, impressed. He thinks about it. "Well, apparently, it's not working, right? Can't someone explain that to them? World peace is a lot less likely than a whole city powered by methane gas extracted from human shit, your holiness. Believe me. They should take the money, find another convent, and pray for something else altogether!"

The outer gallery is full of people and busy with reverent murmuring, stifled tears, and even some grateful laughter. Lola is running the day-to-day business in and outside the convent. She guides Marie out of the inner gallery and moves to the stairwell.

"Sister, it's time for you to relieve Sister Therese at vigil."

"Yes, Sister Lola. Thank you," the teenager replies, dutifully.

"You don't have to say thank you after everything you say in English," Lola explains kindly.

"Okay," Marie agrees, "thank you."

"Come, this way. To the basilica."

They skip down the stairwell.

"You know the prayers," Lola asks.

"Yes. I practice always. Thank you."

Reaching the basilica, Lola leaves the girl at the doors and prepares to return to her other tasks. "Go on. I have to get back outside with more beer."

But she hangs back and watches as Marie practically dances across the large empty space to where Therese lies before the altar. With unalloyed delight, the young sister lowers herself to her knees, taps Therese on the shoulder, and ardently dives into prayer as the older woman rises. "Give us this day our daily bread, and forgive us our trespasses, as we forgive those who trespass against us, and lead us not into temptation, but deliver us from evil…"

And so on—for the next two and a half hours.

Marie's English is perfect when she's praying.

Therese approaches the doors and, though still groping her way back into the profane world herself, notices Lola looking on admiringly. She pauses and touches the novice's arm.

"Some day you, too, perhaps."


The garden is abuzz with the friendly, excited, but subdued chatter of the crowd. Lola bangs out from a small door at the back of the brewery, lugging another crate of beer. Leo is there to take it from her.

"Thanks," she says and blows a wisp of hair off her face from out the side of her mouth. They kiss. Then they back away, self-conscious. But then they kiss again before moving off in opposite directions.

Jeff, the aspiring cinematographer, is watching this and his heart is broken in pieces. He hits Charles in the arm. "Did—did you—that guy—Sister Lola—fuck! He kissed her."

Charles is preoccupied. "She's a saint, remember. Be good."

Jenny approaches. "The local TV news is outside."

"This is our big chance," Charles decides, "we've got to do something about this."

Misunderstanding, deep into his own concerns, Jeff backpeddles: "I mean, I don't want to fight him or anything. Not here at the convent anyway."

Lola runs into Jesus' toolshed and finds him at his workbench with the Rule. "Is it ready," she asks.

"Almost. What are these words?"

Lola bends over the book and looks to where he points.

"Latin," she believes, reaching for her mobile device, reading: "*Rhus radicans*."

"Now what the fuck is that?" Jesus complains.

Using her translation app, Lola is alarmed to discover: "Poison ivy?"

But Jesus is not worried. "Oh! Okay. Poison ivy. That's easy," he declares, moving to his shelf of herbs, spices and roots.

"But isn't that toxic?"

"No—well it depends," he explains, calming her. "A little dried poison ivy mixed with lemon juice and some pine tar—and all this other stuff…" He tosses a few flakes of dried poison ivy into a tall jar containing a dark liquid. Lola looks on as he covers it, shakes it well, and holds it out to her. "You soak some bandages in this mess, wrap it tightly around Sister Joan's infected parts, and she'll be better in no time. I've used this on Desmond's leg too when he got mauled by some cats once."

Lola hurries with the jar through the crowded garden and back towards the convent. But Charles stops her:

"Sister Lola!

"Oh, hi, sorry. I'm just—"

"I'm Charles. This is Jenny and that's Jeff."

"Cool," Lola replies, eager to be on her way.

"And this is Elaine," he adds.

"Peace be with you," Lola smiles and starts to go.

But Elaine is knocked out: "Oh, that is so cute and usable! Let me write that down."

Charles presses on: "Have you got a sales and marketing plan in place for this beer?"

Lola pauses, exchanges glances with Leo, who's busy making sales, and decides to give Charles her full attention for a moment: "Well, ah, in fact, no. We are looking for a beverage distributor, though. Can I get back to you in a minute?"

"Sure, absolutely. Thanks."

Lola lets herself in the convent's back door, below the brewery. Watching her go, even the otherwise asexual Charles is impressed: "She's the poster girl for sure."

"Photogenic," Jenny weighs in.

Jeff, still wounded, adds, "And just so sort of nice and holy and everything."

Elaine caresses his shoulder: "Are you going to be okay, Jeff?"

Inside, Lola climbs a short flight of stairs to the brewery. Sister Joan is half passed out on the packing table. Bernadette steps in from the gallery and wipes the sweat from her brow. Rolling up her sleeves, she approaches. "That it," she asks of the jar.

"Yeah."

They douse some clean towels in the foul-smelling concoction and begin rewrapping Joan's arm.

Outside in the garden, Leo, assisted by Xavier, is doing a brisk business at the beer station. He can't help but notice Jeff giving him some attitude. "Jeff, right? From the bar," he asks, trying to break the ice.

But Jeff responds with something he hopes is vaguely like a challenge: "Maybe."

Lola returns and the tension is diffused. She takes a healthy swig off Leo's open beer and then returns to Charles. "Sorry. So, where were we?"

"Well, Lola," Charles begins, trying on his most professionally confident, preoccupied, and world-weary manner, "I've just recently formed a new advertising company and would love to discuss working together."

"Great. Have you got a business card?"

Charles winces, "Ah, no, not yet," he admits.

"This company is really very, very new," Jenny explains.

"I see," Lola replies, trying to soften the blow. But Elaine thinks a little humiliation is good for Charles:

"In fact, it's about twenty minutes old."

"But totally inspired," Jenny rushes to assert, "by what you're accomplishing here."

"Charles has been interning at a public relations firm for two and a half years," Jeff adds, trying to help.

"Thanks, Jeff," Charles sighs, glancing away.

Elaine points out, "Jenny's an ace web designer."

"Jeff has shot some music videos," Jenny continues.

"And I'm a party planner," Elaine concludes. "Here's my card instead."

Demoralized, Charles finally bows to necessity: "Thanks, Elaine."

But Lola is game. These scrambling, competitive, and aspiring ne'er-do-wells do seem like fun. "Well, to start with," she states plainly, "we don't have any money."

Charles brightens up. "Ah! Well, okay then," he happily concedes. "Neither do we!"

## EIGHT

Lola is being photographed in the outer gallery by Jeff and a crew he has put together for the occasion. Charles oversees everything: producer, director, and advertising agency executive all in one. But he's nervous. He is financing all this with two credit cards the charges on which he is in no position to pay.

"I think a little less angelic is better," he decides, biting his lip.

"Like this?"

Lola is not a natural. She tries to look less angelic and the effect troubles Charles.

"No," he replies, perspiring, "less profile maybe."

Jenny looks up over the edge of her laptop. "She should be holding a beer."

"An Our Lady of the Highway beer," Jeff realizes.

"But we don't have those yet," Charles reminds them.

"Any bottle will do."

"Yeah," Jenny points out, "we can photoshop in the label later."

"Here," Jeff says, moonstruck, as he hands Lola a green

twelve-ounce longneck.

"Where do I hold it," she asks.

Jeff has never been more certain of anything in his life:

"Near your face."

"Honestly," Charles decides, "what I think we need is a little more shoulder."

Lola blinks. Where is this all headed?

"Elaine has a few options," Charles continues, raising his hand and snapping his fingers. Elaine eagerly flies in with a variety of Catholic nun outfits.

Peeking out from behind the partition, Sisters Bernadette and Magdalena are concerned.

"This is barbaric," Bernadette states flatly.

Magdalena, more in agreement than she allows herself to appear, tries her best to calm her elder sister down. "Oh, it's harmless," she whispers, adding, "I guess."

Bernadette begins pacing the dim inner gallery. "Okay, so we make beer to support ourselves. I've accepted that. But must we advertise?"

"How else can we let people know it's available for sale?"

"By telling them about it when they come to the convent for our prayers!"

"Oh, I'm afraid we'll need to tell more people than that if we're going to support ourselves," she explains, sitting. "And I'm afraid our prayers of intercession are becoming more and more difficult to manage."

And this is true. It's been six weeks since the first Saturday of intercessory prayer offered by the sisters of the convent and they've become world famous. Just this past Saturday—

Helicopters pass overhead, television crews jockey for the best angles, and crowds of the faithful are lined up and down

Resurrection Avenue. A trio of nuns are strumming guitars and singing "Give Peace A Chance" as a busload of foreign petitioners arrive. A handsome newscaster reports from the scene:

"They come from as far away as the Midwest, Canada, from Europe and beyond. The faithful, the curious, beer lovers from around the globe are descending upon Williamsburg, Brooklyn, each Saturday to ask for the prayers of the good sisters of Our Lady of the Highway."

And the host of a popular and controversial daytime talk show has a couple of senators in the studio:

"And, so, what do you make of all this, Senator; this sudden and furiously popular interest in the nuns of Our Lady of the Highway and their prayers of intercession?"

The first, more benevolent, adamantly conciliatory statesman to answer clears his throat: "Well, I believe that in all inclusive communities of a truly democratic nature, where freedom of religious expression is a right, we need to remember and extend our shared values and respect difference."

His counterpart, an agitated senator from another state, is beside himself: "What!" he protests, incredulously. "I'm sorry, this—this is just like crazy people from all over the place invading Brooklyn! This is what happens when a society comes unglued from rational discourse, when its moral fiber erodes and fantasy takes over!"

Back at the convent, though, while beers are selling briskly near the gallery's entrance, the sisters are receiving petitions and busily writing them down in their chapbooks.

"And for what would you ask us to pray, my friend?"

Magdalena is weary from the day's long effort to listen for real.

"For my brother, Charlie, in the Army, Sister," a young

woman replies. "He's still over there somewhere searching for unexploded bombs."

Further down the line, Bernadette explodes. "Listen, you pervert, we don't pray for that sort of thing!" Then, removing her reading glasses, she calls, "Next!"

The petitioner in question slinks out, pulling his wool cap down over his ears, as someone else takes his place. Sister Therese looks over at Bernadette.

"Sister, are you okay?"

Bernadette cleans her glasses with a napkin and shakes her head. "Nothing surprises me anymore, Sister Therese, nothing." Then, leaning towards the partition, she gets right back to work. "For what would you ask us to pray?"

It's Detective Pena. He's not entirely comfortable being here. "For my son, Sister. I think he's retarded."

Bernadette pauses, takes a breath, and leans back a little. These cases require special care; no one but parents themselves know the realities involved. "Oh. I'm sorry," she says, "What is your name, my friend?"

"I'm a cop, Sister. Detective Pena."

"And your son?"

"Ben. He can do complicated arithmetic better than anyone but he can't do the simplest everyday things like throw a baseball or... or... you know, play computer games and stuff."

Bernadette is suddenly sure the man is exaggerating his fears; his child is probably perfectly normal. She settles on a time-honored and well proven platitude: "Well, God sends us all different kinds of gifts, Officer Pena."

But he's heard all this nonsense before too. "It's *Detective* Pena, Sister."

~

Months earlier, Pena is watching the television mounted to the wall beside the kitchen table where he eats his dinner. As always, he is arguing with his wife, Vanessa, and her two sisters.

"Will you all sit down, for Christ's sake!" he insists.

"Shut up and eat your dinner!" Vanessa retorts.

She and her sisters come and go, back and forth, with dishes and bowls, from the counter to the table and then back again. For some reason Pena can't figure out, these women never sit down to eat. Instead, they chatter nonstop, tasting this and that, stop sometimes to check their text messages, and step out onto the porch for a quick drag off a cigarette. All this as they serve him and his ten-year-old son, Ben. The small home is constantly in motion. There are three televisions on simultaneously. Ben is doing his best to block out the noise and the casual hostility all around him by concentrating on the math textbook beside his plate.

"So why is it I gotta come home to a house filled up with your goddamn sisters," Pena yells, resuming some heated issue from half an hour ago.

"Oh, you got a problem with my sisters," Vanessa says, hip cocked, foot tapping, "then why you gotta go and arrest their boyfriends, huh?"

"Because they're fucking drug dealers in the subway, that's why!"

"Don't use that kinda language in front of Ben!"

Julia, the youngest of the three sisters, switches off the electric potato masher and points it at Pena with fire in her eyes. "Carlos was never no selling anything in the subway, man!"

Pena can't be bothered with Julia. She's hopeless. Instead, he sees an opportunity to contribute to his son's upbringing:

"Ben, what did I tell you: no books at the table!"

But, as usual, Ben confounds his old man. "Hey Dad, you know what algebra means?"

Pena just looks at the kid, threatened. "What kinda question is that to ask your father? You know, I work for a living every day of the week so that you can go to school and learn this crazy shit!"

Celia, the middle sister, cannot get enough of the boy's cute intellectual preoccupations. "Tell us, baby," she encourages him, delivering the boy a second plate of food.

"Don't call him baby," Pena complains.

"It's from Arabic," the kid tells him, "*al-jabr*, which means the reunion of broken parts."

Troubled, Pena looks blankly from his son to his wife. What further evidence is needed to confirm the kid is mentally challenged?

Vanessa shrugs and raises her hands, palms up: "What?"

Unable to speak his mind, to admit his grief, to convey the depth of his disappointment that he'll never be able to watch Monday Night Football with his son, Pena pushes away his plate in disgust: "Why the hell are they teaching him Arabic, for crying out loud! What the fuck is that all about!"

It's all too dark and painful to remember. And now, there at the convent, Pena hangs his head before the partition opposite Sister Bernadette. "No, Sister," he repeats, "I'm sure my son is retarded."


A few days after the burglary at the convent, Detective Pena waits in the conference room over at Magnificent Waste Management Corporation. The place is impressive, he has to admit. It reminds him how crappy the precinct is; how much he resents his own home; how many mistakes he's made in his life, generally.

Gordon Normal arrives. "Officer Pena," he asks, extending his hand.

Pena stands and corrects him, flashing his badge. "Detective Pena."

"Sorry."

"I've got a kid in custody caught busting into the convent of Our Lady of the Highway out there," Pena begins. "Says he was paid to do so by Magnificent Waste Management Corporation."

"That's absurd," Normal laughs, seating himself at the conference table.

"It's also a felony for everybody involved," Pena points out, "if we can prove—like this kid says—that he was issued a firearm by said employer."

Gordon Normal remains expressionless. But deep inside, he's throwing a fit because he can see it all now—


Vincent is half listening as Hubert Jones offers him both an envelope full of cash and a handgun.

"Now, listen son, you don't know where this money comes from or who you're working for, right? I don't know you and you don't know me, correct?"

But Vincent is looking right at Jones' corporate name tag, reading, *Hubert Jones, Magnificent Waste Management Corporation.*

Jones sees this and, cursing himself, removes the name tag. "Understood?"

"Okay," the lackadaisical young criminal replies, taking the envelope and the handgun.

A few nights later, locked up in the police precinct's holding cells, Vincent tells all as he brags to a seemingly simple-minded inmate. There's a video camera recording it all:

"So, this dude I'm negotiating with, Director of Operations or something at Magnificent Waste Management Corporation, Hubert Jones, he's like okay five hundred for the job. And I'm like: fuck that! One thousand for me and another five hundred for my cousin, Xavier! And we get to keep the weapons!"

His skinny, shy, unshaven cellmate, Carl, nods, amazed.

"And he, wow—he went for that, huh?"

"Damn right he did," Vincent declares, striding back and forth all gangsta fashion, "fucking college educated middle management tool!"

Carl gets this kind of work a lot, pretending to be a gullible vagrant held overnight in the precinct. He's actually a member of an off-off-Broadway performance group specializing in contemporary American avant-garde dance theater.

Pena and Detective Oscar, are watching this scene play out on a monitor in Pena's office. "That's it," Pena says, standing, "that's all we need to know."

Though it's all speculation, Normal is pretty certain this little nightmare he's just raced through in his head is correct. He expertly triangulates the likely repercussions and decides some radical gesture is needed. He leans forward and presses the intercom.

"Elise?"

"Yes, Mister Normal," his trusted assistant's voice comes tentatively back at him.

"Fire Hubert Jones immediately. Reassign his parking space."

"Yes, Mister Normal."

Normal leans back and returns to Pena. "Sufficient," he

asks.

"No," the detective replies, not surprised.

"Officer…"

"Detective."

"Detective," Normal tries again, "what if I were to tell you that the convent of Our Lady of the Highway may very well be harboring an international terrorist?"

"I'd ask you why you're changing the subject."

"But, in fact, I'm not."

"Yes, you are," Pena comes back hard. "The subject is this kid who says you gave him a gun and paid him to go scare the sisters in the convent."

"It's related."

"Related to what?"

"Detective Pena, you, being a Catholic I presume from, what, Central or South America?"

"What the fuck does that have to do with the goddamn price of tea in China!"

"More than you know."

"What," the detective stutters, plainly worried now.

"Cuba," Normal suggests, guessing.

"Mexico," Pena responds without knowing why.

"Then I'm sure you've heard of Sister Tatiana-Magdalena dos Santos e Ramirez."

This does the trick. The name simply spoken aloud makes Pena's face go red. He rises to his feet—

Dinner at the Pena home has descended into chaos. There's a news item about Magdalena on the television.

"She's a terrorist," the detective insists, spitting his dinner back down onto his plate.

"She's a saint," Vanessa shouts, spinning around from the

sink full of dishes.

"A psychopath," Pena continues, "they say so on the TV!"

Celia removes some bowls from the table and backs up her sister. "She builds hospitals when the government can't even tie their own shoes laces!" And Julia, too, the youngest, has facts to hand: "She blows up boats full of guns the drug dealers use to keep the government in power!"

"Yeah, right, of course," the man of the house sees fit to remind them, "and she smuggles illegal immigrants into the United States of America!"

"That's right," Vanessa reminds him calmly, "like your father."

Terrified and deeply wounded, Pena stands. "Hey! Not in front of the boy!"

"And our mother and aunts and uncles too!" Celia adds, proudly.

"Fuck them," Pena scoffs, "they're Ecuadorian!"


Pena now sits back down on the couch at Magnificent Waste, trying to control himself. "That nun… that nun is a…" and here he relishes the evil sounding word, "…an anarchist."

"A well-known anarchist," Normal adds, seeing an opening for his aims in the detective's obvious and irrational rage.

"This illegal immigration, I say fuck you to that," the detective stammers. His mom and dad were, in fact, illegal immigrants for years and Pena lays the blame for his low self-esteem and fierce patriotism at their feet.

"As you should," Normal commends him, knowing a borderline psychopath when he sees one.

"How do you know all this," Pena asks, shaking his head in disbelief. "Tatiana-Magdalena over there at that convent?"

"I've made my own investigations."

"Why?"

Normal moves to the window and looks out at his vast domain, marred as it is, however, by the convent. "I need that land."

"For what?"

"The world's first viable industry-standard methane gas manufacturing facility."

"Methane?"

"Cheap fuel from the ultimate source of renewable energy."

"And what would that be?"

"Human excrement."

"Shit," the detective asks, confirming, disliking big words.

"That's right."

"You are a strange man, Mister Normal."

"I intend to be mayor, Detective."

Pena stands and hoists his belt up over his expanding gut. "Good luck."

"My acquisition of the property the convent is on will secure my business aims. The success of my business aims will insure my election."

Pena joins the ambitious man at the window and glances around. He covets all Normal has. "You're like, what: fifty?"

"Fifty-five this month," Normal states, pacing around the conference table, conscious of his youthful good looks.

"You look like a guy who likes his job."

"I like success. I like achieving things."

"Being a cop sucks," Pena makes plain and comes away from the window. "I suppose you got some kind of private surveillance outfit patrolling this operation of yours?"

"Well, as a matter of fact, I just fired my *director* of operations."

Right, Pena remembers, he just witnessed that. "I sometimes think of early retirement," he says.

"Detective, once that convent's gone and I acquire the property and put my plan into action I'll need a revamped and beefy security apparatus—and someone I can trust to run it."

Pena puts his shoe up on the couch and reaches down to retie his lace. "What kind of salary we talking about?"

"What are we expecting?" Normal counters, wondering if the shoe on the couch is some kind of a standard cop negotiating technique.

Pena straightens up, sniffs extravagantly, and removes his notebook from the inside breast pocket of his jacket. He writes something on a page, tears it out, and slides it across the table to Normal who lifts it, reads, and places it back down.

"That's reasonable."

Pena nods and retrieves the paper; no need to leave clues. Still, he kicks himself for not having written a larger figure.

"You sure Tatiana-Magdalena is in there," he asks.

"Practically certain."

"You know, of course, this is a bribe."

"A successful one, I hope."

"Me too."

They shake hands.


And so, the very next day back at the precinct, Vincent is craftily terrorized by the brooding detectives.

"Vincent, I'll be honest," Pena says, "things look bad for you."

The kid is speechless.

But then comes the real pressure: "Your grandmother is outside."

"Fuck no!" the kid wails. "Why did you... Shit!"

And, indeed, Señora Diaz paces in the hall outside. The little girl, Inez, sits doing her homework and the baby, Joseph, is in his stroller, drooling.

Inside, Pena lightens up and puts a hand on Vincent's shoulder: "All we're asking for is a little cooperation."

The popular and controversial talk show host is now happy to have in the studio a Protestant pastor, a law professor from Columbia University, and Bishop Thomas Frank, the Catholic bishop of Brooklyn. The media pro listens with almost believable thoughtfulness as the pastor earnestly unpacks the recent phenomenon at Our Lady of the Highway:

"I think," the pastor begins, "that in the past number of weeks what we've witnessed in Brooklyn is something very much like an awakening of a—yes a spiritualized community, particularly amongst young people..."

"But what about the beer," the host interjects, "the commodification of religious sentiment, the exploitation of an imagined female sanctity?"

This is all a bit heady for the kindly pastor. As he tries to make sense of the question, the female law professor opines grandly: "The whole thing is a disgrace!"

Over at Margaret's, the regulars are watching the show on the television above the bar. Charles bursts in, all fired up:

"You watching this! We're huge!"

"Our twitter presence is off the charts," Elaine reports, scrolling through her mobile device.

"Chastity, can I recharge my phone?" Charles pleads, then, glancing up at the television, he begins to tremble, "Oh, wait a minute! Look! Look! Look! It's Bishop Frank!"

Chet, the aged plumber, who always sits under the television so as not to have to look at it, slides off his barstool and comes around front. "Oh, that guy rocks!"

Chastity turns up the volume:

"Well, there are two ways of being religious in our way of thinking," the bishop admits, "being active and being contemplative. Me, I'm active—I've got to be out there in the world with people, doing things. But other folks are better at prayer, meditation. And the world needs that too."

The studio audience is riveted. The host is jealous of the bishop's common touch. Charles is starting to tear up. His months of frantic publicity and virtual marketing is actually paying off and he's not the loser his relatives believe him to be.

The bishop adjusts himself in his seat, plants an elbow on the armrest, and shifts gears: "You know, say what you will about mysticism and the power of prayer—I could never get behind all that heart and soul myself. But I remember as a soldier in combat I had to say to myself—often—you know, in practical terms, if all these people on both sides were praying, they wouldn't have the time or the inclination to shoot each other with guns or be blowing one another apart with hand grenades. I mean, that might seem simplistic, but damn it—more power to the sisters out at Our Lady of the Highway!" He holds up a bottle of the newly packaged and labeled beer. "And their beer is excellent."

Charles now weeps openly. Chet lays a fatherly hand on the young man's shoulder.

Detective Oscar is projecting a bunch of pictures of fugitive nuns in a room set aside for this purpose. There are both mug shots and surveillance photos. Vincent has been rewarded with all the McDonald's he can eat.

"No. No. No…" the kid recites as faces flash by. Shots of Magdalena, Evelyn, and Veronica come and go. He recognizes them but pretends he doesn't. "No. No. She was prettier. No."

Pena is skeptical.

Oscar is frustrated. He turns back to the boy: "You sure? Take your time. Look again."

"Don't fuck with us, kid," Pena mumbles from back in the shadows.

"Damn, these french fries are gone all cold," the kid complains.

"You telling me you don't recognize any of these nuns!"

"The mean one, the one who beat me up, I didn't see her face too well," Vincent offers, "but there was this other one…"

"A prettier one," Oscar tries to confirm.

"Hey, wait," Vincent points.

Oscar stops the parade of images. Pena steps forward as he goes back a few pictures.

"No, not that one," the kid directs, "keep going. There! That one!"

It is a shot of an unknown nun laboring in some tropical locale.

"This one," Pena asks, outraged, "you recognize this one?"

"No," Vincent relaxes, sitting back, "she was taller. Where is that, anyway, like, Tahiti?"

Pena drops down in the nearest available chair, giving up.


Lola is now in a nun getup that has an improbable bustier feature and off-the-shoulder sleeves. Elaine is helping her attach a garter belt to her thigh-high stockings.

"You sure? Really? Is this okay," Lola worries.

"Adorable," Elaine assures her. "Here, let me…"

But they both look up as the door opens.

Jesus steps in and, seeing Lola all sexed up, immediately turns away, blushing. "Oh! Sorry. Sister Lola, we're outside. Pankaj from the bodega. His brother-in-law, Rashid. The beverage distributor. Sorry."

Lola jumps up in a hurry. "Oh! This is important."

She steps outside, forgetting what she's wearing, and meets Rashid, a busy Muslim business man. All three men are dumbstruck by her outfit and Rashid piously turns his back.

"Rashid," Lola asks politely.

"Hello," Rashid replies, eyes averted.

"I'm Sister Lola. We spoke on the phone."

Rashid hands his card to Pankaj who hands it to Jesus who hands it, shyly, to Lola.

"Mustafa-Said Beverage Distributors, LLC," Pankaj's relative states, "Jackson Heights, Queens."

Lola glances at the card but is disconcerted by Rashid looking away while he addresses her. Jesus removes his jacket and drapes it over her shoulders. "Great," she says to Rashid, though she's still uncertain. "Thanks. I mean, so, do you think we can do business?"

"Oh yes, I think so."

"The beer is okay, right," Lola continues. "We've applied for all the appropriate licenses. You think it will sell?"

Pankaj backhands his cousin in the chest to indicate it's okay to face the young woman. Rashid does.

"I do not drink beer myself, Sister. But my degenerate brother-in-law, Pankaj, here, does and he says it is tasty and refreshing."

Pankaj blinks and drags his gaze away from Lola. "Yes,

my respected associate, Rashid, is only interested in making a sizable profit from the recreational needs of depraved Westerners."

Clearly, these two go way back. Rashid tilts his head and sighs, resuming a decades-long argument with his brother-in-law: "I'm a Westerner myself, Pankaj. I was born in New Jersey.

"An infinitely pious and God-fearing place, I'm sure. Tell the sister what is needed."

"Well, we'll need to start with a minimum of at least one thousand cases."

"Whoa," Jesus exclaims, trying to do the math, "a thousand cases!"

"How soon," Lola asks.

"A month to six weeks," Rashid estimates.

Lola steps aside, projecting costs and scheduling: "That's what: twenty-four bottles a case, a thousand bottles at…"

The sisters are huddled around the kitchen table, making calculations, taking notes, and brainstorming.

"We're doing between five hundred and six hundred bottles a day," Evelyn reports, "depending on how many sisters we have on duty."

"And that depends," Bernadette adds, "on how many empty bottles Jesus is able to 'liberate' from Magnificent Waste Management's recycling facility every couple of nights—"

On any given night over the past few weeks, when a truck pulls up before Magnificent Waste rattling with empty bottles, it's stopped by Jesus and Desmond who are blocking the entrance to the recycling depot. Jesus holds a baseball bat in one hand and the dog's leash in the other.

"Get the fuck outta the way you maniac," the driver laughs.

"Cooperate, and do the right thing," Jesus warns, "and Desmond will leave you in one piece."

"Is that Desmond?"

"Damn right, that's Desmond."

Though Desmond is thick, heavy, and ugly, he is the most laid-back animal on earth. The driver is not intimidated. But when he hears Xavier jump up onto the back of the truck he starts to worry.

"Whoa! Hey, easy! What do you want?"

"Bottles," Jesus declares heroically.

"Fine," the driver concedes, "what kind of bottles?"

"Green twelve-ounce long necks."


Striding through the brewery, clipboard in hand, Lola sums things up for the sisters following her. "If we want to be in business with Rashid a month from now, we'll need to increase production to a thousand bottles a day at least."

"We'll need another bottling machine," Evelyn suspects, "or two—or just a bigger one."

Magdalena wanders on ahead as the others pause. She turns, thinks a moment, then comes to the point: "And, of course, we need more sisters."

But now, coming forward, Lola retrieves six or seven opened letters slid in behind the back pages on her clipboard. "After reading our fan mail this morning, Mother Superior, I'm not sure that will be a problem."


A day or two later, a crowd of nuns of all ages and from different orders file politely into the outer gallery, nodding greetings to one another, waiting for something to happen.

Behind the partition, Magdalena, Evelyn, and Bernadette watch and observe. Evelyn is encouraged. "Outstanding," she whispers.

Bernadette, far more battle-tested, has reservations. "Not so fast, Sister." She crosses to Magdalena, "Mother Superior?"

Magdalena steps forward to the partition and, unseen, speaks: "Sister, you, in the blue habit. Come closer. It's me, the mother superior."

A stout thirty-year-old nun glances around and ascertains she is the only one wearing a blue habit. She approaches the partition.

"What is your name," Magdalena continues.

"Amelia."

"I see from your habit you are of the Order of the Incarnate Word."

"Yes. My convent is in Minnesota."

"And what brings you here?"

"I want to be part of the vigil."

Impressed, Magdalena glances back at Bernadette who is also gratified. Bernadette comes forward. "Sister," she asks, "you would renounce your vows to the Order of the Incarnate Word and become, like us, a sister of the Order of Clementine?"

"I've thought about it long and hard. I've prayed. I've discussed it with our prioress. She's given me leave to do so—if you'll have me."

Concerned the young woman's choices have been well thought through, Magdalena resumes. "And why, Sister Amelia; are you unhappy with the Order's Rule?"

"I want to be where the action is, Mother Superior," the modest nun replies, "and, well, everyone seems to know now:

the action is at Our Lady of the Highway."

Magdalena smiles and catches Bernadette smiling too. But the senior nun hides it. Evelyn lifts a slat of the blinds and sizes up the young nun with an eye to her own concerns—the brewery.

"Sister Amelia," the prioress asks, "are you comfortable around machinery?"

"My father and brothers work in a foundry," Amelia replies brightly, "I grew up on my grandparent's dairy farm."

A week later, Sister Amelia is busy and productive at the new heavy-duty bottling machinery. The place is bustling—

Another nun now stands before the partition and Magdalena asks, "And you, Sister Annunciata, please, where do you come from?"

"Mother Superior, I am from the Augustinian convent of the Blessed Sacrament in Palo Alto, California."

"And you want, instead, to become a Clementine?"

"I have always wanted to be an active nun working in poor communities trying to relieve suffering. But…"

"Go on."

"It's been twenty-two years and, because I'm an academic, I get assigned teaching positions in places where I am of no real use and where I do not have time to pray as I should."

Intrigued, Bernadette sits forward, pauses, and asks:

"As you should?"

"Deeply, continuously, passionately," Annunciata replies.

Bernadette leans back, nodding. "Sign her up."

But Evelyn, once again, is thinking about womanpower hours: "Sister, what is your academic specialty?"

"Languages."

A week later, Evelyn and Annunciata cajole Jesus from the brewery window. He's pacing in the garden outside with the Rule of the Order under his arm, Desmond standing aside, watching.

"Mister Ortiz, please," Evelyn implores again, "we need the book."

"But you ain't, like, needed it for all these years," he moans petulantly, "and now, like, all of a sudden…"

"We'll give it back, I promise."

"We can translate it now, Mister Ortiz," adds Annunciata.

"Who's that," Jesus stops and asks, not recognizing the voice.

"That's Sister Annunciata," Evelyn explains. "She can read Latin and Dutch and many other languages."

Now he's got a different attitude. "Really," he asks.

"Yes," Annunciata assures him, smiling at the prioress who gives her a high five.

"Well, okay," Jesus says, climbing up onto some crates to hand the book in through the window. "But don't lose it, okay? There's other stuff I use in here all the time. Medical instructions and technical drawings for the well and the pump downstairs—"

Over at Bodega Pankaj, Charles and his team are loitering near the coolers studying beer packaging. "We need a catchy slogan," he announces. "Look, like this: 'the king of beers.'"

"Born in the Rockies," Jeff reads off another product.

"How about 'get holy,'" Jenny suggests.

Jeff makes a face and looks to Charles for insight. The pilot of their fortunes answers sagely: "That could be misinterpreted."

And he moves on.

"Really? How?"

"Sounds too gay or something."

Jeff decides the conversation is over his head and wanders away, as Charles continues: "You've got to think about this stuff, come at product presentation from every angle. Use your imagination. Right Pankaj?"

"Are you going to buy that?"

Only now does Charles notice he is halfway through eating a hastily selected powerbar. He offers Pankaj his credit card.


Pena comes down the hall towards his office in the precinct and meets two FBI agents, Proctor and Blakely.

"Agent Proctor?"

"That's right," the man says. "Officer Pena?"

"Detective Pena," Pena corrects him.

"Of course, sorry." Then, turning aside, "My partner, Agent Blakely."

"Detective," Blakely nods, shaking Pena's hand.

"We can talk in here," the detective says, leading them to his office.

Once inside, Proctor continues a conversation they've been having on the phone all morning: "So you have reasonable grounds for suspecting Sister Tatiana-Magdalena dos Santos e Ramirez is hiding in the convent of Our Lady of the Highway?"

Pena sits behind his desk, straightens his back, and folds his hands before him: "Almost definitely positive."


Two days earlier, Pena is with Donna Brown and Jim Little in their offices at the Water Authority.

"Mister Gordon Normal," Pena begins, "of Magnificent

Waste Management Corporation mentioned you actually had a face-to-face conversation with the mother superior."

"Well," Donna begins, skeptically, "we spoke through that—"

"A kind of fence," Jim explains, "an iron railing from floor to ceiling."

"And there were blinds too."

"But we saw her—or, at least, I did, briefly, when she stepped into the room."

"Before the blinds were drawn," Donna concludes.

Pena slides some photos across the table for them to see.

"Would you be able to identify her as this woman?"

Donna and Jim study the few pictures but can't be certain.

"Oh," Donna frowns, "I don't know, officer. It was just for an instant."

But Jim lingers on one of the photos. It shows Magdalena in profile, her wimple askew, handcuffed, and being led into a police van. It could be from five or more years ago. He plays the few moments at the convent back again in his head—

"Excuse me a minute," Jesus says in a hurry, "I gotta get these blinds closed."

Jim now hears footsteps in what looks like a hallway at the other end of the interior gallery. He glances over through the grille just as Jesus lets himself inside the partition and reaches for the ropes to draw the blinds.

The mother superior reaches the door of the gallery thirty feet away, but turns aside, pausing before entering, leaving instructions for her sisters. Her face in shadow but her striking profile, her grace of movement, clear to see and fairly unforgettable.

The blinds are drawn with a snap. She's gone.

Back at the Water Authority, Jim is still lingering on the photo. Pena, watching him, thinks he sees the unmistakable signs of recognition. He's done this for years. He's good at it. Jim Little recognizes that face in the photo.

"Anything," he encourages the man.

"Maybe," Jim admits.

And that's good enough for Pena.


Back in his own office again with Agents Proctor and Blakely, Pena tacks up Magdalena's mug shot. "I hate this son of bitch nun," he declares.

"This crazed zealot," Proctor declares, "poses a grievous threat to US financial interests throughout South America."

"My fucking left-wing, slut, college educated sister-in-law has got my wife out of her mind about this cunt."

Blakely, the statistical guy, nods. "She's popular with feminists, socialists, pacifists and, of course, religious fanatics."

"Right?" Pena rejoices, happy they understand. "It's what I'm saying: let's go get her!"

Blakely points out, sensibly: "We won't be able to get a warrant to enter the convent to find Tatiana-Magdalena with so little evidence."

Pena is burnt. His whole career has been like this, the glory of police work tripped up by bureaucratic niceties. "Fuck. She's in there. I know it. You know it."

"We admire your ambition, Pena," Proctor counsels.

"But advise caution," Blakely adds.

"Restraint."

"Moderation."

"Prudence."

"Discipline."

Pena is visibly beaten up by all this federal wisdom. He slumps into his chair and Proctor lays a hand on his shoulder. "You've got to find some other reason to get a warrant to enter that convent."

Leo enters Margaret's Bar. Charles and his new firm, Awesome Publicity, have taken over the place. It's their temporary headquarters. At her laptop, Jenny is putting the finishing touches on her label design as Charles pins up a proof of their proposed poster. It is a scorching sexed-up shot of Lola showing leg, some bare shoulder, and holding up a bottle of OLHW premium lager.

Leo looks on, impressed. "Sweet," he whispers.

Jeff is in love but not certain with what: "It's my best work," he utters, a tremor in his voice.

Jenny comes up beside Leo and explains; "We photoshopped her chest just a little to, you know…"

"Yeah," Leo nods, smiling, "she doesn't fill out her blouse quite so aggressively in real life."

"Yeah, and what are you trying to say," Jeff snaps, provoked.

"I'm saying she's my girlfriend, pal," Leo decides to make perfectly clear, adding, after a pause, "remember that."

Charles comes between the math teacher and his infatuated friend, steering Jeff away as Leo goes to the bar and joins Jesus and Desmond. And now Father Robert enters and the new publicists all salute him:

"Peace, Father!" they call as one.

"No need to salute," the priest suggests, hanging up his jacket. "And, conventionally, it's 'peace be with you.' But, you know, whatever."

He sits at the bar as Charles stares at the old tin ceiling and has an epiphany. "That's it," he exclaims.

"That's what," Jenny asks, worried. Charles has been having too many ideas these past few days and she's been revising artwork nonstop.

"Our slogan: 'peace be with you!'"

"But I told you that weeks and weeks ago!" Elaine sighs.

"Quick, Jenny," Charles dictates, disregarding Elaine, "text Lola and get approval."

Over at the bar, Jesus, too, is anxious and worried:

"Father Robert, I had to give it to her."

"Give what to who," Robert asks, dragging his mug of beer towards himself.

"The book."

"The Rule?"

"To Sister Evelyn."

"The Rule of the Order," Robert confirms.

"Yeah," Jesus admits.

Robert drinks, thinking, then concludes: "Well, that's only right and fair, seeing as how you stole it all those years ago."

"That book is the only thing I ever stole that didn't belong to me," Jesus insists, but then adds, "I mean, from the convent."

"Look, I'm sure you'll be forgiven," the priest consoles him, "…eventually."

Jesus drinks and looks off wistfully into the darker, cobwebbed regions above the bar. "I worry about purgatory, Father. Really, I do."

"Make amends," Robert suggests, his thoughts elsewhere.

"But God's merciful an' shit, right?"

Robert pauses, lowers his beer, and looks at the man. "You really want to get into this right now?"

~

That evening, Lola and Veronica are working side by side on the assembly line pasting labels onto bottles of beer. All the nuns are busy and industrious, but they're also glancing up to admire the newly arrived extra-large poster of Lola hung high up on the wall. Amelia enters from the hall with a new crate of labels and sees the poster for the first time. She stops, smiles widely, and calls out: "Wow! Sister Lola!"

"They made my chest bigger than it really is," Lola insists.

"It's your smile that makes all the difference, dear," says kindly Sister Catherine.

"Both hot and sweet," teases Sister Amelia.

Meanwhile, Evelyn, stubbing out her cigarette butt by the window, adds: "This beer is going to be the biggest thing since sliced bread." And, by way of an answer, Bernadette sits and opens a beer. "And this convent's going to hell in a handbasket."

Sister Magdalena, who has appeared in the doorway, is concerned about this herself. "Well," she suggests, "though what Sister Bernadette says is a little extreme, it is true: we must keep our eye on the prize. Fame and fortune as excellent brewers of a fine domestic lager is all well and good but, more importantly, we now have sixteen sisters in the convent! That's only an hour and a half once a day for each sister to lie facedown on cold stone and pray for the sins of the world." She reaches Bernadette who hands her the beer. Magdalena takes a swig and concludes, handing it back: "Sisters, I put it to you: This is progress!"

"Amen," all round.

In the productive quiet that follows, Lola glances back over her shoulder to Bernadette. "Sister Bernadette," she queries dreamily, "can I participate in the vigil?"

"You," Bernadette asks in turn. "No, you're only a novice.

You have to be consecrated to the Lord by taking your vows." But she can see that Lola is a little disappointed. "Are you interested?"

"Well, it's kind of," Lola shrugs and gives up, "I don't know—exciting."

"Oh, yes," Bernadette concurs, proudly, "hard core penitence, strict obedience, ceaseless resistance to the allure of the sinful outside world… It's not for everyone but it's the only life worth living if you ask me."

Lola smiles at the label of the beer in her hand: "Sister, I think it should be you on the label."

Some sisters giggle and others are mortified anyone would joke like this with the sharp-edged Bernadette. Bernadette, however, pleasantly exhausted, adjusts her reading glasses and studies the label of the beer she herself is drinking. "You know, Sister Lola," she responds at length, "once upon a time I could have given you a run for the money."

NINE

In her office at the convent, where she is within two weeks of completing her novitiate, Lola dials the Alcohol and Tobacco Trade and Tax Bureau. At a dismal office somewhere in Albany the most dissatisfied and annoyed state employee in the world answers the phone.

"Alcohol and Tobacco Trade and Tax Bureau. Kim speaking. I'm going to lunch in ninety seconds. How may I help you?"

"Hi, this is Sister Lola from Our Lady of the Highway convent in Brooklyn. We submitted our Brewer's Notice and Brewer's Bond three weeks ago and I'm just calling to check on its progress."

Colossally offended by this outrageous provocation, Kim falls back in her chair and stutters: "Oh, oh… really?"

Lola flinches from a small burst of static electricity at her ear and looks at her mobile device. Bringing it back cautiously to herself, she continues: "I'm sorry. But we were told it would take two weeks and we want to make sure we're in compliance with state and federal requirements before we begin selling our beer."

Kim shakes her head, amazed once again at the self-centered, entitled, and ignorant manner of people generally everywhere. "What—hey, listen, Sister: do you think you're the only bunch of nuns trying to open a brewery!?"

Lola closes her eyes and wishes she didn't have to inform this obviously unhappy person of the facts. But she has done the research. "Well, yeah, I think so. At least in Brooklyn."

"Look, I'm going to lunch," Kim declares. "I'm switching you over to Mister Drake." And she puts Lola on hold.

The name Drake gives Lola pause. She holds.

On her way out to lunch, Kim calls across the office to the slippery looking forty-year-old Richard Drake, who used to be Lola's boss at Rutledge Insurance. "Richard, there's some nun called Lola on line five wanting to know about the approval of her Brewer's Bond! Deal with it!"

Likewise, the name Lola quickens Drake's pulse a little. Though he's busy scanning archived licenses from before the digital age, he follows orders and takes this call. "Richard Drake," he announces. "How may I help you?"

Lola knows this voice. "Mister Drake?"

"Lola?"

As the attentive reader may recall, months ago—

Drake is watching from the Rutledge Insurance conference room doorway as Lola grabs her coat and starts to leave. He intercepts her. "Lola," he asks as he motions to help her on with her coat, "how's it going with policy 17,834?" But she flinches and steps aside. He's been expecting this. She's touchy, a little prudish, but a tightly wound sexual time bomb—he's certain.

"That would be the Wilson family, Mister Drake," Lola replies, apparently more upset than usual after one of his departmental pep talks, "and their five-year-old daughter with multiple sclerosis."

This, too, of course, he can count on: sentimental identification with the insured. It's boring. But he'll put up with it in her case. "Don't let it get personal, Lola. It's just a policy."

"I quit."

"Easy. Come on. Lola, you're up for a raise soon," and he goes so far as to lay his hand on her waist. "What are you doing after work? Let's have a drink and discuss."

"Don't… touch me," she practically screams under her breath.

Drake falls back in mock alarm. But as he does so, he sees Meg, another policy adjuster, looking on in real horror, clutching a stack of policy files and protecting herself behind the watercooler—

"You're no longer at Rutledge Insurance," Lola now asks Drake over the phone.

"Seems the whole company was owned by some hedge fund that went bust and then, well, you know how that goes down." Sadly, yes, Lola understands all too well: thousands without coverage and grave financial loss in all directions. Drake is less cynical than he is perfectly oblivious. "Don't worry, Lola. The taxpayers will foot the bill and, in the meantime, I landed this sweet job in state government. Are you really a nun now?"

"Yes. Kind of."

But now the man has what might be called a crisis of conscience. "Shit, that's—God, Lola, I hope it wasn't me that…"

Lola rolls her eyes to the ceiling and prays for patience. "No, Mister Drake, your attentions were undesired but they did not drive me into a nunnery."

"Oh, good," Drake sighs, genuinely relieved, "because I do like you, Lola. If there's anything at all I can do, just say so."

"Well, Mister Drake, I do need our Brewer's Notice and Brewer's Bond approved immediately."

He swivels in his chair and faces the computer. "Let me call it up. What's the brewery's name?"

"Our Lady of the Highway."

"Got it," he says as he calls up the necessary information. "Oh," he reads, "the Trade and Tax Bureau need to approve labeling, marketing, and recipe."

"Yes, that's all been submitted," Lola informs him.

"Oh! Correct again! Here they are. Wow, hey, that's a nice shot of you, Lola. I mean, on the label."

"Thank you, Mister Drake. Can we now consider these things approved?"

"Sure," Drake confirms, "I'm ticking all the appropriate boxes now." And he does so. "You'll have confirmation in a few minutes. But..." he starts again then falters, reading further down the online form.

"Yes," Lola asks, anxious to sew this up.

"It seems that under certain conditions the Alcohol and Tobacco Trade and Tax Bureau will want to perform an on-site inspection of the premises."

"Exactly," Lola replies. She's read the instructions for the application backwards and forwards a number of times and understands that a duly authorized representative of the Alcohol and Tobacco Trade and Tax Bureau needs to certify in writing that the on-site inspection is waived.

"That would be tricky."

"Yeah?" this representative of the Bureau asks.

"This is a cloister."

"A what?"

"This is one of those convents where the sisters have re-moved themselves from the secular world and no one ever sees them."

"They never leave the convent," Drake asks, sitting back in his swivel chair, aghast.

"Never," Lola has some fun rubbing it in.

"What about you," he now inquires, growing worried.

Lola is forced to admit: "I'm a novice. Not a nun. I'm only here temporarily."

Encouraged, Drake sits forward again, "Oh, very good," he says warmly, "because, look, Lola, I'd love for us to hook up and, you know, discuss all this—privately. Maybe a nice restaurant. Perhaps a show beforehand? I'd come down to New York City, make a weekend of it."

Lola rests her brow on her free hand, elbow on the desk, eyes closed, desperate. She's willing to confuse the issue just a little for the bigger aim of saving the convent: "Well, sure, Mister…" she begins but, adjusting, "Richard… in the mean-time can you waive the requirement for this on-site inspec-tion?"

Delighted to help but still uncertain, Drake looks around himself at the nearly empty communal office of the Bureau and rashly assumes: "Well, yeah, sure."

"You are a duly authorized representative of the Alcohol and Tobacco Trade and Tax Bureau, aren't you?"

"Of course," he assures her, clearing his throat, reaching to the name plate on his desk identifying him as R. Drake, Junior Assistant, Accounts & Licensing, and turning it face down.

"Oh, good," Lola says, gratefully. "When I can I expect to receive it?"

"By the end of the day," Richard surmises. "If not, by lunchtime tomorrow without fail."

"Thank you, Richard."

"No sweat, Lola. Now, ah… is this the number I can reach you at?"

Leo comes down from the street into the subway station and swipes his MetroCard. Pushing through the turnstile, he sees a poster of Lola as the OLHW girl. He enjoys it and smiles. Then he notices a couple of junior executive types ogling the sexy nun.

"Smokin', huh," one calls over to Leo.

Leo makes no comment. The guy's friend cups his balls and gives them a little tug. "Yeah, I'd know how to make this little sister pray!"

Leo turns away, suddenly dizzy with conflicted feelings, trying to think about arithmetic as the train roars into the station.

Pena tacks up Magdalena's mug shot again. He does this in his sleep. He is a man obsessed, on fire with righteousness so fierce he's prepared to step outside the law to fan the flames higher. And it's always the same, the two FBI agents, Proctor and Blakely, calmly pacing his office, frustrating his pursuit of justice.

"There in this convent of Our Lady of the Highway which is where nobody can see the nuns," he reiterates in his dad's clumsy English, "is this pain-in-the-ass anarchist Sister Tatiana-Magdalena dos Santos e Ramirez who I would like to strangle with my own bare hands if I could."

"Your professionalism is not in question, Pena." And the stolid, plain speaking, federal agent elucidates further: "This crazed zealot is a documented obstacle to US financial interests throughout South America. But I need to know if we have a positive ID on Tatiana-Magdalena before I commit federal agents to the mission."

Pena is no longer sure he's dreaming. "She's in there, I know it. You know it."

"We admire your ambition, Pena."

The walking computer, Blakely, advises, "Caution."

And Proctor elaborates, "Restraint."

"Moderation."

"Prudence."

"Discipline."

It goes on and on and on until Pena sits up, awake, sweating, alone on the couch because it's been months since he's slept with his wife. He reaches for his cigarettes and steps out onto the back porch in his underwear. He, too, believes he's just had an epiphany. And Proctor's patronizing motivational shot in the arm is still ringing in his ears: "You've got to find some other reason to get a warrant to enter that convent."

The sisters are busy brewing, bottling, and packing up crates of beer. By now the place is a small industry. More sisters have been arriving weekly from all over the country and the vigil is secure; enough nuns so that each of them do only a half an hour of prayer each day. On average, they're producing six thousand bottles of beer per week.

Up front, in the relative quiet of the gallery, Vincent comes in from the garden with the stolen candlesticks. He's followed by Señora Diaz and the children. He dawdles and his grandmother hits him with her umbrella.

The sisters are waiting in the inner gallery and Magdalena winces as the boy is threatened with another blow. Finally, skipping out of swinging distance, he approaches the partition.

"Good morning, Vincent," Magdalena says. "Thank you for coming."

"Yeah, well, I'm sorry for breaking into the convent and scaring you sisters and everything."

"Ha," Bernadette scoffs, "you scared us about as much as a cockroach."

Vincent's machismo is a little bruised and Magdalena shoots Bernadette a reprimanding glare. "Sister, please!" Then she comes closer to the partition and returns to the boy. "Thank you, Vincent, your apology is accepted and we wish you well."

"Here's the candlesticks." He kneels down and places them inside beneath the partition.

"Vincent," Evelyn now says, "Mister Ortiz can use regular help around here and we can pay you a salary now that we're in business making beer."

Standing back up, Vincent wonders if this is a trick question. "Really?"

"There's a lot to do," the prioress explains, "mostly shipping and receiving. Long hours. Heavy lifting."

"You mean, like, you know, a regular job?"

"You are eighteen, aren't you, Vincent," Lola asks, opening a folder of tax forms.

"Yeah," he answers cautiously.

"You'll need to fill out this IRS Form W-4 and provide us a copy of your photo ID." She slips the form under the grill and he lifts it.

"Well, yeah, sure, thanks," the boy says finally. But then, speaking quietly so his grandmother can't hear, he steps closer. "Hey, ah, Sister…"

"What is it, Vincent," Magdalena asks.

"They interrogated me and stuff over at the police station and, well, they're all worked up about some nuns they wanna bust."

Momentarily blinded by dark misgiving, Magdalena slowly responds: "What nuns, Vincent?"

"This cop, Detective Pena, man, he's got a hair across his ass about someone called Sister Tatiana-Magdalena dos Santos e Ramirez or something and he thinks she's here in your convent."

Now all the nuns except Evelyn and Veronica look at Magdalena and Lola stares at her feet. None of this is lost on Bernadette who also notices the mother superior clutching a handkerchief, her palms sweating, as she takes a small step closer to the blinds.

"Vincent, did the police discuss anyone else?"

"They didn't say any other names but it was like they know this Sister Tatiana-Magdalena travels with a posse."

"A posse," Bernadette repeats, clueless.

"A gang," Sister Jeanne explains.

Vincent adds excitedly: "They're all supposed to be these criminal nuns who are wanted by the FBI an' shit."

Señora Diaz smacks her umbrella on the bench: "Language!"

Vincent cringes. "Sorry. Sorry, Sisters."

Magdalena turns away and comes face to face with Bernadette's fury and suspicion. Blinking, gasping, she addresses Lola. "Sister, please get Vincent set up for employment. And inform Mister Ortiz. We'll talk later."

Lola looks on, worried, as Magdalena moves unsteadily out of the gallery. Bernadette follows on the mother superior's heels and then, in a flurry of fraught, whispered prayers and oaths, the rest of the sisters return to work.

Seated at the kitchen table, radiating anger, Bernadette is waiting for an explanation. Magdalena is standing at one of the windows, gazing outside at nothing, working out in her mind the various options available to her. It's clear she and Sister Veronica, in particular, should flee as soon as possible. Sister Evelyn is a much more well-known confederate, but there are no charges against her anywhere at present. And she's needed to guide the brewery through its first few months of operation.

But then there are the sisters from Honduras. If they're found out, the convent will be charged with violating the immigration laws. But she and Lola have already established contact with convents in Cuba who can take these sisters without too much intrigue now that the US and Cuba have reverted to more relaxed diplomatic relations. No one is going to ask too many questions about Central American immigrants *leaving* the country.

Veronica, Magdalena has decided, though a little unstable, is a good nun. If caught, she'll receive a lengthy prison sentence for having broken into and vandalized a not-so-secret nuclear arms site. She needs to get the young sister over the border to Canada and find refuge for her in an obliging convent in Montreal.

But she, herself, Tatiana-Magdalena, hasn't felt the heat of pursuit this intensely for some time. She knows she keeps herself as busy as she does simply as a way of not thinking about the consequences of her possible capture. Due to treaty obligations, the United States will have to send her back to Argentina where she will be executed if not tortured indefinitely, for her mind is a storehouse of radical activist contacts throughout Central and South America.

"Sister, who are you, exactly," Bernadette finally asks, interrupting Magdalena's frantic mental scheming.

Staying where she is, facing the window, the younger nun closes her eyes and answers quietly: "I am Sister Tatiana-Magdalena."

Bernadette cannot believe it. Even she, who refuses to follow the news of the outside world, even she has heard of this silly and dangerous nun. "The notorious 'dos Santos e Ramirez,'" the senior, veteran, careworn nun concedes, angrier with herself just now than with Magdalena.

"That is my family's name, yes."

"Why didn't you tell me!"

Magdalena comes away from the window, weak, and sits at the table too. "It was thought the less you sisters knew the better it would be for everyone."

"Thought by whom," Bernadette wants to know.

"Well, me, the bishop, and..." but no longer seeing the point in equivocating, "well, me and the bishop."

Bernadette stands and slaps her hand on the table, "That man is in love with you!"

"Sister Bernadette!"

"You've bewitched him!"

"Sister, be reasonable! I insist!"

But Bernadette can't stand still. She stomps over to the kitchen counter, furious. "Politicians," she exclaims, disgusted.

Magdalena stands, too, and corrects her: "Activists."

"Call it whatever you like," Bernadette shoots back, stopping and pointing at her sister. "It all amounts to the same thing and is not a nun's proper job!"

Her blood up, Magdalena comes around the edge of the

table, knocking over a bench. "And what is a nun's proper job," she demands to know.

"To pray," Bernadette shouts with conviction, "constantly and forever—in Latin!"

How to argue with this?

Magdalena hasn't got the strength. She turns away and sits back down. "Sister, can you really believe that prayer alone can help relieve suffering and spread peace?"

"No," Bernadette declares without emphasis, coming back across the kitchen, "I'm not so vainglorious as to imagine I can do any such thing, like you politicians and activists and whatnot." Then, shaking her head, and stationing herself behind Magdalena who is leaning on the table, she spits out: "Zealots! Fanatics!" When Magdalena turns back to look up at her, she completes her point: "What I can do is keep myself apart from the corruption of this human world and help as many as possible remain uncontaminated by it until such time as the Lord relieves us of our burden. That's a nun's job!"

Although Magdalena admits to herself, again, that she admires Bernadette and sisters like her all over the world for certain aspects of their philosophical conservatism, she resists the allure of standing back from the responsibility to intercede when human cupidity overruns simple common sense. Greed for money and possessions only—always, everywhere, since the beginning of time—requires the subjugation of the less fortunate and the willful destruction of, for instance, the environment. She cannot understand, try as she might, why people don't get this. And, at the same time, she suspects her own faith is not what it should be; perhaps she is an imposter. "Sister, I sincerely wish I was capable of such faith in heaven."

Differences aside, Bernadette knows a punch-drunk nun

when she sees one. She feels bad now to have come on so righteously with a misled but obviously well-intentioned sister. She sighs and leans over to right the bench and set it back on its feet. She sits, pauses, then reaches over and takes Magdalena's hand. "And it breaks my heart to see you have such faith in the ways of this world."

"There is no way to get to heaven except through this world, Sister."

And here, at last, Bernadette sees the one point she is in a perfect position to assert: "Exactly," she concludes, again, without force. "That's why we make convents."


Father Robert and Sister Ellen rush in to Bishop Frank's office and find him, too, staring out the window at nothing, weighing the odds, rehearsing different scenarios, trying to gauge the opposition's resources.

Just like war.

He turns and looks at them.

"Trouble at Our Lady of the Highway, Your Reverence," Robert reports. "We suspect the law knows Sister Tatiana-Magdalena is inside."

The bishop nods and sits. Lola called Sister Ellen an hour ago. Plans are in motion. Action must be taken.

Ellen comes forward. "Now, Bishop, don't do anything rash."

"I've got to go out there and talk to her."

The prospect of this is Sister Ellen's personal nightmare. "Your Reverence, please, remember last time."

"I'm older now, less impetuous," he says. And, in fact, he looks a decade older all of a sudden. He stands and crosses to the framed photo of Magdalena.

The last time: over fifteen years ago, tangled up in some

regional strife between striking workers and the Brazilian military, all because of needing desperately to be near her. They just barely survived. He was nearly expelled from the priesthood. He almost kissed her, for god's sake. Then the three years getting sober in a monastery outside San Antonio. Life, he thinks, is perpetual penance for the sins he hasn't even committed yet.

Ellen pleads wordlessly with Robert and the young priest steps forward: "You know I'm more than happy to be the go-between, sir."

"No, Father Robert. Bless you. But we can't have you compromised. You're too important to too many parishes in the area." He comes away from the picture of his love and rolls down his sleeves, getting ready to go. "No, I asked Tatiana-Magdalena to assess the situation and reduce the target. She's done that—in spades. Now I have to secure her retreat." He checks his jaw in a little wall mirror. "I need a shave." Then, going for his razor: "Sister, please, bring me my good cassock."

Pena is briefing Detective Oscar and the FBI agents: "As far as our intelligence goes, these sisters of Our Lady of the Highway are making beer and preparing to sell beer without any of the appropriate licenses."

Blakely wants nothing more than to capture Tatiana-Magdalena, but his job is to be cautious and skeptical. "That is not, strictly speaking, true."

Pena wants to strangle the man but his junior partner keeps his head.

"Yes, that's correct," Oscar concedes, respectfully, "they have *applied* for these licenses."

"But it will be months before they are issued," Pena adds.

Proctor grasps the plan and approves. "And, in the meantime, this provides us with a plausible excuse for undertaking an investigation of the premises."

"And," Pena points out, "getting a warrant for it."

"And, once undertaken, making an inventory of those individuals therein," Oscar concludes.

"What we find, we find," Proctor nods. He likes this kind of good old-fashioned entrapment.

Blakely is convinced. "Good work, Officer."

Pena stares him down. "De–*tec*tive," he hisses with quiet violence.

It's all lost on Blakely, though, whose attention, just now, is back to abstract probabilities and manpower estimates, while Proctor, still pacing the room, thinks out loud: "This must be a complete surprise, Pena. We don't want Tatiana-Magdalena suspecting anything and getting away beforehand."

Meanwhile, in Albany—


Richard Drake stays late at the office and waits till his immediate supervisor, Kim, wrestles herself into her coat and barks into her mobile phone: "If that kid thinks I'm shelling out for another semester of that fucking art school, he's got another thing coming!" Then, pushing out through the door, spotting Drake still at his desk, she stops. "Richard, get yourself gone. You know there's no such thing as overtime around here."

"I just want to get these scans from 1985 backed up on the drive. I'll be leaving in ten minutes."

"Suit yourself," Kim shrugs and leaves.

Richard waits a moment, then pulls out the waiver for the on-site inspection that he's been working on all day. He copied the standard verbiage from earlier waivers granted over the years and typed up a new one to fit the convent's particulars. At first, he thought to just forge Kim's name, as she is, in fact, a duly authorized representative of the Alcohol and Tobacco Trade and Tax Bureau. But, apart from various other felonies, forgery was close to the heart of the collapse of Rutledge Insurance. Though he himself was not indicted, he was vigorously investigated. If it wasn't for his younger brother who works in the governor's office, he might still be looking for a job right now.

So, instead of forgery, he decided to just criminally misrepresent himself. He doctored a piece of the bureau's stationary to include his name over the designation: *Supervisor, Accounts & Licenses*. But he still needs the official stamp which Kim keeps in her desk drawer, right side, bottom. Even before she returned from lunch, he had gone over and busted the drawer's lock mechanism.

"What the fuck!" he heard her grumble midafternoon. "Why don't they get us some modern goddamn desks in here for crying out loud! Shit!"

He assumes she immediately filled out an interoffice work order. But he knows as well as Kim it will be a week before anyone from maintenance shows up. So, he crosses over to her desk now and stamps his letter appropriately and in perfect confidence. He can't imagine the state paying too much attention to something as cute as a clutch of cloistered nuns making craft beer. This will go totally unnoticed and earn him points with the lovely and enticing Lola—a nun! He's never had a nun. In fact, he hasn't been laid in a month and a half and worries if he's losing his touch.

He signs the bogus document with his left hand and creates a scrawl worlds apart from his own carefully important right-handed signature, just in case he has to insist, in the future, that he was framed.

Awestruck, Jesus leads the bishop into the outer gallery from the garden. Vincent and Xavier flutter around like two trapped squirrels, not certain what or how to do anything. Jesus orders them around with glares and gestures while Bishop Frank slowly, and with beating heart, approaches the partition. At last, Vincent hurries over with a seat for the great man to use.

Inside, in the main hall, Magdalena pauses and prepares to enter the inner gallery. Evelyn and Veronica flit around her girlishly but in dead earnest, smoothing her veil, straightening her wimple, checking her face in the light.

"Sisters, he won't even be able to see me," the mother superior admits weakly, pale.

They back off but linger anxiously as she steps forward and grabs the door's handle. But still, she hesitates. She looks back at Evelyn.

"Go," Evelyn says plainly.

"You're all aglow," Veronica adds, wide-eyed, and Evelyn jabs her in the ribs with her elbow.

But Magdalena is, nevertheless, a little heartened. She takes a deep breath and enters.

Frank looks up at the sound of the latch to the unseen door. Jesus cocks his thumb towards the garden and his two minions scram. He follows them out and closes the outside door softly.

Once in the garden, he stations Xavier in front of the door. "You stay right here and if anyone tries to get in before the bishop comes out you—" He looks around himself and finds a shovel, "You hit 'em with this fuckin' shovel."

"Anybody," Xavier asks, worried.

"Anybody stupid enough to insist," Jesus confirms.

Back inside, the bishop listens to Magdalena's steps as she slowly crosses the inner gallery and sits. He knows these steps.

"Your Reverence," her voice pierces the barrier between them like the edge of a fallen leaf slicing through concrete.

"Mother Superior," he mumbles, breathlessly.

She collapses in on herself a little. "My situation has been compromised," she says finally.

"Understood."

"I ask, please, to be removed from my position as soon as possible. I'm a liability to the community."

This is all the way it's supposed to go. Hierarchy is everything to a church. Affection, respect, even desire has to be filtered through recognized and respected modes of formal address. But it's killing the bishop.

"You've achieved the objective here, Sister," he assures her with effort, grafting his military life of engagement onto his ecclesiastical role as some sort of father, or older brother, or uncle. "The full might of the diocese is at your disposal."

Relieved, she sighs and relaxes. Though, when has she ever doubted his ability and commitment? "Thank you," she says, "we've made arrangements for our sisters to return to Central America."

"Excellent."

"They'll depart tonight."

"Well done."

"You use the same aftershave."

He grins and shrugs. He's willing to die a painful death right now to ensure this nun gets safely away. "If it ain't broken don't fix it," he lets fall, shyly.

"Oh," she laughs, delighted, "how often I've acted on that excellent advice, Your Reverence!"

He moves his chair closer, the ice broken. "It's good to hear you laugh again."

Magdalena inches her chair closer too. "What have the years been like for you?"

"Ah, well," he confesses, leaning back and passing his hand through his hair, "fund raising, politics, crisis intervention of one sort or another—basically, a desk job."

"You've done much good. Everyone knows that."

"I miss being out in the field, though, in the thick of it. But here I am: in the rear with the gear."

Outside, Jesus and Vincent are busy unloading supplies onto the brewery's new loading dock. They've even had a new entrance gate installed, making it easier for large trucks to deliver and receive. But as he pauses to take a swig from his hip flask, Jesus hears helicopters circling overhead. He steps out from under the loading dock's roof and gets a better look at the sky.

Sure enough, there are three helicopters circling in formation above the convent.

"What the fuck is that all about," he mutters. Crossing the garden, he climbs his ladder to look out over the wall. In the distance, a parade of cop cars, black federal agency sedans, and a truckload of fully armed National Guardsmen are approaching.

Inside, the bishop and Magdalena are talking soft and low. "I was naive," she confesses. "Sometimes I think I made mistakes."

"Tactical errors," he consoles her. "Your heart was always

in the right place. And…"

But the door bangs open and Jesus shoves his head in.

"Sir, Bishop, Your Reverence…"

"What is it, Mister Ortiz," Frank replies, standing. But he hardly needs to be told. He's trained to feel—to the very atmosphere—the approach of trouble.


Outside on Resurrection Avenue, Pena leads the parade. Jumping from the lead car, he strides proudly to the little door with warrant in hand. He rings the bell. Jesus opens it leisurely. "Good afternoon, Officer."

Pena flashes his badge, "Detective Pena," he growls. Then, repocketing the badge, "Is this the convent of Our Lady of the Highway?"

"You know it is, dude," Jesus reminds him. "You come here on Saturdays to ask the sisters to pray for your kid you think is retarded."

This is news to all Pena's associates. They look amongst one another and try to avoid the detective's gaze.

Pena carries on. "Who are you?"

"Jesus."

"You're who?"

"I'm Jesus."

Pena makes a mental note to greatly trouble this asshole's life once the raid is accomplished. In the meantime, though, he turns to Detective Oscar who is checking his own notes.

"Yeah," Oscar confirms, "fits with earlier reconnaissance. Jesus Ortiz, janitor."

Now Jesus is offended. "I am the groundskeeper, asshole! I am not a janitor!"

Then Vincent appears. "Jesus, what do I do with these pallets of new bottles if the sisters don't need them yet?"

Pena is shocked. "What the fuck are you doing here?"

"I work here now," Vincent answers proudly.

"Vincent's now vice president of shipping and receiving," Jesus clarifies and Pena knows he's being fucked with; something is going on inside and these two dopes have been sent out to cause delays.

Proctor coughs to indicate things should move ahead. So Pena whips out the warrant. "I have a warrant here to investigate these premises."

"A warrant?"

Pena hands it over. Jesus searches for his reading glasses, patting himself all over, then holds the envelope at arm's length. "Vincent, go get my reading glasses from the toolshed."

Pena bristles, but he and the troops are forced to wait.

"Who's in charge here?" Proctor calls from a few yards back.

"Who's in charge," Jesus repeats pointlessly, delaying still more, "of the convent, you mean?"

"Yes," the FBI man states efficiently.

Jesus looks the agent up and down, takes his reading glasses from Vincent, and assumes a kind of comradeship with Detective Pena. "Who is this guy? Can I talk to him? I don't want to break any law I don't know about or nothing."

Down in the basilica, Bernadette is doing vigil when the sisters all burst in and hustle to get Magdalena and Veronica down into the basement. The mother superior quiets everyone down.

"Sister Lucia, please relieve Sister Bernadette at vigil."

Though in tears at the thought of losing Magdalena, the young sister obeys and kneels. She starts praying and

Bernadette gets up. Expecting the worst, the older nun leaps right in: "What now?"

"Local, state, and federal authorities are outside waiting to investigate the premises," Magdalena admits.

Bernadette steps back like she's been shoved. The sanctity of the convent is, maybe, even actually, her true religion. Fiercely territorial, she's a team player, after all. "Over my dead body," she replies.

As relieved as anyone can possibly be under such circumstances, Magdalena falls forward and hugs her. "They're looking for me," she explains, "but they'll arrest Sister Veronica, too, if they identify her."

Bernadette nods and turns to Veronica: "What'd you do?"

Veronica is still trying to process what's happening.

"Same old, I guess—crimes against the military-industrial complex and so on—I think."

Bernadette squeezes the girl's elbow to buck her up. Then she turns to Evelyn: "I suppose you're in on this too?"

But Magdalena intercedes: "Sister Evelyn will be arrested but there are no crimes outstanding that she has not already done time for."

"Well, that's a relief," Bernadette admits.

"Mother Superior," the prioress insists, "with all due respect, you are not going anywhere without me."

And this is something not to be taken lightly. Tatiana-Magdalena's greatest exploits to date have involved this tough, smart, and selfless ex-bartender.

"Sister Prioress, this is not forever. I name you, now, mother superior of Our Lady of the Highway." And she watches her friend's face and allows this to sink in before adding, "I've discussed it with all our sisters here."

Evelyn looks more afraid than she ever has been: "But,"

she stammers, "can I?"

"Of course, you can," demands Bernadette, taking charge of the two fugitives and forcing them on towards the altar and the pier below.

"Hang on," Magdalena calls to them all, "we'll get through this!"

Out in the garden, Jesus can stall no longer and steps aside to admit the Law. The soldiers enter with weapons drawn and a battlefield stance out of all proportion to the situation. They stop and aim when they discover Xavier guarding the door to the cloister with a shovel. The squad commander, Douglass, raises his hand and signals.

"Cease and desist," he commands.

"Cease and what" Xavier asks, squinting.

"What's that he's holding, Commander," Proctor asks rhetorically.

"A shovel, Agent Proctor. I think."

Blakely is all over this: "That constitutes a weapon."

"And implies resistance," the ambitious junior Detective Oscar points out.

"Which changes the rules of engagement," Proctor announces happily.

But Pena sees where this is headed and won't have it. "Now, easy—easy! I can't just storm the place. If we don't do this the right way nothing will stick and they'll throw the whole thing out of court." He looks around and locates Jesus. "Hey, you, Ortiz, tell this kid to back off."

Moments later, the soldiers burst in through the door of the outer gallery, automatic weapons aloft. They secure the area before Pena, Oscar, and the FBI guys enter. They all come to a stop, though, when they see Bishop Frank standing across the large space in his imposing cassock. They flinch when he steps forward.

"Gentlemen," he welcomes them with the patience and humility of a recognized and entitled superior.

One soldier is jittery and handles his weapon without confidence. He's confused about the various powers in the room—the cops, the feds, the national guard (of which he himself is part) and, now, this guy, the bishop.

Having not expected the bishop, whom Gordon Normal has apprised him of, even Pena is thrown off guard: "Oh, um… are you in charge?"

"I am the bishop of the diocese," Frank replies. "The sisters are praying. How can I help you?"

Pena glances at Squad Commander Douglass. "Stand down," the younger man commands and the soldiers lower their weapons.

"Well, ah, Bishop," Pena proceeds, "we have a warrant."

"A warrant for what?"

"To investigate the premises."

"On what grounds," the bishop asks. But then, aggravated by the jittery soldier's lack of training, he barks, "Secure that weapon, soldier!"

The jittery soldier snaps to attention and settles down. Now he knows who's in charge—the bishop.

Frank accepts the warrant from Pena and looks it over.

"We suspect," Pena elucidates, discomfited, "that the sisters are manufacturing beer with the intention to profit commercially thereby without filing for and receiving the requisite approvals or licenses."

Frank finishes with the warrant, shoves it inside his cassock, and nods. "And this requires a platoon?"

Squad Commander Douglass, appreciating the man's familiarity with protocol, is happy to clarify: "Sir, in fact, just two squads, sir."

This annoys Pena who sees the pecking order in this room falling to pieces. "Will you shut the fuck up," he snaps at Douglass. Then, returning to Bishop Frank, answers: "That's my prerogative."

Frank nods and calls back towards the partition. "Sister Lola?"

The Law looks where indicated. The soldiers lift their weapons.

Outside in the garden, squad two of the National Guard are securing the perimeter and detaining Jesus, Vincent, and Xavier who sit quietly in the door of the tool shed. The squad leader here is a woman named Wilson.

"This is that convent where the sisters make beer, right," she asks.

Jesus snaps out of his trance. He's been trying to think how to get away with—well, everything. It's only now occurred to him how massive the illegal immigrant nuns from Honduras issue is going to be. He also suspects the mother superior has a backstory that brushes up against the criminal. She agrees too readily to his shadiest suggestions. And the prioress? She's got to have a criminal background! She's taught him useful work-arounds regarding all kinds of minor illegalities.

"What," he asks Commander Wilson

"Ain't this the convent where the nuns make beer," she repeats amiably.

"Oh, yeah, this is it."

Another soldier, Private Randazzo, is looking over the

cases of bottled beer. "It any good," he asks.

"The beer?" Jesus lightly backhands Xavier in the chest: "Tell 'em Xavier."

Xavier reads from the label on a bottle: "A premium craft lager balancing a delicate malt backbone with citrus aromas and a lingering freshness."

Lola appears in the outer gallery with a box of filing. She lets herself out of the gate and comes forward. Douglass lowers his weapon and removes his cap.

"This is Sister Lola," the bishop explains, "a novice of the Order of Clementine. She takes care of the bookkeeping and business affairs of the convent." Then, turning to her, "Sister, are we in a position to assist these people?"

"I'm sorry to have caused you all this effort, Officer…" Lola begins.

"Detective," Pena says, respectfully, in spite of himself.

"Detective Pena…" she continues, "but here are copies of the various licenses from the Alcohol and Tobacco Trade and Taxation Bureau."

Pena is shocked and undermined. He takes the papers but is too irate to read them. He hands them to Oscar. Meanwhile, he bluffs.

"We'll have to look these over."

"They were just approved yesterday."

"What about your wholesaling license?"

Lola finds this too and hands it over. "Here it is. That's from the municipality of Brooklyn and, here, this is the corresponding approval from the state."

Pena is embarrassed, desperate, and curses the day his wetback dad crossed over the border into Texas and burdened his son with a lifetime of civic stigma. "Look, I happen to know for a fact that it takes between three and four months to get these approvals."

"Well, Detective," Lola replies politely, "in the published guidelines it actually says two weeks."

"Yeah, but everyone—" Pena asserts with overwhelming conviction, "everyone knows that with state and city offices two weeks means three months."

Detective Oscar looks up from reading the background documents: "That's true," he confirms, "standard op."

"I was persistent," she says.

The bishop feels it worthwhile to point out: "And the licenses were issued."

Pena is stumped.

Proctor steps forward, though refrains from taking control: "Detective, is there a problem?"

Pena is about to answer, helplessly, but Oscar looks up from the license Lola was tendered and announces: "The on-site inspection has not been undertaken."

Pena looks at his partner and hopes to be saved.

Oscar goes on to explain: "An on-site inspection is required before a license can be granted."

"Unless," Lola points out, "a waiver, in writing, is issued by a duly authorized representative of the Alcohol and Tobacco Trade and Tax Bureau." She nods and points to the papers in Oscar's hands, adding: "Page five."

Oscar flips through to page five and reads the document. He is afraid to even look at Pena, but he must, displaying the page. "It's been issued."

Pena tears the page from Oscar's hand and forces himself to read it. "Drake," he sighs.

"Yes," Lola confirms. "Mister Richard Drake. He waived it. We just received it this morning."

Pena now has a moment of blind, violent, inspiration. He shoves the paper back at Oscar and seethes: "Get this asshole, Drake, on the phone right now."

Up in Albany at the Bureau, Drake's phone is ringing at his unattended desk. Kim can't bear it any longer. "Where is that fucking creep," she calls as she stomps over to answer it. "Richard Drake's desk, Kimberly Sotomayor speaking, how may I help you?"

In the interest of moving things along, the author has chosen to assume that you, the reader, can imagine the kinds of things said and discovered in the subsequent phonecall by Kimberly Sotomayor, Detective Oscar, and the two senior agents of the FBI.

Ten minutes later, Kim steps out into the massive hallway and finds Drake making time with two office girls outside the restrooms.

"Mister Drake," she intones in a manner the office girls, for instance, know to mean big trouble.

Back in Brooklyn, Oscar signs off and hands the document to the FBI as evidence, explaining to all: "Richard Drake is a filing clerk at the Alcohol and Tobacco Trade and Tax Bureau. He is not an authorized representative. He's in custody as we speak. This document is meaningless."

Pena shivers with exoneration, imagining throwing the opening pitch of the season at the old Shea Stadium and basking in the loving applause of his fellow citizens—a famous and respected civil servant.

The Law, however, all look around, on edge, as the lights flicker. Then, as Lola takes the bogus document from Blakely and studies it, two of the five lighting fixtures in the gallery explode. The bishop looks from the sparking sockets to Lola and touches her arm. "Easy."

Below the basilica, the sisters all clamber down to the pier where the boat that delivered the sisters from Honduras is tied up and waiting. They help Magdalena and Veronica down into it.

In the garden, Commander Wilson and Private Randazzo wait, chatting, as Jesus graciously pours them a cold glass of beer. He steps around side the toolshed and hands it to them.

"I can't believe they got us out here chasing down some nun anyway," Wilson complains. Then, to Jesus, "thanks, man."

As she drinks, Randazzo concurs: "Yeah, this whole thing's a waste of time."

"Wow," Wilson enthuses, "nice!" She hands the glass to Randazzo who is waving over the other soldiers.

"Hey, Reid, Greco, come try some of this 'delicate lingering freshness'!"

Jesus steps back and sets aside the empty bottle on which is scribbled, in frantically happy handwriting: *Extra Holy!*

Not being able to stall any longer, Bishop Frank crosses the outer gallery and approaches the gate in the partition. He has already confirmed there are no females present besides Lola. "Gentlemen," he begins, "in good faith that you are open-minded to other people's beliefs and the things they hold dear, please remember that for three hundred and forty-seven years no man has entered beyond this gate."

Most of the men present find this impressive, maybe even cause for second thoughts. Pena himself is vaguely troubled.

But he is so entirely and deeply troubled at all times it's hard to tell how much this issue, in particular, contributes. Proctor and Blakely had all sensitivities to other people's beliefs indoctrinated out of them long ago. They walk to the gate as if nothing has been said. This helps Pena overcome his own dim reservations.

Frank opens the gate and stands aside to allow the lawmen inside the cloister. But he stops once more. "Generations of sisters dedicated to peace and resigned to the most exacting poverty have lived out their lives within these walls praying nonstop, twenty-four seven, for an end to war and avarice."

This floats over the heads of the professionals and manages only to hit the hearts and minds of the ranks. Douglass is visibly hesitating as the bishop continues:

"I hope you will excuse me, but I wish to respect their tradition and remain out here. Sister Lola will show you around the brewery and answer your questions."

After this, no one but Proctor and Blakely are immediately eager to enter through the gate. Proctor stops and looks back. "Come on," he says to Pena.

Pena goes through, sweating, and looks back at Douglass.

Douglass hesitates but then mutters into his wireless: "Listen up: reinforcements, squad two."

Wilson gets this message just as she's taking another gulp of the Extra Holy. "Oh, shit," she declares, laughing, then slurs into her walkie: "Oh-Okay, chopy thap." She puts on her helmet and stands, woozy, "Fuck. Squad two!"

Randazzo and Greco are all chilled out, enjoying the sunshine. Reid drains the glass, stands, and follows. But Randazzo is amused to give a kind of order: "Dude, your weapon!" Reid stops, turns back, and cracks up, returning for his forgotten automatic machine gun. They all laugh and stumble off, giggling.

Down below the altar, Magdalena and Veronica are ready to go. Evelyn pulls the chain and the hanging corrugated steel door painfully creaks, scrapes, and bangs its way open.

Up above, Gordon Normal, at this very moment, is watching the action down at the convent with binoculars, delighted. But he happens to spot the boat emerging into the canal.

Inside, the convent appears deserted as Lola leads the lawmen and soldiers down the main hall. "I assume you need to see the brewery," she confirms with every effort to be civil.

But Proctor is already suspicious, looking around. "Where are all the nuns?"

Lola stops and turns back. "They're praying. This is the brewery, which is what you need to see, correct?" She continues on. "Here is the bottling section. The germinating room and kilning are further back. Watch your step please."

The four soldiers of squad two catch up, stumble into the main hall, and bump into one another, giggling. Seeing the others, they try their best to straighten up.

Lola's mobile bleeps and she checks it.

Proctor assumes this is potential treason and, dragging his attention away from squad two, approaches Lola, threateningly: "Who is that?"

Defiant, Lola pauses, sighs, raises the phone to her ear and, before answering, complies, "My boyfriend."

This short-circuits squad two and they fall to pieces with laughter. Randazzo leaning his head against the wall, drops his weapon. "No, no more, I can't take it..." he gasps. And the others are nearly as helpless, in stitches or starting to hallucinate and wandering off on their own in childlike trance states.

Pena's mobile rings now too. Terrified of what he's witnessing, he manages to check it, sees who it is, and answers immediately. "Hey."

"The canal!" Gordon Normal shouts, apoplectic, from his godlike vantage point above the convent. "The canal!"

Jolted from his recent feeling of incompetence, Pena drops his phone and, while scrambling on the floor to retrieve it, relays, "The canal!"

Douglass indicates that squad one should relieve squad two of their weapons and they do so, carefully, gently, afraid. He himself, just following his training, keeps his own gun trained on Lola.

"Give me a break," she says, unimpressed. "You want to see the brewery or not?"

Douglass lifts his hand to his earphone and communicates to reserve forces elsewhere: "The canal—copy—the convent backs onto the canal—over."

Magdalena and Veronica, with approximately two minutes of training, are not experts at steering a small boat with an outboard motor. But they have to go and they have to go now.

"Go with the current!" Evelyn reminds them. "Stay to the side! Fifty yards or so! He's there on the right!"

Fifty yards along the canal, Father Robert is climbing down to a small concrete ledge beneath the roadway. But he steps aside and backs into shadow as two flat-bottomed National Guard cruisers cut through the water towards the convent. Before the two nuns can get more than a few yards into open water, the boats are racing towards them. Seeing this, Evelyn throws them a rope and hauls them back in while the others pull the chain and close the door.

Upstairs, making his way past and through the delirious members of squad two, Pena calls to Proctor. "We have them located!"

Proctor backs Lola up against the nearest wall. "Which way to the canal?"

"Canal? What canal?"

Squad two's Randazzo is dancing to some tune only he can hear.

"Commander," Blakely shouts to Douglass, "what in god's name is the problem with Sargent Wilson's squad!"

But Douglass is relieved not to have to answer this because Detective Oscar has located the stairs down to the basilica.

"Detective," Oscar calls, "a way down!"

The nuns help their sisters back up out of the boat and pause, hearing the Law pounding on the heavily barred doors up in the basilica.

"Sisters!" Pena calls in the distance. "Open up!"

Sister Lucia, face down before the altar, closes her eyes and prays faster. Sister Evelyn emerges from below the altar, followed by the others.

"Sisters," Pena continues, "this is Detective Pena of the New York City Police Department together with Agents Proctor and Blakely of the Federal Bureau of Investigation! We do not want anybody to get hurt! But you must open these doors or we will have no option but to force them open in a violent way!"

Bernadette's faith is shaken. "Men," she sighs, "in the convent of Our Lady of the Highway." She needs help to sit. "It must be the end of the world."

But Evelyn lights a smoke and decides the outside world is as dumb, misguided, and ultimately beatable as it's always been—at least in her experience. She enjoys one deep drag and exhales. "They won't violate this sanctuary."

Bernadette lowers her face into her hands, defeated. "They

have guns," she pleads. "Sister, I've seen it before. And they have, as men always seem to have, badges."

Evelyn nods, agreeing. But she also sees Tatiana-Magdalena, her hero, pale with fear, knowing what's in store for her if she's caught. The prioress nods and embraces one last deep drag of her beloved nicotine, convinced the collective goodwill on their side of this door will demolish the violence and stupidity on the other. "Sisters," she says at last, "move away from the doors and protect yourselves. Cover Sister Lucia."

On the floor, Sister Lucia's eyes are closed tight and she's praying with a vengeance, sobbing, as thirty-five of her sisters come down around her protectively, shielding her with their own bodies so she can continue the vigil.

Out on the stairwell landing leading down to the basilica, directly above and before the entrance, Lola sinks to her knees and hangs her head as the National Guardsmen apply plastic explosives to the massive, old, six-inch-thick doors.

Up in the outer gallery, Bishop Frank listens as best he can to the catastrophe deep inside the convent. He suspects the worst, of course, but puts his trust in God. He sees Jesus and the boys watching anxiously from the door to the garden. He comes to the center of the room and, inviting them, kneels.

"Come, let us pray," he says softly.

Jesus and the boys obey like clockwork.

Making the sign of the cross, the bishop begins. "In the name of the Father and the Son and the Holy Ghost…" he prays as Jesus and the boys follow suit, Xavier watching Vincent for guidance. "Our Father, who art in heaven," the bishop continues as, elsewhere, Father Robert comes back up from the canal, panicked, and hurries away unseen into the wilds of Brooklyn. "Hallowed be thy name," the bishop admits as the National Guard calibrate the radio frequency that will ignite the plastic explosives and blow the basilica's doors down. "Thy kingdom come, thy will be done," he testifies as Lola kneels on the staircase, too angry even to cry. "On earth, as it is in heaven," the bishop accepts as, inside the basilica, Evelyn steps back and places herself between the doors and the sisters huddled over Lucia. "Give us this day our daily bread, and forgive us our trespasses," he implores as the explosives are set and readied, the sign given, and Douglass moves aside to protect himself. "And lead us not into temptation," he begs as Pena imagines tendering his resignation and having a swank office of his own at Magnificent Waste, as Oscar is wondering what new car he'll buy once he replaces Pena, as Proctor assures himself there's a new mid-level desk job for him at the State Department once this goes down.

The button is pushed.

Evelyn waits.

Magdalena presses her forehead against Lucia's and Bernadette, rising, joins Evelyn, whispering along with the unseen bishop: "…but deliver us from evil."

TEN

"No," Lola whispers.

But the doors are blown to pieces anyway.

At the blast, Bishop Frank looks up from his prayers in the gallery and Jesus falls over backwards. The boys dive into the corners of the room.

Down below, the dust settles to reveal Evelyn waiting, cigarette still clenched in her teeth, bleeding a little here and there from the blast of wood fragments, as she supports Bernadette who's been thrown over. The first thing they see through the dust and smoke is Lola kneeling on the landing halfway up the staircase outside—like an angel hovering above a scene of carnage. The novice raises her eyes and looks right at the prioress as Pena approaches, flashing his badge.

"Detective Pena, New York City Police Department. You're under arrest."

Evelyn backhands him across the jaw and he goes down hard—out cold. And before anyone can even grasp what just happened a click is heard, the click of a standard issue police revolver—not firing.

Oscar's startled gaze drops from Evelyn to the weapon in his hands held out straight before him. Evelyn, too, looks from it to Oscar and sees the man is panicked, trembling. Then both she and Bernadette glance up to Lola on the staircase landing where the young novice passes out.

Everyone's heard this little click—this gun that did not fire. Even the giggling soldiers of squad two at the top of the stairs dummy up and try to get a grip. Douglass, seeing Evelyn pick up Pena's revolver, wants to avoid a massacre. "Hold your fire," he commands his squad, backing off slowly, a hand raised to placate the prioress.

Lucia continues praying. The others have flattened themselves to the stone floor. "Is anyone hurt," Magdalena asks, lifting herself up, but everyone seems okay.

"Easy," Douglass whispers, getting his squad back out into the hall without taking his eyes off this armed nun who's just decked an NYPD detective.

"Get out of my basilica," Evelyn commands with easygoing ferocity.

Douglass nods and complies.

Oscar, though, is frozen, still pointing his gun—in shock, unable to breath. Douglass reaches out and takes the man's weapon from his hands and gestures for someone to drag the junior detective back outside the blasted doors.

"I'm... I didn't... it's..." Oscar mutters as he's guided back.

Proctor and Blakely are worried this is now about to become a hostage situation. But Evelyn nudges Pena with her foot. The detective comes to, his jaw dislocated, struggles to his feet and scrambles out. Evelyn—fully aware she's almost just been shot dead—slides the detective's gun across the floor and outside into the hall where a soldier secures it with his boot.

By now the rest of the sisters are at Evelyn's side—a wall of women, Douglass thinks, with nothing but their God on their side. And he, for one, knows that they're now calling the shots.

Lucia keeps praying.

A month later, Brooklyn is in flames.

A smartly dressed female newscaster of impeccably uncertain ethnic origin repeats what everyone already knows and can't get enough of: "Well, it's been over a month since the storming of the convent of Our Lady of the Highway by city, state, and federal law enforcement officials and Brooklyn is still out of control."

In amongst the tumult, a correspondent positions himself before chanting crowds in threatening opposition to state troopers and local police: "Jane, the sisters of Our Lady of the Highway were not just making beer out here in Williamsburg, they were spreading the love," he shouts above the clamor, "smuggling illegal immigrant nuns into the country and putting them to work in their inadequately licensed microbrewery. Still, the population is up in arms about the forcible entry of National Guardsmen into the hallowed ground of the convent a month ago this Friday where for almost three hundred and fifty years an uninterrupted prayer cycle for world peace has been maintained."

Elsewhere, Señora Diaz is randomly interviewed: *"No bueno,"* she shakes her head. "Is not good. Very not good. It is…" She turns to her granddaughter: *"Inez, que?"*

Inez recites as if she were in a spelling bee: "Sacrilege," she suggests, "S-A-C-R-I-L-E-G-E. Sacrilege."

"What she says," her grandmother concurs, "Sacrilege."

Back in the studio, the newscaster provides a new spin on old news: "The mother superior of the convent, of course, is the notorious Sister Tatiana-Magdalena, who has been on the run from US federal law enforcement agencies for almost a decade for the sinking of a US government contractor's ship loaded with armaments destined for a failed right-wing military coup in Venezuela. She was also the mastermind behind an operation that smuggled more than a thousand illegal immigrants, mostly from Central America, into the United States between 2007 and 2012."

The lawyer representing the convent is Steven Levine, a friend of the bishop. Raised without any sort of religion, he is, nevertheless, regularly referred to as an Excellent Jewish Lawyer. Though this frustrates him intellectually, he's not about to contend with two thousand years of highly charged ethnic identification and the belief in magic powers it seems to foster. Personally, he learned the law of the United States of America and loves negotiating its sometimes treacherous but always fascinating freeways and back alleys. He's particularly good at botched police actions. To maintain his physical and emotional health, he spends four weeks each winter at a Buddhist retreat in the Berkshires.

Anyway, he's managed to coordinate this private out-of-court session in Judge Soriano's courthouse offices in downtown Manhattan where His Honor lays down the law:

"Mister Levine, no matter how beloved these sisters are now by the half-drunk hipsters of Williamsburg, Brooklyn, they've committed a major crime against the laws of the United States and they will have to pay the price, reasonably negotiated, that any other convicted criminal would have to pay: time spent in a federal penitentiary."

Levine is not too worried about this case. The cops really

did mess things up for themselves. This, for Steven, will be a small war of attrition, the gradual reduction of the NYPD's credibility, not to mention that of the FBI and the National Guard. "Yes, Your Honor; understood," he replies, "but, for the time being, can we settle for house arrest?"

"Certainly," Soriano agrees.

Detective Pena jumps up out of his seat and kicks a chair. "No," he screams aloud, "that's just... fuck!" And he sits back down, spent.

"Detective," the judge feels it necessary to reiterate, "given the very well publicized and gross ineptitude of these attempted arrests, I think it best we keep the sisters where they are, doing their strange prayers for world peace. They've captured the imagination and the goodwill of the population. We don't want outright insurrection on the streets of Brooklyn before the trial even begins!"

"But this fucking anarchist son-of-a-bitch Sister Tatiana-Magdalena dos Santos e Ramirez must be handed over to the federal government!" Pena shouts.

"In due course, yes," Soriano nods. "The government is under treaty obligations to extradite her. But the others..." He calculates. "I think the term for the others will be fairly mild: three years across the board."

"Why, because they're nuns," Pena asks in disbelief.

"Yes," Soriano replies without sentiment.

Pena can't believe it. Neither can the lawyers for the state. But the judge continues:

"If these god-happy miscreants weren't under vows of obedience to the Catholic Church I'd throw the book at 'em wholesale, Pena! Ten, fifteen years if I could." Soriano stands. He wants to leave. He works his arms into the sleeves of his jacket. "But it's the Catholic fucking Church, goddamn it, the longest living authoritarian organization on earth. It's a formidable outfit, Detective, believe me. I've gone toe-to-toe with them in the past. They make this crowd from the State Department look like a bunch of amateurs."

Pena hangs his head.

Crossing the room and grabbing his briefcase, the judge continues, addressing Levine: "Nevertheless, make no mistake, counselor: we're going after every single one of their accomplices inside and outside the convent!" Stopping in the doorway, he turns around and addresses anyone of the five or six people in the room who still care to listen: "Illegal immigration from south of the border, for instance, is a hot political product these days and I think a number of us want to make a name for ourselves for the future. Am I right? A case like this is a political gold mine! Let's not fuck it up."

No one dares answer.

He didn't think anyone would.

"Now, I'm sorry if I've upset anyone's more tender ethical sensibilities, but I gotta go get lunch."

Some demonstrators outside the convent are dragged off and thrown into a police van as the news correspondent wraps things up: "So for the time being, the sisters are under house arrest. And though there is much criticism and argument about the legality of these arrests, alleged conspirators are being rounded up all over the five boroughs."

Charles and his friends are led into a court building amidst much media attention and he's loving it, waving to the crowd like it's all about him. A little later, the enterprising young ad exec is being questioned by a hastily assembled committee of inquiry made up of six senators.

"So, young man," one of these asks, "you're saying you saw no evidence of this veritable 'underground railroad' operation during your sales and promotion work with the sisters?"

Charles is in his element: the spotlight. "Senator, the only railroad I know of or ride, underground or otherwise, is the L Train to Bedford Avenue, Williamsburg; sometimes as far as Lorimer but under no circumstances further west than Union Square."

Elsewhere in the clamorous halls of justice, Detective Pena is being interviewed:

"Detective, is it true this web of corruption reaches as far up as the Vatican?"

"It's hard to say, Bob," Pena dramatizes, "anything's possible. But, of course, there may be international implications. Bishop Frank of the Brooklyn Diocese has been subpoenaed, and many others…"

Meanwhile, Gordon Normal has three flatscreen TVs set up in his office, all tuned to different news channels. He paces from one to the other, increasingly paranoid: "This incompetent boob, Pena, is going to turn on me, I know it."

"How," Elise asks. "For what?"

"I bribed him with a promise of a job to get him off our backs about issuing handguns to minors."

"And he accepted?"

"Yeah but, you know, he can spin that anyway he wants if they threaten to disgrace him and toss him off the force."

He sits on the edge of the office couch, jittery, wringing his hands, his eyes dodging from one screen to another. In fact, he's been sleeping on this couch for weeks. Elise has never seen him like this, worried and unshaven. He grabs a bottle of OLHW from the glass table beside him, twists off the cap, and drinks. After a good, healthy swig, he looks at the label, shrugs, and admits:

"This stuff is not bad, actually." But then there are developments on screen. "Uh-oh," Gordon quietly shrieks, standing, "now this slippery holy man too? He's bound to be trouble."

Bishop Frank is before the senate committee:

"Bishop Frank, is it or is it not true that the sisters of Our Lady of the Highway asked you for a new priest?"

"They asked if I'd recommend a new confessor."

"And what's a confessor?"

"A priest who visits the convent every so often and hears their confessions."

"Their confessions," the senator asks, worried, sensing dark, cultish, implications.

"It's a sacrament," the bishop explains and the crowded courtroom falls silent.

The senator's job, oddly, is to pretend he is as uninformed as a five-year-old. "And what is a sacrament?"

"A sacrament," the bishop begins, "is a ritual, a kind of procedure through which we focus our attention on God in such a way that God's grace can locate us and impart both judgment and mercy."

Agitated murmurs fill the courtroom and senators from six states consult their notes. This is all being televised and no one wants to look bad back home in their own voting districts. But one brave soul does leans forward to the microphone to inquire plainly: "But how does it work?"

"You honestly admit your mistakes to an ordained priest and you're forgiven, provided you also promise to make amends."

This is exactly what another senator, a woman from Ohio,

has been waiting for—dirt. "So, nuns do sin?"

"We all sin, Senator."

"What are you implying," she shoots back, offended.

"We all make mistakes," the bishop insists, gently.

The woman feels exposed. She's gone too far. How many Catholic constituents does she have anyway? Is this even worth it? But she is saved by the senator from Michigan who asks: "How do you define sin?"

Later that night, Detective Pena is watching the bishop's testimony on his mobile device, back on the living room couch in his underwear, smoking. He switches it off and throws the phone at the nearest bolster.

There are things he doesn't want to remember.

"Being a cop sucks."

Pena looks out the window at the approximately two square miles of corporate endeavor—Magnificent Waste—and envies the man who controls it. "I suppose you got some kind of private surveillance service patrolling this vast operation of yours?"

"Well, as a matter of fact," Gordon Normal replies calmly, watching the detective's tense neck, "I just fired my director of operations."

Pena hoists up his trousers. He stands with his hands on his hips, thinking out loud: "I sometimes think of early retirement."

Gordon makes his way back around the conference table and joins Pena near the window. "Once that convent's gone and I acquire the property and put my plan into action I'll need a revamped and beefy security apparatus, and someone I can trust to run it."

"You're sure Tatiana-Magdalena is in there," Pena asks bluntly, looking down at his shoes.

"Practically certain."

"You know, of course, this is a bribe."

"A successful one, I hope." Gordon admits, and waits for a response.

Pena remains silent.

Normal finally glances over at the cop and Pena turns, offering his hand: "Me too."

Back in Judge Soriano's rooms, however, Pena and the FBI agents are foaming at the mouth. Some people from the mayor's office are screaming into their mobile phones. The state's legal team are fighting amongst themselves.

Steven Levine waits.

"Settle down," Soriano demands, pounding his desk with his fist.

They do. They settle down. After a moment, and with a sigh, the judge continues: "Counselor, state your case."

"Apart," Levine commences, "from the fact the warrant issued to Detective Pena was exclusively for the investigation of the brewery at the convent, and based on the assumption that the sisters were not in compliance..."

"And were they in compliance," Soriano asks.

"Yes, they were. An investigation of the premises was not mandatory unless specifically requested by the state. And, apart from the fact that half of the armed National Guard deployed in this operation were under the influence of some as yet unknown narcotic..."

"That was the beer!" Pena is up on his feet again, red in the face.

The legal team for the National Guard is texting Washington and arranging for flights back home.

"That was the beer the sisters were making and trying to sell," the disgraced detective goes on. "It was Jesus: he drugged them!"

Some of the lesser informed legal assistants present are beginning to wonder when this delusional law enforcement official will be dragged from the room.

"Detective, please!" Soriano shouts, finally shutting Pena up. He now directs his gaze to the federal government's legal team. "The issue is not the beer and who provided it, but that armed US National Guardsmen were drinking on the job!"

Now that it's clear the warrant to search the convent was inadequate, and that the National Guard were loaded, Steven Levine can begin passively dictating the terms of the indictment. A year from now the city, the state, and the federal government will be glad they didn't press their cases further than this and expose everyone's manifest incompetence. The issue for him now is to block any suggestion of conspiracy.


"Where are all the nuns," Proctor asks as Lola leads them towards the brewery.

"They're praying," she responds as civilly as she can manage. "This is the brewery. Here is the bottling section. The germinating room and kilning are further back. Watch your step, please."

But just as she's about to move on, her mobile phone bleeps. She checks who it is as squad two stumble, laughing, into the hall from the inner gallery.

"Who's that," Proctor demands, reaching for his holstered weapon.

"My boyfriend."

This short-circuits the lawmen for a moment as they turn

and stare at the inebriated guardsmen.

At the school cafeteria, mobile in hand, Leo sets down his tray. He's watching breaking news on a television above the lunch counter. "What's going on," he asks urgently. "It's on the TV."

Lola turns away from the pandemonium in the main hall and recites calmly, "*De la cruz*."

Leo knows what this means.

Father Robert now wakes up on a couch in a strange apartment somewhere in Greenpoint as he hears his mobile ring. He's disoriented. He sees his trousers and jacket thrown over a chair and jumps up. Doing so, he knocks over a beer bottle and cringes. Climbing into his pants, he locates his phone and answers.

"Leo?"

"*De la cruz*," his friend relays.

"*De la cruz*?"

"*De la cruz*," Leo confirms.

"On my way."

He signs off and finds his shoes. He looks into the next room and sees Chelsea, his attractive thirty-five-year-old female fan from Teachers. She's asleep on her bed, half out of her clothes. At the foot of the bed is a crib with a smiling infant looking up over its edge.

Robert hurries to leave.


Sooner or later, of course, it's bound to be the young priest's turn to address the commission of inquiry:

"And where were you on the morning of the raid, Father Robert?"

"I was in the parish of Saint Ann's."

The senator is not fooled. "*Where* in the parish of Saint

Ann's?"

"Visiting the sick, shut-ins, and members of the faithful who are unable to attend Mass at least once a week."

"So, you were *around*."

"Yes. Around the parish."

"Father, what are the exact boundary lines of the parish of Saint Ann's?"

Court personnel direct everyone's attention to a map of Brooklyn. Robert sighs and bears with it. How to answer only the questions put to him and say no more, so help me God? But half his mind is elsewhere.


Months earlier, he sweats in the convent's confessional, wrestling with both his claustrophobia and bad conscience. Magdalena enters on the far side and kneels.

"Bless me Father, for I have sinned. My last confession was two weeks ago."

"How have you sinned, my friend?"

"I disobeyed the law which, of course, though often unavoidable, is just as often necessary. Nevertheless, I have put my sisters in even greater danger."

"Sister, bringing the five new nuns into the country was, technically, breaking the law of the land. But it was an act of charity and foresight. Nevertheless, you can make amends."

"Yes, I thought as much. How?"

"Sister Ellen, who works with the bishop, has located a convent in Cuba which will legally accept the sisters if we can get them there."

Magdalena stands to go. "Excellent. I'll organize it right away."

But Robert stops her. "Sister, is there anything else you'd like to confess?"

Alone on her side of the confessional, Magdalena looks at the small ceiling and sighs. So much she'd love to confess. But, kneeling again, she resumes practically: "Oh, well, I'm arrogant and reckless, and I have, still, carnal feelings. But I deal with it, Father. Thank you. I have to get our sisters ready to travel." Rising again, she waits for his closing remarks, perhaps a standard penance. But he remains silent. "Father," she asks.

"You do," the young priest finally asks in turn.

"Excuse me?"

"Carnal feelings, I mean." He doesn't remember ever having had the opportunity to discuss such things with a woman older than himself.

Magdalena recognizes the curious, plaintive cry beneath the formulaic language of the sacrament. There, on the far side of this screen, inches away, she's sure, is a young man who has pledged the impossible and is feeling the strain. She's caught there, halfway to her feet, anxious to get away. But she lowers herself back down and pauses.

"I'm afraid so," she admits softly.

"Hmmm," she hears him murmur.

"We're all human, Father," Magdalena adds, reassuringly.

"Yes, yes," he responds vaguely, "of course."


The front page of *The Daily News* features a picture of Lola as the OLHW poster girl. Under an inset photo of Leo leaving the junior high school, there reads the torrid headline: *Sexy Nun's Boyfriend Willing to Wait?*

Principal MacGillicuddy shakes her head and sets aside the tabloid as Leo appears in her office doorway.

"You needed to see me?"

"Yes, thank you. Please have a seat."

He enters and sits.

"Mister Haroldson," the principal begins, "I'm afraid changes to certain longstanding academic priorities have been implemented."

"I'm being fired," he responds, fed up with the cagey institutional jargon.

"As of next semester," she continues efficiently, "seventh grade mathematics will be an online course. And…" but she's at a loss.

"And what," Leo encourages her.

"Your unannounced field trip with the students: this violated any number of the school's statutes."

"Missus MacGillicuddy, if I may put in a word here?"

"As you wish."

"I apologize for taking the kids for a walk."

"They're students, not kids."

"No, they're kids." If he makes no point grander than this, he's satisfied. But he goes on: "They're some of the brightest students I've ever had the pleasure to teach math to in a public school. But they're kids. And they're sometimes overwhelmed by aspects of this world we don't take the time to tell them anything about or prepare them for."

"Are you suggesting that the reading and writing components of the student's education ought to be taught by you— a math teacher?"

"No. But they should be taught by a person. They already receive their reading online and read it in perfect solitude, taking tests related to that reading online as well, in perfect solitude. There's no communal discussion, no shared experience. They learn writing through the use of a self-correcting computer program and are encouraged not to deviate from the corporately sponsored and state approved mechanized norm. They can't develop a style of their own, a conscience of their own. They're terrified by information they receive and are told is correct but can't understand."

"Mister Haroldson, you're talking like a fanatic."

"A fanatic," he repeats and wonders. Giving the principal the benefit of the doubt for a moment, he tries to imagine if this is what fanaticism feels like. He doubts it.

"Which brings me," MacGillicuddy continues, "to the fact of your quite ill-advised association with this Sister Lola at the convent of Our Lady of the Highway."

"So, Mister Haroldson," Senator Somebody-or-Other begins, adjusting himself in his seat, "please state your relationship to Sister Lola."

"She's my girlfriend."

Lots of murmuring, which the senator allows and appreciates as being in some sense in his favor.

"Do you regularly date Catholic nuns?"

Small laughter in the peanut gallery and the senator is pleased. Leo lets it subside.

"She's not a nun, she's a novice," he points out helpfully.

"And what is a novice," the senator from Michigan asks. He doesn't want to tell anyone, but his seventeen-year-old daughter has taken to going to Mass and has a picture of Tatiana-Magdalena as the screensaver on her laptop.

"A woman who lives with the nuns but who hasn't taken her vows and who, for instance, can assist the convent in secular affairs."

"So, you expected her, at some point, to come back out of the convent."

"That's correct. The novitiate was for three months."

"Has Lola always been religious?"

"Not that I know of."

"Then why did she want to enter the convent as a novice?"

"She was under emotional duress. It was thought that a period away from the world, dedicating her time to meditation and to the service of others would be helpful."

The senator from Ohio lifts a bottle of OLHW and ostentatiously studies its label. "This is Sister Lola, is it not?" She holds the bottle up, label prominently displayed.

"Yes," Leo admits, almost proudly. "But they photoshopped her chest. She's hasn't really got a rack like that."

The courtroom explodes with laughter, then applause. It's all over the news and the internet twenty minutes later. The besieged sisters of Our Lady of the Highway are suddenly, as some pundit puts it, "bigger than the Beatles."

Counselor Levine drives his car as close to the convent as he can get, pulling over to the curb before the protesters get too dense. He parks, gets out, and approaches the entrance, making his way through the sizable crowd to a Federal Marshal who checks his credentials before allowing him inside.

A little later, the sisters are gathered in the inner gallery, listening as their lawyer sums up:

"Anyone," Steven explains, "who is not a full-fledged sister of the Clementine Order, having taken the vows officially recognized by the Catholic Church, is going to get seven to ten years."

The sisters all turn and look at Lola.

Steven can't see them but he suspects what's happening. "I'm sorry, Lola," he says, "it's the best I could do."

"We can say she was a hostage," Evelyn suggests.

"That'll be hard to sustain given her obvious involvement

in managing the convent's affairs during the crime," the lawyer replies, staring at the floor.

Sister Amelia remembers how her own family greeted her desire to become a nun: "We can say she was brainwashed!"

"By who," Bernadette wants to know.

"By us," Amelia announces happily.

"Then they'll think we're crazy!"

"They already think we're crazy," Evelyn says, pacing.

"No," Steven insists, "they think you are dangerous criminals, probably terrorists."

"And besides it's not true."

The sisters all stop. Lola has spoken softly, studying her hands folded in her lap.

Levine is trying to imagine what's happening inside, leaning closer, listening carefully. He provokes further discussion by asking for clarification: "What: that you're all crazy fanatics or that you're all dangerous terrorists?"

Lola raises her head slowly and stands, taking a step closer to Magdalena. "I was not brainwashed," she states flatly. "I'll go to jail if I have to."

Magdalena is made faint by this and now needs to sit down herself. Veronica helps her. "Lola," she insists, "this is not your battle to fight."

Lola comes down beside her. "I love it here. And the way you see the world makes sense to me—at least a lot of the time. Out there..." she struggles to continue, "out there for me, the world is... broken."

Hearing this, Levine looks over at Father Robert, who is leaning against the far wall. The priest meets his gaze but slowly glances aside, remembering—

As the G train barrels through the tunnel under Brooklyn,

Father Robert makes his way to a seat further up the subway car where he finds Leo seated with his briefcase, brooding.

"How's it going," the priest asks.

"I'm lonely," Leo answers without drama, without emphasis, just stating the obvious.

Robert nods, blinks, and responds, super positive: "Yeah. And?"

Leo looks up and across at his new friend and wonders, again, what makes this guy tick. "What do you mean, 'yeah and...' what?

"You love Lola more than ever now, right," Robert suggests with simple, boyish enthusiasm.

And, in fact, maybe the guy's right. Leo sits back, sighs, and glances to the middle-aged Hindi woman seated beside him. She glances up from her fashion magazine, curious to hear his response.

Moments later, the train pulls out and Leo is left alone on the platform with Father Robert.

"Understand this," the priest reminds him, "you're being tested. Bear with it. You'll be happier in the end. Stronger. Lola will come back to you."

Leo hopes so. He watches the priest hustle off to work, dodging commuters on his way up the subway steps. He wonders why he's gratefully accepting advice about his love life from a guy seven years younger who has probably never been intimate with a woman to begin with.

Back in the convent, Robert is thinking this too. What has he done? Who could have foreseen this? He can't let the love of Leo's life go to jail for a minimum of seven years. So, he bites the bullet and moves to solve one calamity with another, smaller one.

"Well, Mother Superior," Robert asks, stepping up close to the partition, "what's to be done? Can Lola take her vows? We can't let her do seven to ten years in jail."

"Must it be decided now," Magdalena pleads, terrified of the implications.

Robert looks across to Levine.

"If she's a nun," Steven explains again, "she'll do her time with the rest of you for three years, which I can easily get knocked down to two. And if you ladies behave yourselves inside, you'll probably be out and back in the cloister in twelve months."

The mother superior stands, paces, and thinks a moment. She then stops and looks at Lola, who has returned to a seat at the back of the room, surrounded by seven or eight sisters. "Lola, what about Leo," Magdalena asks frankly, woman-to-woman.

Lola glances at the floor. Finally, "He loves me," she replies simply.

"Exactly," mutters Bernadette, facing away into one of the corners, holding her forehead.

"So… he'll understand," Lola suggests.

Bernadette finally addresses Magdalena. "This is…" she starts but falters. "This is downright unorthodox! It would commonly require her to complete a year, at least, of the novitiate in order, well, in order…" But she's lost her certainty and can't go on. She looks to Evelyn for help.

The prioress crosses to the partition. "There are no hard and fast rules, counselor."

"Well, then, what are we waiting for," he asks.

Veronica falls to her knees before Lola.

"Easy, Sister," Evelyn cautions the excitable girl, "easy."

Magdalena looks to Bernadette who passes out and falls

into the arms of those nearest her.

Out in the garden, Jesus is up on a ladder listening to all this through a small window into the outer gallery. He comes down, troubled. Vincent and Xavier are waiting for him.

"You gotta go get Leo."

"Where," Vincent wonders, confused.

"At the junior high school," Jesus barks.

"But I can't get outta here," Vincent reminds his boss. "We're under house arrest, dude!"

"Fuck that," Jesus says. "Sister Lola's going all the way!"

Vincent knows what this means. "All the way," he repeats, a year or two older all of a sudden.

"Yeah! She's gonna take her vows!"

"No way!" Xavier complains.

"This is fucked up," Jesus says to no one, walking around in circles.

"She's smokin' hot," Xavier sighs, heartbroken.

Jesus smacks him in the head. "Don't talk that way about the sisters." Then, taking a few steps away: "We gotta go tell Leo to get his math teacher ass over here pronto!"

The boys are all fired up. "I'm going," Xavier declares, but Vincent pulls him back.

"No, I'm going!

"Yeah, like how when there's hundreds of white guys with guns outside keeping us in," Xavier insists, as if this addresses anything at all.

Vincent, getting the upper hand, points out: "They ain't all white."

"They ain't all men," Jesus adds, for what that's worth.

"Yeah, but, still, you know what I mean," Vincent concedes.

The argument seems to have exhausted itself. They all sit on the stoop and try to think. Jesus looks at Desmond and the dog looks back at him wisely.

"Okay, I got it," Jesus decides "Come on."


Leo enters Margaret's, newly unemployed, and sits, listlessly, at the bar. Chastity, Chet and a few of the regulars are watching the ever-present TV news coverage.

"The monthlong standoff in Brooklyn," the on-air anchor explains, "is coming to a close today as federal authorities decide to remove the sisters of the convent of Our Lady of the Highway to a minimum security prison to await sentencing."

"Can we turn this off," Leo asks.

Chastity turns it off. She gets him a beer. It's an OLHW. He cracks it open, sips, and looks at the label.

Chastity watches him, then, "I could tear it off the wall too."

"The TV," Leo asks.

She climbs up on the bar, grabs the flatscreen from either side, and viciously, expertly, wrenches it off its armature. Everyone crowds into the doorway and watches as she steps outside and tosses the TV into the street. It is immediately run over by a black school bus with barred windows and *US Federal Penitentiary* stenciled across the side.


Over at the convent, Jesus storms into the toolshed and makes for the fridge. "The one thing Desmond hates more than anything is a uniform. It don't matter: a policeman, a fireman, a mailman, it don't matter." Opening the old fridge, he's disappointed: "Those damn National Guardsmen drink all our Extra Holies or what?"

Vincent points: "No, there's one there. Look."

Way in the back, behind some vegetables, is another of the bottles with *Extra Holy!* written across it in the hand of a madman. "Okay! Xavier, get Desmond's water bowl over there."

Inside the convent, the sisters lead Lola to the little chapel off the main hall. But they remain outside. Evelyn's in charge. She's edgy and needs a cigarette. Someone hands her a half-smoked Camel and she lights up. Then: "Listen, pray," she advises Lola, exhaling. "Think it through. We'll come back for you in an hour."

Lola waits as the sisters all slowly drift away. Then she comes forward to the little altar and kneels. "Oh God," she begins, "by who's light the hearts of the faithful are instruct-ed, grant me the desire to relish what is right and to rejoice in your consolations."

Desmond laps up a bowlful of the dreaded Extra Holy.

"Thata' boy," Jesus says, scratching the pit pull's back. Then, to the boys: "Now, when the commotion starts, those soldiers at the other end of the street are going to have to run down this way…"

Magdalena sits beside Bernadette who is recuperating on her narrow bed in the room behind the kitchen.

"You okay, Sister?"

"That girl, Lola, is a saint," Bernadette insists, still riled up, eyes closed. "She made that policeman's gun not work. That's the short and long of it."

"Relax," Magdalena says, lightly touching Bernadette's hands where they lay folded on her breast, her rosary beads entwined in her fingers. "It's been a tough few weeks."

To put it mildly, she adds to herself.

And this issue of the gun that did not go off has threatened the sanity of the community which, in most particulars, is doing just fine under house arrest. It's not that different from their normal life. But even the most levelheaded sisters get weird in the presence of one suspected of receiving graces. These days, half the sisters won't come within ten feet of Lola, out of fear and trembling, while others dote on her hand and foot.

Their lawyer has confirmed that Detective Oscar's gun was inspected immediately after the incident and that it worked. There was nothing wrong with it. Meanwhile, the poor man himself has been given a leave of absence. His nerves are shot. He didn't mean to pull the trigger, he said—there was no need to—but he was nervous and he did. And he regrets this deeply. He might have shot that unarmed sister. But that nothing happened is somehow even more troubling. Scared out of his wits, they sent him home on temporary leave.

"Also, you gotta understand," Levine's contact at the precinct explained, "a cop's gun is the ground he walks on, the air he breathes. You check it twice a day, you know every piece of it and can take it apart and put it back together again in the dark!" The man just shook his head in sympathy. "Something like that happens—fuck, Oscar's faith in reality crumbled."

"Mark my words," Bernadette repeats, "Sister Lola is a saint."

"Try to sleep."

Magdalena passes quietly out through the pantry and moves slowly across the wide expanse of the kitchen. She herself has never witnessed a miracle. If pressed, she would say miracles don't happen. True, when Lola first came to the convent saying she possessed undesired supernatural powers, Magdalena and the prioress decided not to dwell on it, convinced as they were, through experience, that delusions like these are rapidly got rid off through regular labor and prayer.

But Lola is different, she admits. The exploding bottles of beer in the brewery that night was easily explained. The broken pane of glass could have been anything, the ancient building itself, Jesus suggested, settling and putting pressure on the old window frames.

Though the spoons were alarming.

And now she's learned from Levine the bishop witnessed electrical short-circuiting in the outer gallery when Lola learned she had been undermined about the on-site inspection.

"Grant, oh merciful God," Lola persists down in the chapel, "that what is pleasing to you I may ardently desire, prudently examine, truthfully acknowledge, and perfectly accomplish for the praise and the glory of your holy name."

Desmond is passed out beside the tool shed. Jesus and the boys look on. Xavier is afraid. "Did we kill him?"

"Impossible," Jesus says.

"Is he breathing," Vincent wonders, reaching out carefully and poking the dog with his finger. But he jumps back in a flash when Desmond bolts up like a rocket and barks, a provocative new gleam in his tired old eyes. Moments later, he is tugging powerfully at the end of his leash, dragging all three conspirators along towards the exit.

"Desmond, hold on!" Jesus begs.

Desmond barks defiantly and jumps at the door. They open it a crack and he bolts, disappearing in a spray of saliva, kicking up dust, his tongue wagging obscenely—a loose cannon shot straight off into the crowd.

A young soldier is watching all this and hesitates before reaching for his two-way radio. "Ah, something's happening down here," he reports, nervously, while Desmond staggers around like a lunatic, spotting all these uniforms. Which way to go, the dog asks himself. Who to attack? I'm delirious with choice!

"Yeah," the soldier resumes, "we got an angry and suspicious canine. Please advise. Over."

The protesters are cheering Desmond on as he runs around in circles, snapping at anything in his path.

"Oh God, author and love of peace," Lola prays, "shield me, your suppliant, from all assaults of the enemy, that I may trust in your protection and fear no foe."

At the other end of the convent a separate squad of soldiers are guarding the walls as their commander receives orders over his radio headset: "Copy. On the way." He signs off and calls to the others: "This way! Come on. Trouble down the street."

"Thank fucking god," says one of his men, bored out of his mind and eager for action.

Desmond, meanwhile, is terrorizing Resurrection Avenue. The soldiers would love to just shoot him. But the likelihood of accidentally wounding a protester is too high. They scramble up onto the hood of their SUV to get a better shot.

"Oh God most high, who would have all men be saved and come to the knowledge of the truth, send me as a laborer into your harvest and grant me the grace to bear your message."

Vincent and Xavier slide down a low part of the roof, jump the four feet to the wall, kick their legs over the top, and drop to the recently abandoned sidewalk. "What the fuck are you doing," Vincent snaps once the younger kid lands beside him.

"I'm coming," Xavier insists.

"No, you're not! Go back inside!"

"I can't now!"

"Shit. Why you always gotta be hanging around with me!"

But a shot rings out in Resurrection Avenue and the boys press themselves back against the brick wall. The roar of an angry crowd rolls like thunder over the rooftops.

"Uh-oh," Xavier whispers.

"They shot Desmond," Vincent decides.

And the boys run for their lives.

But, in fact, Desmond is having the time of his life, dodging around in all directions, chewing on people's shoes, tearing their trousers, pissing on lost iPhones. It seems the soldiers standing on the SUV fired a shot in the air to disperse the crowd and get better aim at this rabid animal, but it has just made the crowd louder and less predictable.

"We got a definite kinda' situation down here, sir. Request reinforcements. Over."

Vincent and Xavier run across empty lots and backyards, dodging traffic and jumping fences.

Back at the toolshed, Jesus gets himself a beer and shakes his head. He's crying a little. "Go get 'em Desmond," he mutters.

In the convent, most of the forty-eight nuns who live there now gather from all directions and fill the main hall outside the chapel, letting Veronica step forward to the entrance.

Lola finishes her prayers and turns to look at them all.

Veronica waits.

Lola nods in the affirmative—she's ready.

Over at the school, Mrs. MacGillicuddy looks up in alarm as the front doors bang open and Vincent and Xavier run past her office. She steps out into the hall and looks across to the secretary, Missus Walsh.

"Should I call the police," the secretary asks.

"Yes, by all means, call the police."

Vincent and Xavier barge into Leo's math class and stop.

The kids are just sitting around, dejected.

"Where's Leo," Vincent demands.

"Mister Haroldson," Derek asks.

"Math teacher."

Distraught, Sasha lays her head on her desk. "They fired him."

MacGillicuddy arrives, huffs and puffs with authority, and glares at Vincent. "What's the meaning of all this? Who are you gentleman?"

"How dare you call him that," Xavier protests, folding his arms across his skinny chest like some rapper he saw online.

"Let's go, Xavier," Vincent concedes majestically, head held high. "Wrong house." They walk across the room like emperors, open a window, and climb outside.

Leo's students look on, impressed, as the dignified young thugs stride purposefully across the playing fields. One by one, they get up and follow.

"Students," the principal calls, panicked. "Students!"

But they pay no heed. They're all out the window in no time, sprinting across the field to catch up with Vincent and Xavier.

Lola comes down the stairs from the main hall and is met by the crowd of sisters on the landing. She kneels and bows. Bernadette steps up with an actual crown of thorns and places it upon Lola's head. "Oh Lord," she recites, "bless this crown of thorns and grant unto she who will wear it faithfully, the peace, generosity, and humility your suffering and death for our sake allows us to seek. Our Lord, who lives and reigns in perfect unity. One God. World without end. Amen."

Vincent, Xavier, and Leo's whole class of Advanced Math students burst into Margaret's Bar. Leo looks over, startled.

"Dude," Vincent demands.

"Move," Xavier adds.

"What," Leo asks.

Sasha runs over and actually grabs him by the arm: "Sister Lola's going all the way!"

On the stairwell landing, Lola rises from her knees and proceeds down to the basilica. The sisters make way and follow in procession, reciting, "Lord grant the prayers of your people. Prepare the heart of your servant for consecration to your service. By the grace of the Holy Spirit purify her from all sin and set her on fire with your love. We ask this through Christ Our Lord. Amen."

At the bottom of the stairs, before the blasted doors of the basilica, Lola meets Veronica. Veronica is flanked by two nuns who, together, hold a simple chain with a pewter crucifix. "Holy Lord," Veronica recites, "Almighty Father, Everlasting God, bless this crucifix, that it may be a help to she who wears it. Let it be a support to her faith, an encouragement to good works, a consolation, protection, and a shield against the cruelty of the enemy. Through Christ Our Lord. Amen."

The two nuns take the chain and, together, pass it over Lola's head, laying it upon her shoulders as all the sisters repeat the incantation: "Lord grant the prayers of your people. Prepare the heart of your servant for consecration to your service…"

While Leo runs to the convent, encountering the outer fringes of the protesting mob, Lola rises from her knees and proceeds further into the basilica. She reaches Evelyn and kneels yet again.

"Oh God, the preserver of the human race and giver of all spiritual grace," the prioress intones, "send forth thy blessings upon this ring, that she who will wear it may be protected with heavenly strength and keep a perfect faith and sincere will to persevere in her promise of holy virginity, through Christ Our Lord, Amen."

Lola holds out her right hand and Evelyn places the silver ring upon the third finger as the community recites the incantation yet again. She proceeds to the altar, stops, and lays face down on the floor in the sign of the cross. "By the grace of the Holy Spirit," the assembled sisters conclude, "purify her from all sin and set her on fire with your love. We ask this through Christ Our Lord. Amen."

Leo reaches the convent just as the penitentiary bus pulls up before the door on Resurrection Avenue. Arrested protesters are being taken away but the crowd has become solemn. A corridor of chain-link fence has been set up running the distance from the convent's small garden door to the bus. Leo forces his way as close as he can.

In the basilica, Magdalena is seated up in front of the altar. "My Sister," she asks solemnly, "having completed the period of profession required by our Rule, what is your desire?"

Rising to her knees, Lola responds with the appropriate formula: "With the help of God, I have come to know in this community the difficulty and the joy of a life dedicated completely to peace and the relieving of suffering. Mother Superior, I now ask to be allowed to make perpetual profession in this community for the greater glory of God and for service to the faithful and the enduring."

Magdalena studies Lola. In the three months she's known

this young woman she's never seen her more confident, graceful, and calm. Can she ignite candles simply by desiring light? Can she disable firearms by insisting on peace? Or is she a well-intentioned but emotionally challenged psychotic?

The mother superior stands, hesitates, but finally concludes the ceremony: "May God, who has begun the good work in you, bring it to fulfillment before the end of days and the judgment of all."

As Lola lays face down on the floor again, the nuns repeat in unison: "Lord grant the prayers of your people. Prepare the heart of your servant for consecration to your service. We ask this through Christ Our Lord. Amen."

Out in the street, the people wait. Reinforcements of police and soldiers arrive and take up positions as Pena and the FBI agents are ushered into the convent.

Candles are being lit.

Leo tries to see through and over the crowd.

Inside, police and federal agents line the walls of the outer gallery. Pena looks on as a policewoman officiates.

"Sisters, place your hands behind your heads."

They do as they're told. Lola too. Handcuffs begin snapping into place around each of their left wrists.

"Now, bring your hands down in front of you."

The sisters obey and with both hands before them, the corresponding handcuffs are applied. As each nun is manacled, a chain is fed through a wide link in each set and passed along to the next arrestee, stringing the whole community of women together while another policeman recites: "You have the right to remain silent, anything you say may be used against you in a court of law…"

Leo is close enough now to the chain-link cordon to see the puny little convent garden door. He knows, he believes, he insists Lola must be being forced to take her vows. Otherwise, she'd be just telling him it's all over.

Or is she telling him it's all over?

Has she found God?

Has God found her? Has the supernatural torn a hole in reality and snatched the light of his life away from him? He hasn't seen her since the raid on the convent as no one has been allowed access to the sisters. But he thinks, now, he saw the change in Lola over the three months of her novitiate. She was affectionate, of course, but increasingly calm in a way that made him suspect she had found some other peace that didn't necessarily require him.

It's starting to rain.

The air itself is getting darker. Although there are, by now, several thousand people surrounding Our Lady of the Highway and dozens of domestic and international television trucks with radar dishes positioned for optimal coverage, everything is weirdly quiet. The candles are increasing, contributing to the strange unearthly dimness of the late afternoon. Leo muscles his way closer to the bus and the cordon leading to it. Then, from inside the convent walls, there's a sound he knows: the outer gallery's door being tugged open. Everyone's heard it. An even deeper hush falls over the crowd, a collective intake of breath. He hears the small rattle of weaponry, heavy soldier's boots, the clink of handcuffs, the crackle of radio communication, and the smaller splash of women stepping into mud. A second later it's a quiet stampede of feet making its way through the garden.

The garden door is opened and the first of the nuns is revealed being led by a woman officer and guarded by two soldiers.

At the sight of this, the sisters cuffed and chained together, one after the other, the crowd is stunned into immobility. For months the object of their adoration, their fan worship, has been a bunch of nuns they have never laid eyes on. Beer making religious virgins were their heroes. Pop singers had written songs about them. A new fashion line was introduced. A television series was planned.

But here they are, now, just regular human beings.

The crowd lift their candles higher.

And Leo sees her.

Lola is fourth from last, followed by three women Leo can not possibly know are the infamous Tatiana-Magdalena and her accomplices, Evelyn and Veronica.

Lola searches the faces in the crowd and locates him in seconds. Though the Law is far from being brutal or hurried, this elaborate and unwieldy ceremony has Lola tugged and jostled forward and up into the bus before she can even whisper Leo's name.

He fights his way back through the weirdly silenced throng and gets closer to the rear of the bus. He can see through the wire mesh-covered windows the sisters being organized into their seats. Once inside the bus, though, all the Law's attempts at an orderly seating arrangement of forty-eight women chained together in a line proves a farce. Lola bolts for the window at the back of the bus and her sisters try to accommodate her, tangling up the guards in their handcuffs and chains.

Outside, Leo claws his way forward.

Pena is at the door of the bus, still in the street, watching the expectant multitude uneasily. He looks up at the driver:

"This crowd worries me. Get out of here now."

As the bus closes its doors and shifts into gear, Leo lunges at the rear window and slaps his hand against it as, inside, Lola reaches out her hand to meet his, palm to palm, through the glass—her new wedding ring glinting in the fading light.

The two of them gasp, seeing it now for the first time, startled at this emblem of some greater and more complex separation.

And the rain starts falling hard as the bus pulls away. Leo stumbles, the wind knocked out of him, blinded by the glint of that ring. Policemen secure a path for the vehicle's progress. The crowd, their candles guttering now, follow ten or twenty yards, but gradually fade away. Only Leo keeps striding along behind the bus, Lola glimpsed, increasingly remote, inside. Reaching open space, the bus accelerates and Leo starts running all out. But there's no way he can keep up. The vehicle recedes into the distant grey landscape and pouring rain till Leo falls to his knees in the mud. Inside the bus, as it rumbles away, a female corrections officer shoves Lola back down in her seat. Stunned and uncertain, Lola raises her eyes to meet those of her sisters and she's met with a potent brew of conflicting feelings running like sparks from face to face—love, suspicion, respect, and even fear.

Leo stayed where he was for a while, kneeling in a puddle in the center of Resurrection Avenue. For how long, he couldn't tell. But the show was over. The crowds had gone home. The journalists and the camera crews dispersed. Even the soldiers and the cops moved on.

Evening descended.

He stood up, wet and muddied, and tossed aside his briefcase. He removed his soaked jacket, too, and dropped that into the mud at his feet.

And then he started walking.

Where to, exactly—again, he wasn't able to say. But he was walking there in a rage few honest men can be expected to survive for long.


THE END

www.ingramcontent.com/pod-product-compliance
Lightning Source LLC
Chambersburg PA
CBHW072054190726
48294CB00005B/1504